THE CULT OF TIAMAT

THE CULT OF TIAMAT

DRAGON'S DAUGHTER™ BOOK 5

KEVIN MCLAUGHLIN

MICHAEL ANDERLE

DISRUPTIVE IMAGINATION®

LMBPN Publishing
PMB 196, 2540 South Maryland Pkwy
Las Vegas, NV 89109

First US Edition, March 2021
eBook ISBN: 978-1-64971-624-8
Print ISBN: 978-1-64971-625-5

THE CULT OF TIAMAT TEAM

Thanks to the JIT Readers

Dave Hicks
Daryl McDaniel
Wendy L Bonell
Dorothy Lloyd
Veronica Stephan-Miller
Diane L. Smith
Jeff Goode
Deb Mader
Paul Westman

If we've missed anyone, please let us know!

Editor
The Skyhunter Editing Team

CHAPTER ONE

The storm bands of Hurricane Marduk had already begun to batter Galveston. The storm had intensified quickly as it moved across the Gulf of Mexico and was currently at the bleeding edge of a category four. The only reason it had not reached category five was because it was making landfall.

Thousands of people had evacuated when the governor of Texas had declared it a disaster. But tens of thousands had thought there was no way the hurricane would race across the gulf overnight and pound into the barrier island that held the record for the deadliest hurricane in US history.

Hurricane Marduk had proven them all wrong. The winds were too intense for the ferry to aid in any more evacuations. They were all grounded, except for the one at the bottom of the channel. An RV had already blown off the Highway Forty-five bridge and the winds wouldn't abate for hours, maybe days.

There was nothing humans could do to help the people stuck there. It was too dangerous for helicopters, planes, or ships. The bridge might hold long enough for a few fire trucks or busses to get onto the island, but no one thought there was any way it would last long enough for people to get off again.

The monster storm was poised to become the most deadly in history, barring some kind of magical intervention. Fortunately, those with the power to help had heeded the call. Kristen Hall, the Steel Dragon, had sent a team of her best Steel Guards to the coast via a teleportation spell the moment that the point of the storm's collision with the gulf coast had become clear.

Dragons flew evacuees over the channel between the barrier island and the mainland while those with the ability to control water used their powers to hold the ocean back. Mages used their dozens of abilities—super speed, strength, telekinesis, and control of the elements themselves—to get people to safety.

And yet, despite spending the entire summer interning for the Steel Guard, Kylara Diamantine—a mage with the uncanny ability to turn into a dragon and a girl who could control the weather itself—was stuck in Detroit operating the radio, exactly like she had all. Summer. Long.

She had thought that when Kristen made her an honorary member of the Steel Guard, her life would change when she graduated from the Lumos School. She had girded herself to be patient. After all, she still had two more years to go.

When she had been contacted in May about spending the summer in Detroit to train at the Steel Guard's international headquarters, her carefully cultivated patience had evaporated like a storm over the Sonoran Desert. Dreams had blossomed of rebellious dragons being put in their place, of mages causing destruction with uncontrolled powers in need of help, of pixies in peril, and of dwarves in distress.

But no. The summer had been spent learning the ins and outs of radio operation. Even now, with hurricane Marduk forcing the Steel Guard into action, Kylara was stuck with it. She had tried to protest, to explain that she could control the weather and maybe hold the hurricane at bay, and that she was ready to do something besides what she had done all summer long.

Melissa Heartsbane—the abrasive but beautiful dragon charged with supervising her internship—had disagreed. She had told her that her time working the radio had prepared her for exactly this— a real emergency. They would need her skills now more than ever. But she had not meant the young dragon mage's ability to control shadow and light, her diamond skin, or her power over plants or heat and cold. She had meant her ability to operate a freaking radio.

So it was that despite being the perfect dragon to help save people from Hurricane Marduk, Kylara sat at the offending device, patched calls through, and took notes on the check-ins of various Steel Guard forces.

"SGHQ, SGHQ, come in. This is Marduk task force. Over." A voice almost drowned out by wind crackled over her headset.

"SGHQ here. What's your issue, Marduk? Over," Kylara asked and tried to not sound tired or bored as she made a note of the time and ID of the caller.

"The wind shear is picking up and—" The wind was blowing so fiercely that she could barely make out what the speaker was saying. She had to admit that had she not worked the radio all summer, she doubted she would have been able to understand one word in ten. "...completely grounded! Already lost...wings torn to hell. Requesting immediate..."

"Marduk, do you need backup?"

"Back...evacuees...thousands left."

"Marduk. Come in Marduk! Marduk, I didn't get that!"

There was no answer.

Kylara paled. It had finally happened. The dragons in Galveston were calling for help and she had been the only one to hear their call.

She checked her ledger—as she had been drilled to do a hundred times over—saw her notes confirming what she had heard, and stood in a moment of panic before she remembered that she was at the communication center for the entire Steel

Guard. The crisis notwithstanding, she could not simply run off and abandon her post.

"Heartsbane. Come in, Heartsbane. It's Kylara."

"What is it, Diamantine?" the dragon asked, her tone brimming with umbrage for being interrupted.

"I couldn't make out every word as the wind was too strong, but they're in trouble. They still have thousands to evacuate and they said something about wind shear."

Heartsbane cursed. "I'll be down in a minute. I want three dragons to meet me out front, preference given to specials with wind or water control as well as any mages we have left."

"Yes, ma'am, but...uh—"

"Don't uh me, dammit! What's the problem?" the dragon snapped.

"All the dragons with wind or water powers are already there. And we only have a handful of mages, all novices."

Her supervisor cursed again, more colorfully this time.

"Send every mage we have, regardless of magic levels. We'll need to open a gate. For dragons, prioritize specials with extra mass—stone skin, metal skin, that kind of thing. Maybe they'll do better in the wind."

"Yes, ma'am, but—"

"No buts. I'll be there in forty seconds. I want to be the last one to arrive."

Kylara's fingers flew over the controls of the radio and she contacted every dragon she could. It was early in the morning so those who were at the base and not working security were asleep. Still, they were trained professionals and every single one of them—the paltry few that they were—answered her summons.

A minute later, they all stood outside the front of the Steel Guard base. Even she could tell that the assembled force was not exactly the best the Steel Guard had to offer.

The three dragons were all rookies and hardly more experienced than she was. One of them could turn his body to granite, which might prove useful, and the other was a vanilla with massive front claws who claimed her digging abilities made her more than a common. The third was straight-up vanilla with plain sprinkles. Still, it was all they had left at the base besides Heartsbane and Kylara.

The mages were more experienced than the dragons but not in the skills that were needed most. As far as the dragon mage knew—and she had spent her summer seated at a radio, desperate for any snippets of gossip, even if it was only the power profiles of the people she saw walking past with cups of coffee—none of them had ever opened a gate on their own.

"Diamantine, what the hell are you doing away from the radio?"

"I woke Zed early to take over. You need me!" Kylara said before Heartsbane could shut her down.

"You're an intern. You aren't qualified to wake Zed, let alone fly into a hurricane. Now get back inside."

"You can't get there without me!" she blurted.

The dragon raised an eyebrow but she didn't tell her to get lost. She knew that for Heartsbane, that was the same thing as telling her to please continue elaborating on her plan if she would be so kind.

"None of these mages have ever opened a gate. Even if they can, there's no guarantee they'll be able to get you back. I can open pixie gates and get everyone there and back no problem."

"Fine. You'll take us there, then evacuate back here and wait for my call to extract us."

"The radios are barely working. I think it's the storm." Honestly, she had no idea why the radios were breaking up so badly but she knew that Heartsbane had far less experience than she did when it came to technology. "I'm not sure you'll be able to call for extraction."

"Then you can open a portal to the same location every thirty minutes to check on us."

"There's no guarantee that the same location will even exist after thirty minutes! Besides, I can help. I have diamond scales and way more mass than a regular dragon. Plus, I have storm powers. You can use me there. I swear I'll follow your every command. At the very least, I can use my portals to ferry people to safety."

Heartsbane chewed her lip for the briefest of moments before she nodded. "Fine. Open a gate and get us there. You will obey my commands or you might as well consider your internship terminated."

Kylara agreed with a full-throated, "Yes, ma'am!" It wasn't a choice, though, and the dragon knew it as well as she did. If they wanted to help the team in Galveston in time, they had to portal there and only she could do that.

"Are you waiting for a pat on the back for knowing how your powers work? Open the damn gate—now!" Heartsbane barked.

She obeyed, opened a gate from this world to the pixie realm, then another from there to the shores of Galveston. As soon as the portal opened in the storm, the wind raged through and almost buffeted her off her feet. She turned her skin to diamond —a skill she had perfected over the summer thanks to the Steel Dragon's tutelage—and stood strong against it.

The dragons shifted to their dragon forms, the mages put shields up against the wind, and the team pushed through the gate into the teeth of the storm.

CHAPTER TWO

Despite growing up in the desert, Kylara was very familiar with storms. She had seen them drag massive boulders down mountainsides or transform dry sand into a mudslide of debris. They had carved the Grand Canyon, after all. You could see them as plain as day in the landscape of the desert, easier even than in forests where the plants endeavored to hide the destructive power of storms with their roots.

She had never experienced anything like this, though.

The winds were so strong that she had to lean forward to almost horizontal to even walk into them. The mages could not move at all and had to shelter behind the bulk of the granite dragon.

To her, it seemed to be a miracle that the city still existed at all. They had come out near the base of the Highway Forty-five bridge. Already, the top of the high-arched structure was gone—lost in the cloud cover and driving rain or simply demolished by the wind. Kylara could only guess.

The roofs of a few hotels and houses had already been stripped away, and she stared in mute shock as the winds tore the shingles from another as if it were nothing but wrapping paper on a gift that the hurricane wanted. A palm tree flew past high above and toppled end over end like it was nothing but a twig. What was more surprising was that other nearby palm trees were still rooted in the ground, their trunks bending as the storm lashed their leaves.

A mage whipped a shield up as a bush of some kind hurtled toward them. It bounced off the magic barrier and was immediately lost in the wind and rain.

Heartsbane leaned into the wind, her head tilted almost like she was listening to something only she could hear. She looked at her hastily assembled and somewhat hodgepodge backup force. "They've split into three groups. Two are nearby. I've sent aura pulses to them that we're here and ready to get evacuees to safety. Can anyone go out in this?"

Everyone shook their heads—it was hard to talk over the roar of the wind—except for the digging dragon, Dreida. "I can tunnel down and head toward one of them while I make a path under the storm."

"Do it!" Heartsbane ordered and the dragon dug into the street with her huge front claws. In a moment, she was gone.

"The rest of us need to dig in and be ready when they get here," their leader ordered. "I don't want to drain Kylara's energy opening a million gates, so we'll need a holding area to group people together while we wait."

"We can spin up a shield!" one of the mages volunteered and the others nodded and got to work.

"Are you sure we don't need to go out?" Kylara asked. She worried that one or more of the groups might be in more trouble than they could handle on their own.

"Damn it, Diamantine. I told you that you were under my command on this mission. That means you shut up and do what I say!" The dragon's eyes flared with rage, but when she met her steely gaze and nodded, she only snorted and moved into position beside the granite dragon to serve as a windbreak behind which the mages could perform their spells.

"I've never seen anyone resist her when she's like that," one of the mages muttered to Kylara—or more like yelled which turned into a mutter with the wind. "I could feel her aura and it wasn't even directed at me. You truly are as tough as diamonds."

The young dragon mage suddenly remembered why Melissa went by Heartsbane. She had incredible control of her dragon aura, more so than almost any other dragon, in fact, and could control the emotions of humans and mages as easily as she could turn to diamond. Because of her unusual power, she could also control dragons' emotions to some extent.

She could not influence Kylara however, because she wore a pendant around her neck that her dad had enchanted to protect her from dragon auras. That was a weakness in Heartsbane's ability that the dragon had tried to remedy by being especially verbally brutal with the intern.

No doubt the dragon had felt the auras of the other dragons and used that to ascertain their distance. She had probably made her emotional state one of safety and security so the other dragons would know to come to where she was. All of this was unaffected by wind or electricity, of course. It was a not-so-subtle reminder that there was still much that set Kylara apart from other dragons.

Not all those things were bad, though. She was a mage with the ability to absorb dragons' powers. Heartsbane could control auras, yes, but she had a bevy of powers that no other dragons had—like the ability to control plants.

Nearby, she noticed a hedge of some kind of woody plant with twisting, gnarled twigs and waxy leaves. While the storm ripped up houses and palm trees, this low, densely intertwined hedge did little more than sway in the wind.

"Can we get to that hedge?" Kylara yelled over the storm.

The look on Heartsbane's face said that she had already tried to answer with her aura. "Why?" she demanded when the girl failed to respond.

"I think I can grow it out and use it as a windbreak."

"That's our goal. Let's move, people!" the dragon ordered.

It took much longer than she had imagined. If there had been no storm, it would have been a negligible distance. The hedges were so close that to walk to them would not even qualify as a stroll. But in the raging hurricane, it took much longer. The problem was it required everyone's full power simply to avoid being blown away.

The granite dragon would move forward a few paces and dig his claws into the concrete of the street, and Heartsbane and the vanilla dragon would follow. They tried not to let their wings be ripped apart as they shielded the mages from wind and debris.

The mages would then set up a shield, and they'd repeat the whole painstakingly slow process all over again. It was maddingly slow but they did manage to cover the distance and reach the hedge. They only had to deflect three palm trees, the bed of a pickup truck—the cab was nowhere to be seen—and a couple of dozen shopping carts to do so.

But now that they were there, Kylara got to work. She had changed to her diamond-scaled dragon form as soon as they'd stepped beside it and she used her diamond claws to dig into the ground as she called on the plants. She made their stems thicken as the hedge doubled in height, then extended outwards to form a half-circle bulwark against the wind.

It helped considerably. The hedge shook and moved with the wind, but it bent rather than broke. A moment later, Dreida's head emerged from the hole she dug at their previous position.

"Mages, can you make a shield tunnel to get her and the humans here?" Heartsbane demanded.

Kylara didn't know how the dragon had known there were people in the tunnel too until she remembered that—duh—she had probably sensed their auras.

"We should be able to thanks to Kylara's shelter!" the mage who had bolstered her confidence against Heartsbane's beratement said with a wink at the dragon mage.

"Then stop coddling the intern and make it so!" Heartsbane snapped, doubtlessly reading the mage's emotional state like a book.

They clustered together against the granite dragon and spun their arms in gestures until a path appeared between them and the entrance to Dreida's tunnel. Normally, the telekinetic shield would have been almost impossible to see. The only indicator of its existence would be a faint blue shimmer but in the storm, its existence was as plain as day. Water pounded against one side of it and made it obvious that a magic tube connected the mages to the mouth of the tunnel.

A broad-shouldered man with a stubbly chin and a little girl cradled in his arms emerged from the tunnel and raced toward the mages. He moved with surprising confidence given that he had to sprint through a magic tunnel in an insanely powerful storm.

When he reached them, he came to a stop and put the girl down, who immediately stopped crying with a glance from Heartsbane. He grinned at Kylara.

"Holy crap, Lara! Sorry. Ky-lara. Fancy meeting you here." It was Drew. He had escorted her on one of her rogue missions but she had not found out until later that he was one of the Steel Dragon's most trusted guards—human, mage, dragon, or otherwise. She had told him her name was Lara and because of it, he still often shortened her name. If he didn't, he put far too much emphasis on the "Ky" because he had not learned it until later. From anyone else, it would have been annoying but it made him endearing like they had a secret code.

"Cut the backslapping and tell us how many more you have in that tunnel," Heartsbane said with a scowl.

The man didn't so much as flinch at her hostile attitude. If anything, he seemed to appreciate her being so direct. "There's about a hundred in that group. Maybe another couple of hundred with the other Steel Guard teams. I have to say, I didn't think we would get out of here. It was a smart move to bring Kylara and her portals."

Heartsbane grunted at the compliment unintentionally given to the dragon mage. "Diamantine, once they're all here, open a gate and get them to Detroit. Drew, you and me are going out to get the others."

"That sounds good. I could use a shower." Drew grinned and gestured at the rain.

"The rest of you will stay here. Diamantine, that goes double for you."

"Yes, ma'am."

"I know you think you have special powers, but we need your gates to get people out of here."

"Yes, ma'am."

"Gerard is in charge. I'll communicate via aura if I need to and you'll listen to what he says."

"Yes, ma'am."

Heartsbane glared at her—anytime she looked at anyone it was a glare—but for her, it was a gentle one. She finally seemed to realize that Kylara was not arguing and agreed that the priority was to get the people who could not help themselves to safety.

The dragon nodded again and bounded into the storm. The winds snatched her slender frame up and hurled her into a building, but she landed on her talons and used the momentum to propel her along. In moments, she was lost in the storm.

Kylara turned her attention to the people at hand.

"Move in here against me, folks. We want as many in here as we can before we get you all out of here," Gerard said as he gestured at his massive, stone-flecked belly. The people crowded closer and seemed to have decided that a dragon was less threatening than a hurricane. The mages expanded the shield around them and let the plants she had grown hold their own against the gales of wind.

Drew emerged from Dreida's tunnel again and cupped his hands over his mouth to be heard. "That's everyone from this group! We'll get you all to safety, all right? It's very important that when you go through the portal, you keep moving. There are many people here and more coming. We can't have a traffic jam on the other side. Questions?"

"How are we supposed to know what a portal looks like?" a man yelled, his words almost snatched away by the wind.

"Kylara?" Drew raised an eyebrow.

She nodded and opened a gate. The mists swirled around the circle that seemed to cut a hole in the air itself to reveal the front of a steel and glass building. The man who had asked the question recognized it easily as anyone else.

"Oh, right," he said somewhat sheepishly.

"Let's go, people! Keep moving!" Drew yelled and they listened. Kylara could see through the portal and the skeleton crew that was still at the base were all there to help. They moved people out of the way, got those who needed medical attention the help they required, and tried to find places for people to wait for their friends and family.

The teams repeated the process a few more times. Heartsbane led evacuees to Dreida, who took them through a tunnel and back to where Kylara and the mages had made a shelter from the wind. The dragon mage felt like she was getting the hang of the flow and rhythm of the work when Gerard and the vanilla dragon looked at each other with panic in their eyes.

"What is it?" she asked and suspected that it was a dragon's aura she was unable to sense.

"Heartsbane's in trouble," Gerard said. "She's calling for help. It feels like…like she's drowning maybe?"

"It must be the storm surge," the other dragon said.

"We have to help," he replied.

Kylara nodded and desperately wanted to volunteer, but she remembered how crystal-clear Heartsbane had been about her expectations for her to stay put.

"That's it for the evacuees," Drew said as he stepped from the tunnel. "Or the ones I saw anyway. Hernandez found others. Did she show up yet?" He looked around and got his answer. "I thought I didn't detect any profanity."

"Kylara, I want you to go," Gerard said.

"Me? But you weigh more," she said.

"I do, but there are no more people to evacuate here with your portal. The only ones left are with Heartsbane. At least, I think they are. Auras aren't my thing. You have powers the rest of us don't. You can do this."

"Heartsbane—"

"Said I'm in charge and I'm telling you to go. Unless you're scared?" His smirk said he knew damn well she wasn't.

"Do you want me to get you all home first?" She grinned.

"Over my granite body. Now go. You're wasting time. They should be near the beach. I'll signal that you went to them."

Kylara still did not understand how auras worked exactly but she had no desire to get into a technical discussion on the topic now.

She stepped into the hurricane.

The first thing she learned was that she had to keep her wings tight against her body. Every gust wanted to rip her into the sky, even with her diamond scales. With them tucked securely, she pressed forward and each step demanded that she dig her claws into the street to stay anchored to the earth. She had no idea how she would see anything in the storm. If she had aura powers, maybe she'd be able to tell where Heartsbane and the others were but without them, she could only hope that someone would signal her in some other way. Even without her pendant on, aura powers seemed to be one dragon ability she couldn't quite grasp yet.

When she saw a bright green flash about two blocks up and a block over, she took it as a sign. She cut across first and used a building as a windbreak before she entered another wind tunnel. A moment later, she saw them through the storm. Heartsbane and a dragon Kylara knew by sight but not name were sheltering a group of people. The dragon had the ability to control water and had made a bubble around them. It was an odd sight because it looked like it was rising from a street made of water.

Kylara understood then what the problem was. The storm surge had finally hit the island. There was no way these people would be able to walk to where she and the others had been.

Resolute, she started toward it but panicked briefly when the bubble seemed to pop and get whisked away in the wind. One of the people threw something into the air that exploded in another bright flash of green light. Hernandez maybe? Drew had said that one of his long-time teammates had an obsession with explosives.

She tried to hurry but she now battled not only the wind but water as well. A few curse words drifted to her on the wind before Heartsbane led the humans inside a building to escape the floodwaters. The winds were far from the point where they might begin to dissipate. She didn't see why the top half of the building they'd all gone into couldn't be ripped away like so many others already had been. It could, of course, which meant she had to hurry.

Unfortunately, she couldn't move at any kind of speed, not with the storm being what it was.

That gave Kylara an idea, though. She did have storm powers. Could she use them to simply dissipate the hurricane? She had never heard of a dragon doing that—in fact, she had heard that it was impossible—but she had to try.

She reached out and felt the wind currents and the moisture

in the air. But that was akin to saying dumping a bucket of salt on your tongue was the same as tasting it. The wind was so strong that she could not feel individual flows. The rain fell so intensely that she could not grasp any particular trace of moisture before it was gone.

It was obvious—painfully obvious—that she would not be able to do anything to stop this hurricane. That would be like expecting an ant to build a skyscraper simply because it had made a mound of dirt with holes in it. She could try to harness this storm, however, and in doing so, she would be drained of what power she had. Once that happened, it would hurl her through the air like she was nothing more than another shopping cart.

But there were some currents she could feel, she realized.

They were weaker than the major bands of wind that tried to level any plants or structures foolish enough to exist in this part of the world at this particular moment, but they were there. Off the sides of the buildings, tiny currents rippled and ebbed. Could she do something with those?

Kylara reached out but made no effort to redirect the main force of the storm. Instead, she tried to touch the tiny enclave of relative calm behind the building Heartsbane and the others were inside.

It worked after a fashion. The wind did not stop blowing and the rain did not stop falling but in that space, at least, it was calmer. The water was pulled away by the wind and the intensely low pressure of the areas outside. She emphasized these effects instead of trying to make new ones. It would be tough but this could work. She could provide them with a path to her and get them out.

Kylara wished she could signal with her aura the way the other dragons could. She needed to tell them that she was there and could keep them ahead of the storm surge if only they hurried. For the first time, she felt the full disadvantage of having no aura.

She did, however, have powers that were not affected by wind or rain. She opened her mouth and launched a beam of light at the building Heartsbane had entered. A flash of green light came in response. A second later, a window shattered and Heartsbane's head poked out. She crawled out and into the tiny area of relative calm, then gestured for the humans to follow and use her body as an escape ladder.

The storm intensified as if it had discovered that some mortal peon was interfering with its destruction and wished to end the insubordination. Kylara could not stop it but she could feel it, and she knew that the people would not reach her position. After a moment's thought, she opened a portal at the base of the building in the calm space, even though opening the gate at such a distance while she also controlled parts of the storm felt like being tugged in five directions at once.

Heartsbane ushered the humans through it as the dragon mage's nose started to bleed.

The water dragon stepped in to help keep the storm surge at bay and one of Kylara's ears added a gusher of blood to her nostrils. She was barely holding on but she couldn't fall into the voice in her brain that demanded she pass out and rest.

Her scales rippled as she held the storm at bay and kept the portal open. They had to hurry. She would not be able to keep the storm back much longer. It was too much. Even making this one pocket of calm was too much.

Kylara felt her power fail her. The portal closed. Most of the humans had made it through but Heartsbane, the water dragon, and Hernandez had most definitely not. And, she thought desperately, there were the dragons and mages she had left behind.

She felt like she had failed them all. Her power was too weak and she did not have what it took to save them. She simply didn't have enough.

"Why did you stop?" a high-pitched voice asked over the roar of the storm.

She turned—she was already experiencing tunnel vision—and saw a pixie inside a bush. "Why would the Big Pixie stop?"

"I'm too weak. I can't do this alone." Even those words were exhausting to say while she maintained the pocket of calm around the Steel Guards.

"But why would you ever try to do anything alone?" the pixie asked and suddenly, the pocket of calm around the Steel Guard expanded.

"I…thank you!" Kylara blurted.

"Did you hear that?" the pixie chirped. "The Big Pixie thanked me."

Three more of the creatures popped out of the bush and the space of calm solidified. "Thank us too. Thank us too," they chorused.

"Of course. thank you." She wiped the blood from her face. "Can you open a portal and take them to Detroit?"

"Detroit?"

"That's where the Steel Dragon lives, right?"

"No problem."

A gate appeared but when it did, the bubble of calm vanished. Heartsbane and the others barely made it through with scant seconds to spare before the storm surge would have washed them away.

"Now I need to get back to the others," Kylara muttered.

The ground in front of her erupted.

Dreida grinned at her. "How are you doing, Diamantine? I thought you could use a way out."

She crawled into the tunnel and scrambled after the dragon before the rising waters of the storm surge found the entrance.

They raced back and her rescuer moved so quickly that she could barely keep up.

The two of them reached the other end seconds before the flood did and crawled out as the tunnel filled with water.

Kylara opened a portal but it didn't work.

She was out of juice.

"Kylara?" Gerard asked and fear fractured his granite features.

"I'm…trying." She grunted with effort but the magic didn't respond. Her mind raced but couldn't think of a single thing that she could do.

Before she could confess her failure, the pixies moved beside her. Instead of opening a portal, they poured their power into her. She felt it flow alongside her inner magic and she managed to open a gate to Detroit.

Everyone scrambled through as the storm raged at the gate and tried to force itself across hundreds of miles into the streets of the Motor City.

She limped through last and was barely able to make out Heartsbane's sardonic smile before she crumpled and her tunnel vision finally closed in completely.

CHAPTER THREE

Kylara had no idea how much time had passed because it was hard to track these things with a massive headache and blood dribbling from your nose that refused to clot.

It was morning so there was that, but whether it was the same day or not was anyone's guess. She had fried her cellphone in the storm—she had vague memories of lightning striking her when she'd tried to redirect the hurricane but she honestly didn't know if those were hallucinations or memories—so she couldn't check the time on it.

Even if her phone was working, now was not exactly the time to take it out and look. She was in the Steel Dragon's office, seated across from Kristen Hall herself. The most influential dragon in the world had her hands steepled in front of her and an inscrutable expression on her face. Behind her was nothing but a bank of windows overlooking Detroit. Between them was a massive desk made of what appeared to be reclaimed barn wood. It looked odd in the glass and chrome office. Out of place, much like Kylara felt.

"Heartsbane has already given me a report," Kristen began after a period of time that Kylara could only describe as painfully long. "Is there anything you'd like to add before I tell you what she said about your actions?"

There was something decidedly unsavory about the way she had said "your actions," but she didn't know what to do about that. She thought she had done well—or more like well enough. No one had died thanks to her gates. It was somewhat embarrassing that she had passed out in the middle of a storm given that she could control the weather, but she had only gone out because Gerard had told her to.

Finally, she settled on answering with a non-committal, "No?"

Kristen's inscrutable expression shifted into a slight smile and a tiny nod. "You've learned a measure of humility too. Very good."

"So Heartsbane said I did all right?" she asked and her curiosity effectively ruined her poker game.

"She used the word 'acceptable.'"

Kylara nodded, but couldn't stop herself from wilting at the lackluster praise.

The Steel Dragon raised an eyebrow at the young mage. "I'm the leader of the most powerful dragon council in the world and I've saved her life more times than I can count, and she's never said anything I've done is acceptable. From Heartsbane, that's high praise. You should be very proud."

"I should?"

She smiled broadly. Kylara wondered if her aura reflected the same feeling but of course, it was hidden from her.

"You should. You followed orders, used initiative, and wielded your powers effectively in a manner that helped everyone. You saved lives, both those of your teammates and the people you were there to help."

"Heartsbane said all that?"

Kristen snorted. "Hardly. But everyone who came back returned through your portal, so your work speaks for itself."

"Thank you, ma'am, I appreciate it, but the pixies helped too. I would never have gotten the team back without them."

"There's that newfound humility again." The woman winked. "There is nothing wrong with accepting help, especially when you need it to help others."

Kylara didn't know what to say to that so she mumbled another, "Thank you," and hoped there wasn't a but coming.

"I'm quite pleased with your progress over the summer. Your actions during the evacuation underscore how well you have done."

"How well I've done?" she blurted, her tone incredulous.

"You don't want to accept the praise your boss is trying to give you?" Kristen looked amused, not annoyed, thank God.

"I do...of course I do. It's only that... Well, I didn't do anything all summer but train and work the radio." She gave her a lopsided smile. The training sessions hadn't even been that hard, not compared to fighting Lord Boneclaw in the void or facing Mortimer Smith. Of course, she knew better than to admit that to Kristen.

"Your training and familiarity with the radio both paid off. When the chips were down, your performance exceeded expectations. You found a way to innovate while still prioritizing following the chain of command and helping people who could not help themselves. That's exactly the kind of traits I look for when hiring Steel Guards."

"Wait, are you saying that I can join your team as a full Steel Guard now?" Kylara asked.

Kristen chuckled. "Wow, when you decide to take a compliment, you certainly run with it."

"So that's a...yes?"

The woman snorted and stood, then turned to look out the window. "Drew's right about you, you know."

"About what?"

"You remind him of a younger version of me. I had thought that with your new sense of humility, that might not be true, but I can see it now."

Now that felt like a compliment, especially coming from Drew. Kylara was surprised that he would say such a thing—and even more surprised that Kristen would relay the tidbit to her—but immensely flattered at the same time. "Is that yes?"

Kristen guffawed and turned away from the window to pierce her with her steely gaze. "That's a no. For now, anyway. You're still in school, after all."

"I've done things that none of my classmates have." She regretted it as soon as she said it and knew it sounded arrogant.

"From the reports I've read, you've done things with some of your classmates—"

"That's true, ma'am." Kylara could not believe she had interrupted the most powerful dragon in the world, but she couldn't take credit for beating Mort or Boneclaw. She would never have been able to do either without her friends. "But the five of us could join—"

"When you finish your schooling, I hope you all apply but until then, you need to keep attending the Lumos School. The five of you are making waves in the dragon world. Three dragons —one of which is a Midnight and another a Lumos, no less—plus two mages working together as equals is something the world has never seen."

"Th-the world?" she stammered.

"Boneclaw and a wizard using pixies to fuel his magic are big deals. Word gets around, especially since most dragons are terrible gossips."

"I...I didn't realize." Kylara knew that all the dragons at the Steel Guard base knew who she was, but it was the job of security forces to know things. She hadn't realized her reputation extended beyond the people she had met.

"It looks like keeping you busy at the radio worked." Kristen winked again. "We normally don't offer this to interns, but would you like to take the last week of summer off? There's only a week before the Lumos School reopens and I thought you might want to spend some time with your mom before—"

"That would be great!" she answered before she realized that she had now interrupted the most powerful dragon in the world not once, but twice in a single conversation. It had been a good summer but she'd missed seeing her mom on a regular basis.

"Excellent," Kristen replied and didn't seem to mind the excited interruption. "Unless there's anything else you'd like to add about your mission at the coast, you're free to go."

Kylara had nothing to add. She had earned an "acceptable" from Heartsbane and a genuine compliment from Drew. Honestly, she did not want to ruin the goodwill she had somehow earned by putting her foot in her mouth.

She left Kristen's office at the top of the building and hurried to the apartment she'd used for the summer. It took only moments to gather the few things she had brought with her and open a portal, and she left before Kristen could retract any of her compliments.

As she stepped through the gate and saw Hester Diamantine smile at her arrival, she decided it was well worth the headache that opening it had triggered again.

CHAPTER FOUR

Fire so hot it charred her diamond scales.

Wind that threw her around like she was nothing but a piece of trash.

Bones…bones everywhere, clawing at her with talons stolen from corpses.

A lake of lava she couldn't fly away from until she splashed into mud.

But the mud was worse than all of it. It didn't cool after the heat of the flames or lava. It didn't anchor her after the wind. Worse, it was filled with the bones of the dead. It pulled her deeper, filled her lungs, and drowned her yet didn't kill her, not quite. It was taking her somewhere deep down. Boneclaw was there, but the mud was not taking her to him. He was merely a part of it, eager to pull this prize into the waiting darkness.

She fell ever faster through the slime until finally, the sensation forced her to wake up.

Kylara blinked her eyes open from the nightmare and immediately cursed. She was still dreaming. She was supposed to be in her bed in the house her mom had rebuilt after the fire elemental had incinerated it. Instead, she was on the shore of the pool where Boneclaw had tried to kill her to steal her powers.

This was a staple location of her nightmares ever since he had tried to drown her there. Even Mortimer Smith and his immense power hadn't been able to make much headway in her bad dreams. He made appearances, of course, but it was Boneclaw, this place, and the horrible sensation of despair that emanated from its depths that were the mainstays of her nightmares.

At least she knew she was dreaming this time. That wasn't always the case. She turned one of her fingers to a diamond-tipped claw and pricked her leg. It hurt and a spot of blood welled before her dragon healing powers healed the wound.

Unfortunately, she did not wake up.

She pricked herself harder and felt the sharp jolt of pain that should have woken her. Again, nothing happened.

Her heart hammered in her chest as she looked around the mossy shore of the pond. Was she dreaming? Usually, in her nightmares, everything about this place tried to drag her into the pond. If she found the shore, it collapsed into water. If she grasped a branch, it became a skeletal claw. Tentatively, she reached out with her plant powers and tried to make a nearby flower bloom. Astonishingly, it did. That never happened in her dreams, which could only mean…she wasn't dreaming.

Kylara felt the blood drain from her face. The last thing she remembered before her regular slew of nightmares was saying goodnight to her mom, the grit of slightly undercooked black beans still in her teeth. She had stretched in bed, read a book about mage history until she was too tired to keep her eyes open, and passed out.

She had not opened a gate to enter the pixie realm. And she would never open a gate to the very place that haunted her dreams.

Somehow, she had gated herself to the pixie realm in her sleep. It was a terrifying realization. Activating any of her powers

—even turning into her dragon body—in her sleep was bad news. But opening a gate that took her there was unthinkable. What if she somehow tore the rift wider as Boneclaw had and some of the swamp water poured out to taint her dimension? What if... what if that entity she felt deep beneath the water awakened from the pixie-induced sleep it was trapped in?

Having nightmares about this was bad enough, but taking herself there while she slept? That meant she had lost control over much more than her imagination.

She pushed to a seated position, still hoping she would wake up although she knew that she already had. There was nothing to be done about it there, though. She reached inside herself for her inner pixie magic and was about to open a gate to take her home when she heard something.

It almost sounded like a voice calling to her, but she heard no words she knew or anything that sounded like any language she had ever heard of.

Instead, the words and warnings of the pixies raced through her mind. The last time she had been anywhere near this place, she had arrived accidentally and even then, she had been in the meadow, not the swamp at first. The pixies she had met had run off to lull whatever slumbered below the swamp back to sleep.

Which implied that it might have woken up.

Had she been the one to awaken it? And if she had, then how? The pixies said some things were better left buried and she had taken their advice—at least she thought she had. But she had come there in her sleep. If she had done that, what else could she have done?

She shivered as the voice—was it a voice? Kylara didn't know —called out again. It was a long, low moan, like someone or something was experiencing a personal nightmare. She could almost feel something too. It was as if a vibration flowed through her very soul.

The pendant on her neck began to heat. She looked around

and used dragon sight to pierce the gloom of the dank, mossy woods, but she saw no other dragons. That was odd. She'd felt the pendant warm before but only in response to a dragon trying directly to influence her emotions.

When Heartsbane talked to Kylara, she sometimes joked to herself that she could use her pendant to heat a cup of tea. But no one was there. She saw no movement in the woods and no tell-tale shadows that did not belong. Plus, this was the pixie realm. The only dragon who could come there of her own accord was her.

The pendant sensed something, however, and it continued to grow warmer. In moments, it went from warm to scalding hot. It burned her chest but she did not dare to take it off. The magic protected her from dragons trying to sway her emotions. If it was this hot, it meant a dragon was trying to influence her harder than any other ever had.

But where was this dragon? There was no one in the woods and no one flying overhead. The only movement was the surface of the pond, which had begun to bubble as if the water were coming to a boil.

Kylara stared with wide eyes at the surface of the pond that was now placid again. It did not become placid, nor did the ripples from the bubbles dissipate. It was as if they had simply never been.

She shuddered, no longer certain if this was a dream or not or if she wanted it to be one, and opened a gate to her home in the mountains of New Mexico. With a sigh of relief, she stepped out of the oppressively humid air of the swamp and into the cool, dry air of the desert and immediately closed the gate behind her.

She was awake.

Without a doubt, she knew she was awake.

For a moment, she simply stared at the wall. She had never had a dream like this before. All her nightmares since she'd faced Boneclaw had been messy, chaotic experiences. Images of the dragon, the swamp, and the other battles she had been in all vied for dominance. She had never been able to use her magic to change the conditions of the dream or to use her magic to escape.

Either way, Kylara was not about to even try to go back to sleep. The sky was beginning to lighten in the east. Her mom would be up soon if she wasn't already.

Cautiously, she called on her shadow powers and used them to blanket the floor with a thin layer of interlacing tendrils of darkness. She stepped on these to muffle her footsteps as she walked to her mom's room. With her breath held—although she had no idea why—she opened the door and peeked inside, hoping to the powers that be that her mom was still asleep and ignorant about what had happened to her daughter.

Hester Diamantine lay in bed, her eyes closed and mouth open, and a thin line of drool worked its way down her chin. "Lara..." she mumbled as she slept. "I don't care about them...kiss me..."

The dragon mage closed the door and resisted the urge to yank it shut. She was a little grossed out that her mom was having a dirty dream about the mage she had named her after but was more relieved that she was asleep. After the snafu last year where she had been forced to wear a magic-inhibiting bracelet when the headmaster of the Lumos School had thought her gate powers were malfunctioning, she didn't want to let anyone know that they were now doing exactly that.

She knew her mom was different. Although a member of Dragon SWAT, she had taken a baby mage and run from a respected career. But ever since Hester had been captured by Cassandra, Kylara's aunt, she had been different. She didn't think she would try to get someone to put one of those cursed silver bracelets on her but she also knew about as much about pixie magic as anyone else—nothing. She would likely talk to the headmaster about it, who would talk to Kristen Hall. And if the Steel Dragon told them to put a bracelet on her, both Hester and

Amythist would obey. They were dragons and they were loyal to their council.

Kristen might not order such a thing, of course. She had praised her work this summer and knew how much she had hated wearing the cuff, but she didn't want to risk any of that without a damned good reason.

This was something she had to resolve on her own. She was the only person who could open gates to the pixie realm. That meant she was the only person who could possibly answer the questions that raced through her mind right now. Well, maybe the pixies could help, too. She'd need to ask.

Satisfied that her secret was safe, she went back to bed to try to get a little more sleep but it did not come. Every time she nodded off, she thought of the pond and snapped awake.

Soon, the sky was light enough that she knew that even without nightmares, she wouldn't be able to get back to sleep.

Besides, she liked mornings in the desert. She snuck past her mother's room again, scribbled a hasty note and left it on the kitchen counter so her mom would know where to find her, and went out into the desert to be as far away from anything remotely resembling a swamp as she possibly could.

CHAPTER FIVE

There truly was nothing like the desert at dawn. The chill was still in the air but the first rays of the sun already tried valiantly to warm the atmosphere into something scorching. Every living thing there knew this and had known it for thousands of years.

Cactus blooms that had been open all night to invite bats and moths to visit for nocturnal meals closed almost as fast as the sun slid over the horizon. What little dew had formed—precious little—was diverted down waxy leaves and thorny stems to be sucked up by ever-thirsty plants.

Tiny mammals like mice, shrews, and voles scurried about, trying to fill their bellies, cheeks, or nests with food before the heat made it too oppressive to move. Larger mammals chased the smaller ones. Kylara saw two foxes and a bobcat prowling in the dawn.

Birds sang and filled the desert with melodies that wouldn't be heard again until the first few moments of the next day. They chose the time when the light was bright enough to show off their dusky feathers but not so bright that they would be blind to the soaring hawks that would use the heat-baked sand to rise high into the sky.

A family of Harris hawks surveyed the scene below them from the top of a cactus and the talons on their long yellow legs looked even more intimidating than the thorns they grasped. They must have eaten well the day before as the two adults pushed the mottled one off the cactus to go and hunt. If they were hungry, the more experienced adults would have led the family in the hunt.

Kylara saw all of this from above and she reveled in it. She missed this place with its quiet dramas and its constant feuds over water and shade. There were times when she wished she could remain there, but the landscape was also a reminder that she could never return to those days of isolation. There were still blackened stumps from when her aunt Cassandra had sent a fire elemental to capture her mom.

She was just about to reach out with her plant powers to move some of the growth along when she heard her mom roar into the morning light.

"Don't you dare!"

In an instant, every animal she had been watching was gone—whether frozen and camouflaged or hidden in a shelter, she did not know.

"I only wanted to make them grow a few twigs."

"The desert's doing fine," her mom replied. "Are you? You stopped coming out here this early when you became a teenager."

"I'm…good," she lied.

"Good enough to train?"

Before Kylara could answer, her mom dove at her.

Hester collided with her like a meteor. There was a time when the strike would have knocked her to the ground and ended the duel before it even began, but she was no longer a little kid.

Unable to break free of her mother's hold, she sent shadow tendrils between her and her dragon claws to force them to expand and release her.

"You've learned a new trick," Hester said and sounded proud

before she exhaled a great blast of flame at her. Kylara used shadow to make a shield that absorbed most of the heat and let her diamond scales take the rest. She flared her light powers and left the other dragon temporarily blinded.

"Do you give up, Mom?" she asked.

"Never!" her mother shouted and struggled to right herself as she plummeted toward the earth.

She briefly considered opening a portal beneath her mom and another high in the sky to confuse how far from the ground Hester expected herself to be, but she thought of her nightmare and decided against it.

Instead, she reached out with shadow powers again and lashed her tightly.

"You don't have to cradle my fall!" Diamantine protested.

"Oh, I'm not," she said as she let her land heavily and made a couple of twisted trees extend their branches over her and pin her to the ground.

The dragon struggled but she was laughing and tried to be careful to not damage the plants. "I guess I can't fault you for growing some of the vegetation in a fight," she said as her daughter landed beside her.

Kylara made the plants reach skyward, and Hester Diamantine was free.

"Are you all right?" she asked her.

"Hey, just because you can hold your own against me these days doesn't mean I'm some vanilla. I still have diamond skills."

"Oh. Speaking of which…" She transformed into her human body but left her skin shimmering with diamonds.

"Kylara, you've done it! Great job, sweetie." They hugged in the morning light of the desert and it was nice.

When they pulled apart, the girl sighed. Sometimes, she wished she could go back to when everything was simpler.

"Are you sure you're all right?" her mom asked.

"Yeah, I'm fine."

Hester nodded but Kylara didn't think she believed her. Yet again, she wondered if an aura would give her more insight into what the woman truly felt.

"I don't have anything to do today. Well, there's a water pump in the aquaponics that's clicking for some reason, but I can deal with that tomorrow. Do you want to hike up the Straits and run some drills? I bet I'm still faster than you, even with your fancy education."

"I'd like that, Mom," she said.

They took their human forms and started up the mountainside. Hester jumped from boulder to boulder and her dragon powers fueled her legs and propelled her in great arcs. The dragon mage tried to keep up and push last night's nightmare from her mind. For a time, she was able to and fell into the rhythm of the exercise—leap…float…land, repeat. The two climbed steadily higher until they reached the mountain stream that had carved a zigzag pattern through the rock.

They took turns racing down the Straits, pushing themselves to increase their flight until they reached speeds that not even they could handle without pounding into a cliff face. It was the best Kylara had felt yet since she'd woken up. It was impossible to focus on anything but tight turns while actively flying the Straits.

Any time she rested, however, her mind seemed to wander again. The last time she had been there, it had been Sam that she had outraced. What would her life look like if he had never appeared on her land? It was an impossible question, she supposed, with an answer that had no bearing on the world that was. It had been back when she thought she was simply a dragon with an overprotective mother instead of a mage who could absorb dragon powers and also the Big Pixie. Those were certainly simpler times.

"What's on your mind, Kylara?" her mom asked after she careened into a cliff on one of her runs.

"It's nothing," she lied.

"It's not nothing. You shouldn't have crashed on that run. Come on, I know the last two years have been…hard but I'm still your mother. If something is bothering you, I'm here. You can tell me."

She considered telling her the truth, she truly did, but she chickened out and asked something tangential instead. "Do you have any idea why I never picked up any aura powers?"

"Is…that's what's bothering you?" Hester seemed a little taken aback. She had never put much stake in aura powers and was a combat person, through and through.

"I merely think it's odd. I got your ability to turn into a dragon and to breathe fire. I even got your diamond scales but why not aura powers? Did you simply never use them on me?"

Her mother chuckled. "Oh, I certainly tried to use them on you. Believe me. I tried quite hard to make my little Ky-ky want to use the potty instead of doing her business while in flight."

"And it didn't work?"

"Not really, no. But you know I've never been very good with auras. Oh! I know what this is about. It was that bitch Heartsbane, wasn't it? Talking to her for five minutes always left me doubting that any of my feelings were my own. Did she use her powers to make you feel bad? Because if she did, I promise you I am not above kicking her butt even if she is a Steel Guard. We used to work together, you know, a long time ago, but still. She might have given you a hard time on my account."

Kylara shook her head. "No, Mom. It wasn't her." She did make a mental note to ask her what exactly Hester Diamantine had done that would have merited retribution against her kids. "In fact, she never affected me at all."

"Well, that's odd." The dragon frowned in thought. "Heartsbane uses her aura practically without thinking. She used to use it on our boss. It's hard to believe she never tried to use it on you."

The dragon mage chewed her lip. "I guess that's the thing. I don't know if she even tried to use it on me." She fingered her amulet.

Hester facepalmed. "I can't believe I forgot about your amulet. That's why she never used her aura on you. You know, I never let you take that off. Even during potty training. I was too paranoid that another dragon would discern you if you didn't wear it. I still tried to use my aura, though, but it never worked. Even she couldn't get through though, right?"

"No. I don't think so anyway," Kylara said. She did not think the being deep in the pond had gotten through the pendant's protection either, but it had certainly come closer than anything else ever had. She had never felt it get as hot as it had while she had been seated on the edge of the pond. And she hadn't even been all that close. It was good to know that the pendant was far more powerful than she had realized, but it was frightening to think that if it failed, she would be at the mercy of any dragons around her.

"Then what's the problem?" her mom asked somewhat blithely.

"I guess I don't know what I would do if it broke. I don't have any aura powers. If something happened to the pendant, I have no innate defenses. I don't think I can afford that anymore."

Hester nodded and looked relieved. "I understand completely. That's the same reason why I had you train so hard in martial arts in your human form. Yes, your dragon body is more powerful but that doesn't mean you should be defenseless as a human. You want a backup."

"Yes!" Kylara said, pleased that her mom understood her while she also thought it was adorable how she related everything to fighting.

"Well, how did you get your other powers? You got mine when I touched you the first time."

"I think that was because of the cold in the north, though," she said. "All the others have come in combat. I absorb powers when I need to, I think. Like it's a defense mechanism."

"You don't simply take them any time you're hit with them?"

Kylara shook her head. "No. To be honest, I haven't absorbed any new ones in a while. I got pixie powers but nothing from dragons. I think it's because the other students have stopped trying to hurt me in battle."

Diamantine nodded. "That makes sense in a way. But what about the Lumos boy? Didn't he heal you or something?"

"His name is Sam, Mom, and yeah, he healed me, but I think I needed to be healed."

Her mom raised an eyebrow at the way she had said Sam but she moved on. "Well, maybe the reason you never got aura powers is because they've never been a threat. Even the powers you got from Ruby were because you burned yourself. No one has even come close to doing anything to you with their aura because of that pendant."

No one except that entity in the pond. Kylara kept that thought to herself. "I think you're right. I always wear this."

"But you don't need to anymore," Hester said with a slight smile. "Your grandfather made that—and I used it—to keep you safe and secret, but the world knows about you now. Here, I have an idea. Take the pendant off."

She complied and had an idea of where this was going. Suddenly, she felt an overwhelming sense of love inside her. With tears in her eyes, she scooted closer and hugged her mom tightly. In an instant, the feeling was gone.

"Did you use your aura to make me hug you?"

Hester grinned devilishly. "You're still my little girl."

"I don't think love will make it activate."

"Try to defend against it, though. Dragons always push and prod against each other with our auras. Even me and I quite frankly suck at auras. One of the things that makes that pendant so powerful is that it replicates the feeling of emotional pushback so to a dragon, you merely feel like another dragon."

"How do I defend against it?"

"Try not to feel what I make you feel."

Again, the overwhelming desire to hug her mom flowed through her and Kylara was powerless to resist.

"Mom!"

"Sorry, but I don't want to try hate or sadness on my daughter."

"Okay, so…try fear, all right? That should trigger a defense, shouldn't it?"

Hester nodded but didn't look particularly excited about it.

An instant later, she had the overwhelming urge to run. She had never realized how terrifying Hester was. The dragon was so strong and the burn on her hand looked frightening—like the woman would do the same thing to her. Kylara scrambled back and tried to get away. Every instinct told her she had to escape.

"Fight it, Kylara!" Hester roared at her. Why did she roar? Did she intend to push her off the cliff? Would she kill her since she was nothing more than a mage?

The feeling vanished and left her breathing raggedly with panic although she no longer felt it.

"Kylara, are you all right? I'm so sorry."

"No…I…it's fine."

"You couldn't fight back?"

"I tried but…no. Not at all."

"Do you want to try again?"

She nodded. Suddenly, she was overcome with hatred. She hated the woman in front of her and that she had stolen her from her family and kept her hidden. She hated how she made her fight every damn day of her life. She hated the way she cooked beans. Part of her knew what was happening but it was like a candle compared to a bonfire. The hate was so much stronger than the voice questioning it.

Kylara got to her feet, clenched her fists with diamond knuckles, and shot shadow tendrils out across the ground to strangle the woman who had taken everything from her. She slid the tendrils around her neck and brought her close enough to land a blow across the temple with one of her crystalline knuckles. Hester's head lolled and the feeling vanished.

"Oh, my God, Mom! I'm so sorry!" She dropped the shadow tendrils and hugged the woman. "Are you all right? Oh, Mommy, I never want anything to happen to you. I love you so much, Mommy! Can we please go home and snuggle all day long? Can we watch cartoons like we did when I was a little kid, Mommy? Please?"

"Anything for my snookums!" Hester laughed.

Suddenly the feeling of wanting to simply snuggle and care for her mom was gone.

"You...that was you too?"

The woman nodded and laughed. "I thought that if hate didn't get you to rebel against it, making you want to snuggle with me would. Wow, we should have taken that pendant off you sooner. You're like a kite in the wind."

"I know." She slumped despondently.

"Oh, Kylara, don't get upset about it."

"But you tried all kinds of different emotions and I couldn't defend against them at all."

"But I'm your mom. Deep down, you must know I would never hurt you, so you must not register me as a threat. Plus, I'm not great at auras anyway. Heartsbane might be a better instructor. I bet she could make you fear for your life."

"Heartsbane's a Steel Guard, though. I have to go back to school." Kylara put the pendant on again but the heavy feeling in her chest didn't go away. "Maybe this is a power I can't absorb."

"You might simply need to practice. Isn't that how it was with your plant powers? Tanya had to help you, right?"

"I guess so..."

"Oh, hush. That is how it works. You did things with shadow that I've never seen you do before. For all we know, I might have activated your aura and now, you only need to work on it. It'll take time and a study partner. This...Sam seems to have a hold on your emotions."

"Mom! He's a friend."

Hester held her hands up in mock surrender. "Of course he is. I'm only saying that I believe in you and I'm sure your friends will help."

Kylara nodded. Her mom was probably right. She had practiced with all her powers, but time was one thing she felt she was short of. The being in the swamp seemed strong—far stronger than anything she'd felt before. Had it made her appear at the pond where it slept? If so, could it do it every night? And if not that, what had? She didn't know but she had a feeling her aura would be central to all of this.

Still, it was clear that her mother wouldn't be able to help. Hester Diamantine protected herself with diamond scales and grit. She would need someone else to help her. Fortunately, she'd go back to school soon. She could practice there with Tanya, if no one else. Or with Sam. That wasn't so bad, either.

But for now, it could wait. She tried to push thoughts of the pond from her mind. "I'll race you home. Winner cooks lunch."

"Winner? Don't you mean loser?" her mom asked and transformed into her dragon form, thus accepting the challenge.

"I know I can beat you and I don't want your black beans again. Loser does dishes."

They raced down the mountainside. By the time they reached the house, she could almost pretend she believed everything would be all right.

CHAPTER SIX

The week with her mom had been great. Although Kylara still had nightmares, she hadn't reappeared at the pond in the swamp. By the time she had to leave for school, she could almost tell herself it had all merely been another dream.

Still, it hadn't happened again so she felt like she had regained some measure of control. It was also easier to forget about the strange presence she'd felt with the reunion with her friends on the horizon. She hadn't seen any of them all summer and was beyond excited to reunite with her crew. They had all joked about how much they wanted boring summers after everything that happened with the wizard, but she hoped someone had something more exciting than a radio and wind and rain to talk about. Although she did want to brag about saving those evacuees.

These thoughts and a hundred others filled her head as she bid Hester farewell, transformed into her dragon body, and picked her clothes up in a talon.

"Remember to beat up anyone who looks at you funny," her mom said as she waved goodbye.

"I will not, mother," she responded jokingly and opened a

portal to take her through the pixie realm. For a brief second, she was terrified that this power might no longer be hers to control and might have been co-opted by whatever had made her wake up in that place, but the gate appeared as usual. She flew through a patch of pixie sky that was nowhere near the swamp and opened another gate that took her to the Lumos School.

Well, almost to the Lumos School. Kylara had no reason to think that the staff had slackened its defenses and she could still remember all too well what it felt like to port inside the magical barrier that enveloped the campus. She knew it was impossible for mages to use their teleportation spells to get in. Although she still could if she wished to, the pain the shield had caused had stuck with her.

Instead, she appeared outside the front gates of the school.

It was odd to see the front like this. From there, it looked like the most prestigious dragon and mage school in North America—and maybe the world—was protected by a flimsy chain-link fence topped with razor wire. Overgrown hedges and cactus grew on either side of the fence, blocking any view of the interior. The gate was the only part that wasn't completely overgrown, and it had a dilapidated sign on it proclaiming that there was severe danger of nuclear radiation on the other side. She found the threat of radiation poisoning a particularly deft touch. Either that or the old fence on its own might be enough to deter most people but together, it practically screamed *STAY AWAY*.

The only thing out of place was a beat-up truck parked on this side of the fence. A man sat in it and watched her approach with neutral attention.

"Name?" he asked. He wore a denim shirt that didn't quite cover the swirling tattoos that traced up his neck.

"Kylara Diamantine."

"Do you mind waiting for the next group?"

"Uh...sure?"

The mage nodded and leaned back in his unimpressive vehicle.

Barely five minutes later, a black Escalade pulled up and Tanya Fastwing stepped out.

"Oh. My. God. Ky!" her best friend gushed as she emerged from the vehicle and hugged her in an embrace so tight she had to use her dragon healing powers to mend her bruised ribs. "Ahh-hh!" she squealed. "What are you doing here?"

"Going to school?" she managed with the dregs of oxygen still in her lungs.

"In those jeans? Seriously?" Tanya—as usual—wore an elaborate dress that looked amazing even though the dragon had presumably been seated in the massive SUV for at least an hour. She hadn't reached for her signature matching parasol, but Kylara knew that was only because she had wanted both arms free to crush her properly.

"It's nice to see you too, Tanya."

"Did your mom dump you here or something?"

"No, I gated."

Tanya rolled her eyes as if this was to be expected. "God, of course you did. Still, there's no reason for you to walk in. Do you want a ride?"

"I'd love one." She climbed in and sat on leather seats that probably cost more than all the furniture in Diamantine's house.

The driver waved at the mage in the truck, who nodded and gestured at the fence. It opened of its own accord despite the hinges that looked like they were only one more rainstorm away from rusting through. The fence transformed and revealed its true nature.

Instead of chain-link and overgrown desert scrub, the border that protected the main entrance to the campus was a twenty-foot-tall stone wall. Every ten paces or so, the statue of a gargoyle leered at them. Kylara knew from personal experience that those statues did far more than look intimidating and that they were repeated around the entire campus. Also, they weren't limited to gargoyles but ran the gamut of mythical figures and beasts. Dragons, not being mythical, were absent, of course.

The gate itself was a thing of true beauty. All copper and iron, it was wrought into amazing patterns and designs that suggested that if any dragon tried to barrel through, they would leave quite an imprint on their face.

As they drove, Tanya regaled Kylara with tales of shopping, divine meals, and drama that belonged on a soap opera. Although it was a world she had never been a part of—and not one she particularly wanted to be a part of—she still loved every minute of Tanya catching her up with what she had been doing.

"But listen to me talk. What about you, Ky? How was your summer? I never thought I'd see anything go viral from the weather channel, but you saving those people was seriously legit. Was the rest of your summer that awesome?" Leave it to Tanya to explain what someone else had been doing.

"That was certainly the highlight. Other than that, it was radio operation and training all summer long."

Her friend grimaced as if she had told her she had endured torture.

The car stopped moving and the two girls climbed out into the U—the central green space nestled between the three main campus buildings. The driver asked Tanya something about her luggage and she sent him to take it to her room. He took Kylara's as well, which she thanked him for as he hurried away. Other cars stopped and students unloaded.

Most of them greeted classmates they hadn't seen over the summer but a fresh batch of first-years had the wide-eyed look of people out of their depth. Kylara smiled at the thought of how she had felt when she had first arrived. Overwhelmed would be putting it lightly. She was so thankful to have her friends. They made it feel like home.

"Did you see anyone over the summer?" Kylara asked Tanya.

"Yes, I did. Sam and I met up once or twice," the girl admitted.

Kylara didn't know why that made her stomach flutter but flutter it did. "How did that go?"

"We ended on good terms," her friend said, uncharacteristically succinct.

"Ended on good terms? Ended what?"

"I'll tell you later. There's Sam now."

Sure enough, the golden-haired, broad-shouldered boy who could make himself glow walked toward them and smiled his perfect smile. "Kylara!" He waved and hurried closer. "How was your summer?" he asked as he came to a stop, panting lightly until he used a pulse of dragon energy to stop himself from looking out of breath.

"It ended on good terms," Kylara said with a pointed look at Tanya.

Sam paled visibly but shook it off a moment later. "Tanya, greetings." He bowed formally.

Her roommate guffawed at that, which at least earned a smile from him. "Give me a hug, you dolt."

He did and hugged Kylara as well, squeezed her tightly, and gave her a pulse of light energy. It was merely something he did but it always felt great. She felt like she had just taken a quick nap.

"Have you seen Karl or Jasmine?" she asked him. He was a textbook goodie-goodie and helped first-year students with orientation, gave tours to visitors, and the whole extra mile. She assumed he had been on campus for a few days already.

"I saw Karl yesterday," he said with a shrug. "We dueled and I kicked his butt. Well, I would have but he has this new thing he does." Sam wrinkled his nose in annoyance. He evidently hadn't thought of a technique to thwart whatever new method of attack Karl had devised. Kylara made a note to learn both new things from both boys. "Anyway, I haven't seen him since Jasmine arrived this morning."

Tanya looked at Kylara and raised an eyebrow suggestively, but she scoffed. Karl and Jasmine were the two grumpiest people on the planet. "They're probably off complaining together somewhere."

Her companions laughed at that.

A second later, Karl appeared behind Sam and stepped out from his shadow. "Who was doing what where?"

Sam startled and cursed, which made the other boy laugh. "You jerk. Stop that." The golden dragon flared his light and the now too-dark shadow behind him puffed into nothingness.

"I thought you said you would find out how to beat it," Karl quipped. As usual, he wore all black—dark jeans, a black t-shirt, and long black hair that hung past his shoulders. Only his skin was light, so pale it looked like he might tan in Sam's presence.

"I'll work it out and you'll be sorry when I do."

"I don't think he will be." Jasmine approached wearing a mage's robe like she always did. Despite being one of the first mages to ever attend the Lumos School, Jasmine Patel was very traditional.

"What is that supposed to mean?" Tanya asked with another waggle of her eyebrows.

"Only that Karl's never sorry about anything," the other girl said a little too quickly.

Tanya darted a look at Kylara that could have killed a wild boar but she shook her head. Her roommate thought everything was a teen drama.

"I'd be sorry if I'd never met you," Karl said, which made Kylara stare at him.

Sam pretended to dry-heave. "Oh…gross…two goths being nice to each other. Yuck."

"Because we would have had our butts kicked a hundred times over. Jasmine saved us against that fat wizard," Karl said with scorn in his voice.

"I've helped you fight too. Would you be sorry if you never met me?" Tanya asked sweetly.

"Growing flowers is not the same thing at all." Midnight wrinkled his nose in disgust. "The same goes but double for you, Sir Flashlight. I've saved your glowing hide way more than you've saved mine."

"Only because I take hits while you skulk in the shadows. That's practically our strategy. Of course you'll have to fish me out now and then. I'd do the same for you if you ever joined the action."

Kylara smiled at the familiar teasing and jabs at each other. It was amazing that in a school setting, the five of them argued more than they did anything else, yet when push came to shove, they worked together like a well-oiled machine.

"Hey, hey, that's enough." She held her hands up to try to get the two boys to settle. "We all know I've saved all your butts far more than you've ever saved mine."

That brought laughs from Tanya and a fresh round of complaints from the other three. The five of them argued about whose powers were the best, who had trained the hardest, which one of them had the easiest summer, what they would have done when faced with a hurricane, and a dozen other things as they helped each other unpack and headed to dinner.

Kylara couldn't wipe the smile off her face the entire time. It was so pleasant to be back with her friends. She hoped the feeling would last but suspected that a normal year at the Lumos School was simply too much to ask for.

CHAPTER SEVEN

The first few weeks of school made Kylara appreciate her internship with the Steel Guard a little more. If she had not spent her entire summer working a radio, she might have found lectures on dragon history, the proper blend of ingredients needed for enchanting objects, and esoteric and seemingly useless mage and dragon abilities boring. Luckily for her, homework was a delightful change of pace.

"You are killing it this semester, Ky," Tanya complained. They were in their dorm room and the dragon mage had just finished an essay on the origins of pixies and dwarves, a subject she was now rather familiar with.

"Do you need help?" she asked. Her roommate's paper was on the origin of dragons, a much more arcane topic. It was well known that pixies and dwarves were made by mages to be used as weapons. The origin of dragons—and mages, for that matter— was steeped in myth.

"Ugh. No. I still have a week so it's fine. I wanted to write a paper about where dragons truly came from. Instead, it'll have to be an analysis of different legends." The girl sighed.

"Well, the origin of dragons is way older than pixies or dwarves, so that makes sense. But don't be too hard on yourself. If the world's best dragon and mage scholars don't have a definitive answer about where dragons come from, it's too much to ask a third-year student to have the answers. No offense," she finished lamely and hoped she hadn't come across as too judgmental.

Her roommate didn't take offense, though, and simply laughed. "I guess that's a good point. I hope our history professor sees it that way."

"I'm sure he will if you include references to a long list of dusty books."

"Oh, I have those." Tanya patted a stack of leather-bound volumes that looked like they hadn't seen the light of day for decades. At least they didn't smell bad and instead, filled the room with the pleasant aroma of old leather and dry paper.

"Did you find anything good in there?" Kylara asked as she crawled into bed.

"Unfortunately not. It's merely a collection of...what's the human expression? Cow turds?"

"Yeah, something like that. None of it makes sense?"

Her friend shrugged and slid into bed. "No, it doesn't—most of the time—but we're talking about the origin of fire-breathing beings who are almost invulnerable—and, oh yeah, we can transform our bodies. It's not exactly natural selection."

"What's the weirdest one?" she asked.

The young dragon plumped her pillow and turned the light off. "There's one about an old dragon named Tia-mat...Tio-mot. Something like that." Tanya yawned. "It's something about how she's a dragon of the deep or something. It's so dumb, though. Most dragons have fire breath and fly. What does the deep have to do with anything? You'd think if that was the case, dragons with water powers would be far more common." Another yawn punctuated the statement.

"That's all cow turds, though, right?" Kylara laughed nervously into the darkness.

Her friend was already asleep.

The wind blew so strongly that Kylara could not fly and the light was so bright she could not see. She struggled over ice that would not melt under her fire breath.

Boneclaw laughed and gestured for her to come closer. For some reason, he knelt at a throne on the beach and strangely muddy seawater lapped over his robes. Terror showed in his eyes before he bowed so low, the human skull he wore as a mask pushed into the filthy sand.

She woke with a start. Although school had been going well, the nightmares still came at least a few nights a week. She drew a deep breath and reached for the light switch but couldn't find it. Come to think of it, the air smelled all wrong too. She had fallen asleep to the smell of leather and old paper. Now, she smelled rotten vegetation, saccharine flowers, and the filth of creatures long decomposed into humus.

Startled, she sat in the darkness and felt moss under her hands, not sheets.

"No," she whispered. "No, no, no."

She was in the swamp again at the edge of the pond. Foreboding cypresses towered overhead. Vines hung from them to block out what little light there was from the few stars she could see in the sky.

But Kylara did not need to fear the dark. She ignited her body with light and drove the darkness back. It was immediately clear that was a mistake. Her light drove the darkness back, yes, but it also called attention to her.

The center of the pond began to bubble. The reaction was

small but the water was the only thing moving there and it terri-fied her.

Was it only the bubbles and the darkness that made her feel this way, though?

Instinctively, she clutched the amulet at her neck and realized that it was already warm and getting hotter. Was her terror self-generated or was it caused by whatever was deep within the pool? The name of the legend Tanya had said came to her mind, but she did not dare to speak it aloud. If this…this entity truly was sleeping down there, she thought it would be foolish to it address by name.

The sense of dread built and became increasingly stronger until she began to sweat profusely. The surface of the pond didn't change, the trees didn't move, and no skeletons unearthed them-selves, yet she felt terror in her chest. The amulet grew even hotter—so hot that she turned the part of her chest it touched to diamond and used the heat powers she'd absorbed from Ruby Firedrake to dissipate some of the heat.

She didn't need to be scared. It was merely a trick from what-ever was down there. The fear wasn't hers. It was this being's aura, that was all.

"I'm not scared of you!" she shouted and put as much force as she could behind the words. "Without your aura, you're nothing!"

They were bold words, especially since Kylara felt she was the one who was nothing, but she tried to push the sense of inade-quacy away. All she wanted was to fall to her knees and cry or curl in a ball and hug her knees to her chest but she would not. She had to resist this, exactly like her mom had taught her. Although she could not fight back with her aura, she had many other powers.

First, she turned her skin to diamond, then ignited every facet of crystal with light. Where before, a warm light had pushed the darkness back, a thousand facets of brilliant light now shattered the shadows. Any that were left were hers. She sent tendrils of darkness into the pools and made them her own. Anything that approached her would be snared like an insect in a spider's web.

The plants obeyed her as they always did. They extended their roots through the mud of the swamp, intertwined, and grew thicker to create a cage of roots that would keep any subterranean foe locked underground.

Above the swamp, the sky filled with clouds. Kylara called upon the wind to make the clouds spin above the pool. If the surface of the pond so much as burbled, she would call a tornado down and direct bolts of lightning to electrocute anything that broke the surface. She had that kind of power there in the pixie realm and would damn well use it against this entity plaguing her nightmares.

"Those pixies who have made you nap down there? I'm their big sister!" she declared loudly. Thunder cracked as she spoke and the wind blew so hard it knocked a tree into the water. She made it sink and grow new roots to choke whatever was hidden in the muck at the bottom of the pool.

The bubbling ceased and the swamp seemed to grow still—as if whatever was down there was retracting into itself. Kylara allowed herself a small smirk. This was her realm. She would not be intimidated there and certainly not by some dumb beast that pixies were able to control with lullabies.

A few seconds later, she felt a single pulse of energy come from deep in the earth.

It wasn't an attack, not even remotely so. It felt more like a heartbeat or someone standing straight.

Despite the seeming lack of aggression, it was terrifying.

It was as fast as an atomic bomb detonating or an asteroid hitting the earth. In that moment, Kylara realized that all her powers were nothing compared to what was down there. It was like she was a gentle breeze trying to move a mountain or a candle trying to evaporate the ocean. This being was epic, far beyond anything she had ever encountered before. The scale of it was almost incomprehensible. She had faced elementals who could use the forces of nature as easily as a human could use their fingers. Her powers had vanquished hordes of undead, revenant dragons who knew no pain. She had faced and defeated the power of multiple pixies condensed into one angry, bitter man.

This was far beyond all of that. To compare any of those to this was like comparing a human's power to that of a dragon, or worse. Humans could kill dragons with the right tools. She didn't believe there was anything she could do against whatever this was.

Worst of all, it felt like it was getting stronger—like it had taken hold of her presence there and now used it to become more solid and more real.

Kylara understood in that moment that there was nothing she could do against this force. Not there in this place it knew so intimately and certainly not by herself with nothing to defend herself with except the powers she'd absorbed from her friends.

She opened a portal and fled to her room without even a thought for the shields protecting the school.

Of course, she immediately slammed into those shields. They pinned her like a fly in amber, trapped between worlds and unable to move in either direction. The pain was excruciating and for a moment, she thought she was well and truly trapped.

Her brain, fortunately, began to function. She had somehow managed to portal out of the school into the pixie realm, so that meant she must have the ability to punch through the defenses and get in, right? Kylara strained and pushed her magic to its limits. Fortunately, she was flush with the energy she'd drawn in from the pixie realm, which gave her more than enough power to work with.

The dragon mage pushed with her will and felt something snap. Suddenly, she was through. She reappeared in her bed, her stomach tied in knots and threatening to vomit what was left from dinner. But compared to what she had sensed in the pond, she practically welcomed the pain.

As she held her stomach and tried to keep her last meal down, she looked around her room. It was as if she had never left. Tanya still slept, undisturbed by the disappearance of her roommate. The stack of books was still on her desk.

She sighed, not at all sure what to do next. Had her travel been noticed by campus security? She wasn't sure. Her instinct said it was good that Tanya hadn't woken up. She did not want to explain any of this to her—or to anyone for that matter. It would sound insane. How could they believe her if she told them that a hidden being beneath the pool in the pixie realm somehow communicated with her? It would sound insane.

Although if anyone would believe her, it would be her friends. They had faced her aunt—a mage with the ability to control elementals, an ability not seen in hundreds of years. With her, they had faced the skeleton of Boneclaw and a wizard who could use pixie powers as easily as humans used food to fuel themselves.

They might believe her—if she found the right way to tell them. And the pixies would likely know more about this threat.

Kylara clung to these thoughts as she lay in bed and waited for the dawn to come, too terrified to sleep in case she experienced more nightmares.

CHAPTER EIGHT

Sam Lumos was excited for his third year at the Lumos School primarily because of a new class. It was called Cross-Species Magical Inclusion and Theory, and despite the long name, was awesome. In it, dragons and mages were expected to form heterogeneous groups of four to six and work on ways in which their powers could augment or strengthen each other in various situations.

It was essentially custom-made for Sam, Kylara, Tanya, Jasmine, and Karl—although he only included the last one some-what begrudgingly.

Professor Sharra taught it and although he did not know her as well as the other four did, he respected her, exactly as he did all his professors. It also didn't hurt that the class was project-based. The professor would give them an assignment and the students had to find a way to solve the issue.

Their current challenge was to see how long they could keep a one-ton pallet of bricks elevated without touching it. Their team was leagues ahead of the other groups. Between Jasmine's telekinesis, Karl's webs of shadows, Tanya's plant growth, Sam's ability to heal and replenish other dragons' powers with his light powers, and Kylara having all those abilities, they'd already kept the pallet of bricks off the ground for twenty minutes. No one else had come anywhere close to that.

With them all able to take turns and relieve each other, he had time to think. He was currently on standby and the inactivity dragged his thoughts to the fact that he finally wanted to act on his crush on Kylara.

Not that he had any idea how to do that as there was so much between them. There was their history of fighting alongside one another, which he considered a plus. But then there was the fact that he'd trespassed on her mom's land—which he usually thought was negative but it was also a memory they shared, which seemed positive, so he mostly considered it neutral.

Unfortunately, he had to throw in all the stupid bickering he and Karl had resorted to last year when they both tried to woo her. That was a big negative and an extremely embarrassing one. Finally, there was the fact that he was from an ancient and fairly well-known dragon family and she was a mage.

Sam didn't want that to be an issue. He knew it should not be an issue and yet it was. He had grown up in a house where mages were considered inferior to dragons. His grandfather hadn't felt that way, but he had lived his life as an officer of SWAT and mostly kept his distance from his family. The young golden dragon didn't feel that way at all and yet those old, horrible prejudices hung over him. Although, if he never told Kylara how he felt, there was no reason to think she would ever have to meet his parents.

Plus, she could turn into a dragon. He hoped her unique abilities might help dragons who still clung to the old racist mindset break those barriers down. Mages could be more powerful than dragons. Period.

But did it make sense for him to try to start a relationship with her at all?

The thing was, he didn't know if he could forgive himself if he didn't say anything. Kylara was brave, smart, open-minded, and honestly, plain awesome. He couldn't help but like her.

"Uh, Lumos? Are you going to give me some strength or do you want me to drop this pile of bricks on your head?" Karl asked.

"Right, yeah. Sorry," Sam said and realized that he had been staring at Kylara while he'd thought about her. *So not cool.*

He put his hand on the other dragon's shoulder and infused him with healing energy. Even though he wasn't injured, he could still use the energy to fuel his dragon abilities—in this case, the web of darkness he used to support the bricks.

"All right, I'm good. You can go back to creeping." Karl winked to make it clear that he knew exactly why Sam had been staring.

"Shut up, shadow boy."

"Hey, man, no worries." Midnight shrugged, which had the unintended effect of sending a ripple through his shadow web that toppled the pile of bricks.

"Sam, you were supposed to give Karl more energy," Tanya protested.

"Yeah, Sam," Karl said.

"I did!"

"He's right, he did. The transition wasn't as smooth because he was distracted. Weren't you, golden boy?" The dark dragon smirked devilishly.

"Distracted by what?" Jasmine asked.

How he wished Kylara had asked that. Maybe, if she'd noticed him looking at her the way he had, she'd say something? It was not the most chivalrous way to start a relationship but he didn't know what else to do. As it was, she hardly seemed to notice him at all. She currently looked like she was half-asleep.

"Yeah, Sam, what's so distracting?" Karl pressed.

"Is there something in Kylara's teeth?" Tanya asked sweetly. Sam half-regretted going on dates with her at all this summer. He had thought he might have feelings for her after their battle with the wizard but after only a couple of times hanging out, they both knew that neither of their hearts was in it.

Which was truly a bummer because Sam and Tanya being a couple would have been easy. They were both dragons and both from fairly typical dragon families. His was more prestigious since they had light powers but Tanya's new plant abilities more than compensated for the difference. Unfortunately, he didn't feel that way about her and at least she didn't expect him to, which simplified things.

"My what?" Kylara straightened and wiped her face with her sleeve. It came away wet, which made her realize she'd been drooling. Sam wondered why he wasn't annoyed by that and instead, merely found it endearing…and a little concerning if he was honest with himself.

"Are you all right, Ky?" he asked.

"Yeah, fine. Why?" she said, leaned back a little, and rubbed her face.

"You seem a little…tired."

"Ky has nightmares," Tanya said matter of factly.

"That's none of your business!" the dragon mage snapped.

"It is too!" her roommate countered. "You wake me up every other night. Don't get me wrong. I have nightmares as well about half the crap we fought and I didn't go into that creepy void place with you and Boneclaw. I don't know, maybe you need someone cuddly to help you sleep. Someone with healing powers, maybe."

Sam reddened and tried to keep his aura calm and the color from his face before Kylara noticed. She didn't and simply chewed her lip and tried to wipe the sleepy expression from her face.

"I'd do anything at this point, honestly," she said. "Tanya, I didn't know you knew."

"We've all noticed," Jasmine said. "You've been a walking husk. Is there any way we can help?"

Is there any way I can help? Sam wanted to ask her but it did not all seem like the right time to make a move.

"I don't know. I think it might be my aura powers or something," she muttered.

"But you don't have aura powers," he said.

Kylara's look of annoyance almost broke his heart. "I think that's the problem. My pendant...I don't know. Maybe it's busted or something."

"Perhaps Professor Sharra can take a look at it?" he suggested, even though what he wanted to do was try to use his healing powers to help her sleep.

She nodded. "That's a good idea, Sam. Thanks. Do you all mind if I stay and talk to the professor after class?"

"Not at all," Jasmine said.

"I bet Sam can get your lunch for you and y'all can eat in the U," Tanya suggested. Sam didn't know if he wanted to throttle her or thank her. His head said thank but his gut said throttle.

"Yeah, that'd be cool." The dragon mage nodded. "Does everyone want to meet there?"

"I have...uh, other things to do," her roommate said.

"That reminds me, Karl, did you want to work on that... thing?" Jasmine asked. She sounded about as nervous as Sam felt. He looked at the two of them. Had the shadow boy made a move on her? Was there something there? The idea that he might have made him feel foolish. He was supposed to the charismatic one, and although the dragon mage was certainly intimidating, she was not as prickly as Jasmine Patel.

"Oh, yeah. I love that thing," Karl said. He made no effort to hide his grin or the excitement in his aura.

"Great. It'll only be you and me then," Sam said to Kylara.

She didn't seem to have heard him at all. Her attention was already on Professor Sharra, her aura as inscrutable as ever thanks to the pendant she wore.

CHAPTER NINE

"How can I help you, Miss Diamantine?" Professor Sharra asked from behind her desk and didn't look up from the ledger she was working on.

Kylara did not exactly know how to begin as she didn't want to tell the professor everything. She knew that much, but she didn't know what to say. It was possible that the woman knew something about dreams. Mage powers were far more diverse than dragon ones were, but even if she did, that wouldn't help. She thought she could deal with the nightmares. It was the gating to the pond and the entity in the deep that worried her.

She decided she should stick with what her mom had said, that maybe she needed help with her aura. "Do you know much about magical artifacts?" she asked.

"If you think I'll give you clues about the next project, you're out of luck, Kylara," the woman said and still didn't look up.

"No. I like the challenge of the projects, to be honest. It's a fun distraction."

"Distraction from what?" Professor Sharra looked at her for the first time.

Her indecision might make the woman suspicious, she realized. She wanted to answer honestly but she didn't think it was a good idea. Professor Sharra was in charge of field trips to the pixie realm for first- and second-year students. What if she said something that inadvertently resulted in a complete ban against being able to go to the pixie realm?

"I'm not absorbing powers like I used to," Kylara blurted.

Professor Sharra nodded. Thankfully, she appeared to have bought it.

"I wanted to talk to you about dragon auras, though."

"What do auras have to do with magical artifacts?" The woman put the ledgers aside.

In answer, she removed her pendant and put it on the desk in front of the professor. "I don't know if the headmaster told you about this. My grandfather made it for my mom. It—"

"Blocks dragon auras...yes." Professor Sharra picked up the silver-and-turquoise pendant and turned it carefully in her hands. "If your grandfather made this, he was quite a craftsman. It's both powerful and beautiful. I detect hardly any degradation. Do you know how old it is?"

"Uh...not exactly. I was told it was made when my mother and aunt were young. I'm sorry, degradation?" Kylara asked.

The woman nodded, pushed her hair back to reveal the sides of her head that were shaved into intricate geometric patterns, and switched into lecture mode. "Magical artifacts have a certain shelf life, even exquisite examples like this one. Eventually, they run out of juice. Although, from what I can tell of this one, it should have years left if not decades."

The girl nodded and tried to not chew her lip. "But it has become weaker?"

Professor Sharra shrugged. "I couldn't honestly say. There are tests we could do to see but they take time. But something tells me you're not here to talk to me about this amulet."

"No, ma'am. It's...well, it's like I said. I don't understand why I absorb some powers and not others. I'm especially concerned about dragon auras."

"Mages don't have auras and we get along fine," the professor pointed out.

"I know, but dragons treat me like a dragon and part of this is using an aura to communicate. I'm worried that if this pendant runs down or breaks or whatever, I'll be bulldozed the next time I try to talk to a dragon."

It was true although certainly not the whole truth. Kylara was far more concerned about the pendant burning to a crisp next to the cursed pond than she was about it running out of power in twenty years. "My mom thinks that maybe because I've always had this to protect me, I've never had to absorb aura powers. Do you think that makes sense?"

"That makes some sense to me but I'm a mage, not a dragon. I can't honestly say."

She nodded. "Do you think you can…augment this pendant so I can be sure it won't break?"

Professor Sharra smiled and shook her head. "I'm afraid not. The workmanship that went into this is far beyond my level. I was never very interested in fabrication."

Kylara slumped.

"But Ky, if it's your aura you're worried about, you should talk to a dragon. Maybe the Silver Bullet? He certainly throws his around enough—but no, he's too impatient, I would think, for emotional work like that."

"Can you think of someone else?"

"I could guess but I believe this is something you should bring to the headmaster. She'll know the best dragon to tutor you."

"Do you think she'd do that?" Kylara felt hope blossom in her chest. If Lady Amythist could set her up with a tutor, she could defend herself against the creepy being in the depths of the pond and not have to tell anyone about it. She would have to thank Sam for suggesting she talk to the professor.

"Of course. We all want you to be as strong as you can be. If you think you have a deficiency, we should investigate."

"Do you think you would mind…"

"Would you like me to go with you?" Professor Sharra asked.

"If you don't mind. I am still a little nervous after the decision to use the bracelet on me last year."

Professor Sharra bristled at that. As a mage, she had likely worn one for her entire life until the Steel Dragon had changed the relationship between dragons and mages—emancipated them, most mages would say. "I'm so sorry that happened to you. It was a disgusting overreach of power and shouldn't have been done. Even Amythist agrees with me on that now. But of course I'll come with you."

"Thank you, Professor."

They walked up the steps of the classroom and into the hallway of the building. It never ceased to amaze Kylara that a classroom that felt larger than the entire building could fit inside it, but magic was a strange thing. She doubted she would ever fully get used to the things it could accomplish.

They went outside and cut across the U to the main administrative building.

"Kylara, I have your lunch," Sam said as he jogged to catch up to them and adjusted his pace to theirs. "I didn't know if you wanted a salad or pasta so I got both. You can choose whichever you want."

"Oh, Sam." She shook some of the exhaustion from her head and tried to clear her thoughts. In her current exhaustion and stress, she'd forgotten all about meeting him for lunch. "I'm sorry. I need to go with Professor Sharra to see Amythist. Raincheck?"

Sam stopped with boxes of food in each hand. She looked at him over her shoulder. His grin had faded and his shoulders were hunched. It didn't take a dragon aura to tell that he was upset. But why? It was only lunch and it wasn't like he couldn't eat without her. Sam had acted weirdly since the school year had begun. She had intended to talk to him about it but between homework and fending nightmares off, she never seemed to have the time.

"Sure thing, Ky. Catch you later," he replied.

She tried to think of something she could say that would cheer him up but nothing came quickly enough to her tired mind. Instead, she flashed him the best smile she could muster and continued beside Professor Sharra.

They entered the main building and approached the office door. Her companion knocked sharply and they heard the clink of china.

"Come in!" the headmaster said. The woman pushed the door open to reveal Amythist Skyjewel. At a glance, one would never guess that the tiny, wrinkled old woman with a twinkle in her eyes was once one of the dragons mages had feared most in the world. That was a long time before, of course. In the centuries that followed, she had become a friend to all the magical races, especially the pixies.

Kylara respected the woman, although she was still wary around her. She had put a cuff on her the previous year as a precaution. Although she'd reluctantly agreed to it at the time, it seemed like the kind of thing only a dragon who had never had to wear one of the horrible objects would do.

"Greetings, headmaster," Professor Sharra said with a deep bow. Kylara wondered if the bow would have been so deep if the history between mages and dragons were different.

"Greetings professor," Lady Amythist said with a bow that was not nearly as deep. "And Kylara. What brings you to my office? It's a little early in the year to be stirring up trouble, yes? Please don't tell me you've already left campus."

She managed to not pale although she froze for a moment. The old dragon had guessed exactly right. How had she known? Did she somehow know that she had opened a gate in her sleep? But if she had, why hadn't she already sent for her? No, it must be a coincidence. If they'd known she had breached the school's anti-portal defenses, she felt certain she'd have been called in long before this.

"There has been no trouble at all," Professor Sharra said smoothly. "In fact, Kylara and her team are doing extremely well in my class—breaking the curve, as it were."

"Well, that's nice to hear. Tea?" Lady Amythist used her telekinesis to lift the teapot and pour it into a cup.

"Yes, please." Professor Sharra nodded.

"That would be great," Kylara said.

The headmaster smiled and poured three cups, mixed a little honey in each, and passed them on saucers without touching any of them the entire time. "Please sit. Now, if Kylara's not in trouble and doing great in class, what brings you to my office? I would think you'd want to avoid this room more than any other."

The girl couldn't stop a loud, awkward burst of laughter and she covered her mouth hastily in embarrassment.

"Well, I can see I was right about that," Amythist's eyes twinkled.

"Kylara is interested in learning how to use her dragon aura," the professor said.

The old dragon sipped her tea and regarded the girl with a curious expression. "I was under the impression that you don't have one, Miss Diamantine. The pendant has made you all but invisible to our emotional pushes."

"She is concerned that she would be at the mercy of dragons if her pendant was to break," Professor Sharra explained.

"It is a concern that many non-dragons have but I assure you, Lady Kristen Hall is working on legislation to address this very issue. I know it's not exactly a short-term solution but she is working on it." Amythist sipped her tea again.

"Dragons communicate with their auras, though—correct, headmaster?" Kylara asked and thought about her experiences with the hurricane.

"Yes, they do."

"I'm worried that since I can take the shape of a dragon, most dragons will try to use their auras on me and I won't be able to resist. But my inability to read or express myself via an aura also hinders my ability to communicate fully with dragons."

The headmaster nodded. "That is very forward-thinking, Miss Diamantine. But I don't know what to tell you. The simple truth is that you don't have an aura."

"I talked to my mom about it, and we think it might be because I've always worn the pendant. Most of my powers have manifested when I've had to defend myself. I've never been exposed to an aura before, so I haven't had to adapt to it."

"Ah...you need a tutor then." Amythist nodded in understanding.

"Yes, ma'am. My mom already tried to use her aura powers on me and it didn't go so well."

"You were at their mercy?" the old dragon prodded.

Kylara saw no point in hiding the truth. "Completely, ma'am. She could make me love her, hate her, and even fear her. It was awful."

Amythist clucked in understanding. "Hester Diamantine is many things but a master of her aura she is not. I'm not surprised that she couldn't do anything besides bulldoze your emotions. But that didn't activate anything for you?"

"No, ma'am. Not that we noticed."

"You probably need a more subtle touch then. It's a pity you didn't realize this deficiency when you interned at the Steel Guard. Heartsbane is one of the absolute best when it comes to auras. If anyone could make you...adapt, it would be her."

The young dragon mage nodded and tried to stay strong but the despair crept into her again. She couldn't very well leave school and go practice with Heartsbane. For all she knew, the only reason she didn't appear at the pond every night was because of the defenses around the Lumos School.

"Oh, sweetie, it'll be all right. I know a thing or two about auras as well. I'd be happy to train you. We can set up a time to work on it."

Kylara didn't know what to think about that. She wanted to trust Amythist but a voice screamed in the back of her mind that the dragon might force her to tell her about her nightmares and shackle her again.

"Would it be all right if you two practiced a little right now?" Professor Sharra asked. She made it sound casual and even sipped her tea after she said it, but she slid a subtle glance to the girl out of the corner of her eyes.

"That's quite all right with me, but do you honestly wish to spend your lunch watching two dragons try to 'feel at' each other?" Amythist smiled.

"I'd like to know more about auras, too," the woman said.

"Very well. Kylara, would you mind removing your pendant?"

Extremely thankful that Professor Sharra was there, she removed the amulet that had protected her since she was a baby.

"Oh, dear, Kylara—sweetie, you're an absolute wreck!" the old dragon said immediately.

She tried to keep a strong expression on her face but now that she knew Amythist could read her emotions, it was almost impossible. "I've been having nightmares—" She choked around the words. "Maybe because I'm around other dragons? I don't know but I want them to stop."

Amythist nodded. "It'll be all right. We'll find an answer to this. You tried with your mother, you said?"

Kylara nodded and wiped the brief waterfall of tears that had spilled from her eyes. "I couldn't do a thing against her."

"That's likely because she's your mother and you two have a deep emotional bond. You probably already knew what every-thing she made you feel felt like."

"I don't know…" She shook her head. "She made me hate her."

The headmaster chuckled softly. "Every child hates their

parents now and then, Ky. It is the way of things. Now, for this to work the way I think it will have to, I will have to force you into an emotional state so foreign to you that your mind won't have any choice but to rebel against it."

"That sounds painful," Professor Sharra interjected.

"It doesn't have to be but it very well might end up that way. It all depends on how you feel about me, Kylara."

The dragon mage grimaced but remained silent.

Amythist only smiled. "Oh, I can feel bitterness against me, distrust, fear—oh dear, Kylara. I can see why you brought the professor with you. You're terrified."

"Maybe this isn't such a good idea," she said and stretched across the desk for the pendant.

"No, this is good," the old dragon said reassuringly and placed her hand on top of hers. "If you have primarily negative feelings about me, much of our work will be spent trying to force you into a state where you like or even love me. What I will try to do is negate your current emotional state toward me."

"What is Kylara supposed to do?" Professor Sharra asked.

"Simply resist. Try to keep feeling the same toward me as you already do. Believe it or not, this is a trick regular humans can do as well. Dragon auras are not all-powerful. If a strong-willed person hates us, for example—let's say we took one of their family members from them or something—it is almost impossible to make them love us."

"But Professor Sharra said the pendant should last much longer." Suddenly, Kylara didn't want to do this. There had to be another way.

The professor put a hand on her shoulder. "Kylara, I know you're scared, but the headmaster just said that these auras often don't work on strong-willed people. You're the strongest-willed student I've ever met. You can do this."

"Your professor's right about that, child, and you need not worry about feeling any worse. I'll push you the other way. We'll try for a few minutes and see if that works, then you can practice with your roommate before we meet again. But remember that she'll have to make you hate her since you are very close. All right?"

"All right," she said to acknowledge that she understood, not that she was ready to begin.

But Amythist began all the same. Suddenly, Kylara's nervousness was gone. Why had she ever distrusted the headmaster? She had put a cuff on her to protect her. How had she not seen that sooner? This woman was an ally of pixies and she was known as the Big Pixie. They should be friends. In fact, she should come for tea more often.

"Oh dear," Amythist tutted and her feelings of trust and warmth for the headmaster evaporated as quickly as they came. "I fear this will be much trickier than I thought."

CHAPTER TEN

"We've been over this before, but we'll go over it again so we're clear that no one can claim they didn't know the rules."

"Yes, Professor Sharra," the third-year students answered in unison. They all stood in the U while they waited for the security mages to drop the shields around the Lumos School so the professor could open a gate to Austin, Texas.

"Hurting anyone—dragon, mage, pixie, and especially human—will be considered grounds for expulsion. Damaging property will be treated as a serious offense. You are all representatives of a world-class school and your behavior needs to reflect this. We usually go to the closest town. They are much more accustomed to dragon...antics. As we have decided to respect your vote to go to Texas, it means you will be held to an even higher standard. I don't want to hear anything but compliments about all of you. Are there any questions?"

"No, Professor Sharra," the class intoned.

"Remember that you are not to go anywhere by yourself. Stick with someone else at all times."

"Seriously, even in the bathrooms?" Karl Midnight protested, which drew laughter from the assembled students.

"The entire focus of this school is to teach you all to work together," Professor Sharra snapped. "If you think you need someone to hold your hand while you go tinkle, who am I to point out the absurdity of your question?"

A low "oooooh" rose from the students, which silenced him. Kylara couldn't help but chuckle at the reprimand. He had asked for it.

"Remember that I have placed an ink charm on each of your hands. This will identify you as my students to any mages we see, so remember that you are being watched. Furthermore, the charm will carry my voice. If I tell you to return to our rally point, that is not your conscience talking you out of doing something embarrassing, it is me giving you an order. If you get lost and don't know which way to go, simply step outside and look at the sky. Gold sparks mean 'come immediately.' Red sparks mean 'come even faster and be ready for trouble.' All right. If there's nothing else, let's go to visit the live music capital of the world."

The students cheered at this and used magic and dragon-enhanced vocal cords to turn the sound into a cacophony of excitement.

"Okay, okay," Professor Sharra said and gestured for them to settle as she spun her arms to open a gate. A rift appeared immediately in the air. Instead of more well-manicured grass, the students looked down a long street lined on either side with trendy restaurants and cute boutiques. At the end of the long street, across a river and nestled between skyscrapers still under construction, was the Capitol building constructed of pink granite. "We'll meet back here, Congress and Mary, at ten pm. If you get bored or want to come home early, we'll open another gate at three pm as well."

"The loser gate," Karl crowed.

"Mr. Midnight, do you want to attempt to be allowed to stay beyond three or should we simply go ahead and decide that you'll lead the way back to campus this afternoon?"

"I want to attempt to stay, ma'am," he mumbled.

"Very good," Professor Sharra said and although she looked down her nose at him, she didn't seem particularly upset with him either. She gave the impression that she had dealt with exactly this type of student many times in the past and was not about to get her feathers ruffled by yet another one.

The third-years chattered excitedly as they hurried through the portal. When it was Kylara's turn to step through, the professor placed a hand gently on her shoulder. "Do you have your pendant?"

She nodded. "Always."

"Very good. Have fun, Kylara, and if you need any tips, don't be afraid to ask. I hear Emo's new location is almost as kickass as the last one," she said with a friendly wink.

The young dragon mage thanked her and stepped through from the crisp autumn air of the high desert to the surprisingly sticky heat of central Texas in the fall. It had been a few weeks since she'd first talked to Lady Amythist and despite the headmaster saying her lessons were going well, she still used her amulet. She felt it against her chest now, a comforting presence hidden beneath her shirt.

"Where to first?" Tanya asked. "I've never been to Austin. Can you believe that? Everyone says it's the Frisco of Texas, but what does that even mean? Seriously, Texas is guns and brisket. That's about as anti-Frisco as anything."

"Brisket sounds good to me." Sam grinned.

"Well said, golden boy!" Karl agreed.

"I read on the Internet that there's a place called Franklin's that people queue up for," Jasmine said. "It's supposed to be good, I guess."

"I don't want to wait in line for meat on our one day off-campus." Tanya wrinkled her nose. "I want to go shopping!"

Jasmine nodded. "I hear the vintage clothing scene here is top-notch."

"Where did you hear that?" Karl asked.

"The Internet."

"Shall we split up? The boys can get us lunch while the girls go shopping," Tanya suggested.

"No need to be gendered," Sam said. "Even if they do have weird rules about bathrooms in Texas. Kylara, you're more than welcome to come with us." Sam beamed his perfect smile at her.

She was tempted to accept his offer but at the same time, she had a rare opportunity she didn't want to miss out on. "I don't know…shopping with someone besides only Tanya sounds fun. Jasmine, would you want to help me choose something besides ballroom gowns?"

"No problem."

"Why you two insist on dressing as food delivery workers is beyond me, but fine," Tanya said and rolled her eyes dramatically.

"Sweet. It means it's you and me, golden boy." Karl slapped Sam on the back.

"Sure. I guess I'll…uh, see you later, huh, Ky?"

"Yeah, that sounds good," she agreed, unsure why his gaze lingered on her. He and Karl had been getting along much better than they had the year before. Was he worried about the two of them being alone together? "You'll be fine," she joked. "If he gets handsy, blast him with light."

Midnight laughed. "Nothing past first base, dude, I promise. Come on, I hear they pass beers out in line and no one will card a couple of dragons." He transformed and took to the air. Sam cast Kylara one more glance before he took his dragon form and flew to the north after Karl.

Kylara followed her two friends down Congress. If she was honest with herself, she was not exactly excited. She had gone shopping with Tanya before and much of the experience seemed to be finding two or three of the most expensive articles of clothing, then debating which one was the most fashionable. Jasmine had a completely different style and between the three of them, it was a somewhat challenging process but they soon fell into a routine that worked.

They would enter a little vintage boutique and the mage would go directly to whatever was marked discounted and get to work. At first, Tanya was aghast, but after realizing by the third shop that nothing was new at all, she stopped giving Jasmine a hard time. The three shopped well together because their style was so different. Tanya looked exclusively for clothes that Kylara would call gaudy—elaborate ball gowns made of velvet and dusted with rhinestones or wedding dresses or anything of that type.

Jasmine focused on what could only be described as hippy dresses. The dragon mage decided that in a way, they were all robes—which mages often wore—except she had never seen a mage wear a robe printed with sunflowers and matched with a disco ball necklace.

She kept it practical. Her preference was for pants—jeans in particular—and t-shirts. It was exciting to know that buying a shirt in one of these stores would mean she wouldn't bump into someone wearing the same thing. That was one thing about trying to settle on your style in malls that she didn't like. What was the point of buying a shirt if fifty other people in the same town would have the identical one?

By the time they entered the fifth boutique, she had three pairs of jeans and enough shirts to last a lifetime, although some of them felt like their fabric was so thin they would only be able to be worn once before they disintegrated into nothing. She'd also bought a belt with scorpions stitched into the leather, plus a buckle shaped like a diamond.

That was when Tanya saw the boot store.

"Oh, my God. We can all have authentic Texas boots!" she screamed so loudly that some of the tourists across the street stopped eating their cupcakes to look at the three of them.

Kylara shrugged. "Why not? I could use a decent pair of boots."

Jasmine only nodded.

They walked inside and were immediately greeted with the pungent smell of leather and shoe polish and a boisterous, "Howdy," from a salesman with a ridiculous mustache who emerged from one of the many aisles of boots.

"We are looking for your most expensive boots, please," Tanya said to the salesmen.

"Sure thing, ma'am!" He grinned. "Are you looking for exotics or cow leather?"

"What's considered the finest?" she asked.

Jasmine pinched Kylara with her telekinesis. She obviously thought the other girl was being as ridiculous as she did.

"I'll get you a selection, ma'am." He removed his hat and winked at the three young women.

"If you could bring some of the…more basic models as well, that would be great, too," Jasmine said.

The salesman looked at Jasmine's flower dress, seemed to recognize something about it, and nodded. "Of course, ma'am. We have some real respectable leather boots I'll bring over. And we have a great sale this week, too. And for you, ma'am?" he said with a nod at Kylara.

"Something in the middle, I guess?"

"Sure thing. You three wait here or have a look around and I'll be right back."

"Don't you need our shoe sizes?" Tanya asked.

He looked at their feet, then at their face. "I reckon a five will do for the expensive boots. A six for the leather, and a ten for the in-between?"

"A ten?" Tanya gasped.

Kylara shrugged. "I have big feet. You know that. You helped me buy sneakers last year."

"Well, yeah, but I thought you wanted to wear them loose or something."

The man—Williams, his nametag said—retreated.

"Jasmine, if you want fancier boots, all you need to do is ask," Kylara told her. "My mom had money and doesn't like to spend it. I was able to get a fair amount for this weekend, though. Sixteen years of guilt for never letting me leave the house is finally paying off."

"Yeah, what's your deal? The Patels have more money than some dragons. Is everything all right?" Tanya asked.

The dragon mage blanched at the directness of the question, but Jasmine didn't look offended.

"We're fine, honestly. Great. Before the Steel Dragon's revolution, we had extremely lucrative contracts but all that changed. At first, my dad was furious. He started to call every mage he knew and tried to rally them against it and everything."

"It makes sense, I guess," Kylara said and bit her lip. People didn't like to lose what they thought they had earned.

"It did until he found out how much worse off most mages were than we had been under dragon rule. We were comparatively lucky. Most mages—" Jasmine shook her head. "I had some idea but my parents didn't. Once they understood…well, they've been slowly liquidating their fortune."

"Oh, my God! Does Karl know?" Tanya gasped.

"What is that supposed to mean?" Jasmine looked far more offended than when Tanya had asked her about her finances.

"Only that dragons tend to pay attention to fortunes and that if you want to make it work, the Midnights might protest."

"Wait, make what work?" Kylara asked.

Her roommate grinned.

Jasmine reddened.

Williams returned.

"Here we are, ladies." He broke into the conversation, seemingly oblivious to the tension.

"Python for the connoisseur, a blue leather for the lady with the diamond belt, and some nice black leather for the budget-conscious."

"Wait, python. That's a reptile, isn't it?"

"Yes, ma'am. A snake."

Tanya paled. "I would never wear reptile. That's too…" She shuddered.

"I have zebra," the man said. "That's a mammal grown on a farm out east of here, not poached."

"Yes, please. Much better, thank you."

Williams opened another box—he'd come prepared—and the three girls got down to the business of trying boots on.

Kylara loved hers immediately. The turquoise color of the dyed leather reminded her both of her pendant and the subtle shades of color in diamonds. The stitching was beautiful but not too garish. They were, in a word, perfect.

"These aren't exactly comfortable," Jasmine complained.

"They will be, ma'am. You only need to wear 'em every day for a week and they'll fit you like a glove."

The mage did not look eager to have gloves for shoes.

Tanya pulled hers on. The garish black-and-white footwear almost hurt the eye with the bold contrasting stripes. "Oh, my God. They're amazing!" she proclaimed.

"They'll loosen up and adjust to you as you wear them, so they'll become far more comfortable too."

"Oh, who cares?" she said. "Shoes aren't supposed to be comfortable. They're supposed to be divine and these are exactly that. Ring them all up, please. My treat."

"I'd rather not," Jasmine protested. "They're not exactly comfortable."

"I would be offended as a dragon if you said no. Besides, think of the look on Midnight's face. I can see him now." Tanya cleared her throat and prepared her best impression. "Those totally don't suck, Jasmine."

The mage snorted and Kylara laughed.

Five minutes later, they were back on the street in new clothes and fresh boots.

"It's late," Jasmine said. "Do you think the boys got through the line?"

As if in response, a dragon as dark as shadow and one shining like the golden sun appeared above the burgeoning skyscrapers of the downtown skyline.

"Let's go!" Kylara said, transformed into a dragon, and absorbed or displaced or whatever dragons did with clothes when they changed. She made a set of steps of shadow for Jasmine to climb. That earned about a hundred cellphone pictures from gawking tourists and locals in the ten seconds it took for the mage to get situated on her back. Moments later, they took to the skies.

"Do you have lunch?" Jasmine shouted to the boys, who nodded.

"Not Franklin's, though. Forget the line."

"You promised us brisket!" Kylara said, a fake pout to her voice.

"We got some. We flew a little too far and found this place called Smokin' Beauty. It's barbecue sandwiches with Vietnamese toppings. It looks rad." Sam grinned at her.

"Where are we eating?" she asked him.

"We have that covered too. There's this awesome swimming hole south of downtown. It's a spring-fed pool and is supposed to be cold."

"It sounds great to me," she said. She had heat powers after all. Cold meant little and less to her. Everyone agreed and they banked toward the chosen destination.

Somehow, lunch was even better than it looked or smelled. Kylara had never had Vietnamese food before, but it seemed fresh baguettes stuffed with lightly pickled carrots and cilantro was the name of the game. Traditionally, ham or pate rounded out the banh mi sandwich but at Smokin' Beauty, they used slow-smoked brisket or pork belly instead. With a side of fries smothered in more herbs, brisket, and black beans, it was the closest thing to perfection she had ever eaten.

Fed and with the afternoon still before them, the five descended on the frigid waters of Barton springs. Neither the few tourists nor the abundance of locals bothered to fawn over the dragons. It might have been because they had been coming to this spring-fed oasis as long as humans had. Or, perhaps, because it did not feel right to reach for a phone when one wore nothing but a bikini or a speedo. Then again, it might simply be that the people there were too baked in the sun to care about anything but the feel of the warmth of a pleasant autumn day.

Whatever the reason for the indifference, Kylara was thankful for it. They entered the grounds and approached the pool. She stuck a toe in and shivered. "Oh, my God. They weren't kidding about it being cold."

"Let's all go on three, all right?" Karl said with a big grin on his face. "One... Two... Three!"

Jasmine was the only one who jumped. She plunged into the frigid water, surfaced, and yelped at the temperature.

"You nerd!" Karl laughed. "Why did you jump in? I was trying to trick the other dorks."

"Is that right?" Sam said and gave him a shove toward the water. Midnight, though, responded with the familiar odd trick he used so often. Instead of Sam pushing him, his hands seemed to move through shadow and Karl was behind him.

"Smooth move, golden boy, but now you take the plunge." Before Karl could shove the larger boy, he was lifted into the air, levitated over the frigid waters, and dumped in unceremoniously.

"Jasmine?" he sputtered as he pushed to the surface. His long black hair hung wet in his face.

"Only dorks can't defend against mage attacks."

He grinned and tried to dunk her but was instead yanked

underwater by another tug of her telekinesis. "I let you do that," he said as he surfaced again.

"I don't know." Tanya regarded the water a little dubiously. "Karl's lips are already blue."

"We'll hold hands and all go together, all right?" Sam said and took Kylara's hand. It felt warm and strong. He grinned and winked as she met his gaze. Tanya took her other hand. The three of them stepped back a few feet so they could make a running leap and hopefully splash the other two who were canoodling in the cold water.

"All right, three…"

Sam held her hand tighter.

"Two…"

Tanya's grip loosened.

"One…"

The sidewalk in front of them bloomed with green algae growth.

"Go!" Sam pulled Kylara forward as her roommate slipped her hand free. Although she tried to snatch her and drag her in, her feet landed on the slick algae and her momentum carried her out over the water. She and Sam splashed in together.

The water was amazing—cold and crisp and clear. Her body implored her to use her heat ability against the cold but she held off and reveled in the sensation for a moment.

Sam's hand found hers again. "You're cold," he said.

She used her heat powers to warm his hand and his eyes widened as if he hadn't expected to feel something so pleasant and didn't want it to go away.

"Is that better?" she asked him, smiled coyly, and suddenly thought she was very foolish for wearing her pendant. She wanted to know what he felt and had a suspicion that being over-whelmed by his emotions at that moment would be an extremely pleasant experience.

"Oh yeah." Sam grinned. A second later, he was yanked underwater.

"One point Midnight! What-what!" Karl boasted as the golden dragon returned to the surface.

"You wanna go, shadow boy?" Sam grinned and swam after Karl, used his dragon strength to overpower the skinnier boy, get on his shoulders, and dunk him underwater.

"Are you going to get in?" Jasmine asked Tanya.

"In that stinky pond water? As if," the young dragon said. "The aquatic plants growing down there are already complaining quite loudly about the fish and…" She wrinkled her nose. "Crawfish that eat them. I'll be tanning if you need me."

Kylara launched tendrils of darkness and pulled her best friend in.

"Kylara!" Tanya shouted when she surfaced. "How dare you? Do you think that's funny? It's freezing!"

"Oh, whatever. You're fine. You're only mad that I can dunk you and you can't dunk me."

Her roommate smirked and suddenly, plants snatched at Kylara's feet and tried to pull her underwater.

The five of them swam and splashed and played for what felt like forever. By the time they finally pulled themselves out of the water, the sun was already touching the horizon.

"Where to next?" Tanya asked. "I wanted to explore the hill country for my parents. They are thinking about leaving California and have friends who moved out here. I wanted to see how awful it is. Does anyone care to join me?"

"Oh, yuck. Absolutely not. I saw a place that had fried chicken tacos," Karl countered. "Jasmine, do you want to get a bite and find a club with music that doesn't suck?"

"There's supposed to be a heavy metal mage band playing tonight." Jasmine snorted. "They're supposed to slay because they play their instruments with their mind while they mosh."

"I think I love this woman," Karl said. An extremely awkward moment followed. Jasmine's face turned a furious shade of red. Sam looked like he'd swallowed a fish. Tanya smirked mischievously, and Karl seemed even paler than usual. "I'm joking," he said.

Kylara laughed and broke the silence. "I don't know, Tanya. I think I might have to go for the live music over a real estate tour."

"Oh…uh, Kylara, I wondered if you'd want to go to this restaurant at the top of one of the buildings downtown. I read that the food is good and you can see the sunset or whatever. If you want to, that is. Or we could go to the show, I guess," Sam said.

"Ew, no. No nerds. You'd probably start glowing and ruin the show," Karl said.

"As great as it sounds to watch musicians who perform by beating their fans senseless while they pretend to play instruments with their minds, dinner over the city sounds way better," Kylara joked.

Sam looked all the more nervous at her answer. Odd. She had agreed to go with him. Shouldn't he be happy?

"Ugh, fine. You all go have fun being gross," Tanya said and transformed to take off.

"Wait, Tanya. We were told to stick with someone else, remember?" she reminded her roommate.

Tanya chuckled. "I think I can handle myself for a while. Go enjoy yourselves."

"Every group has a dragon. Will auras work over these distances to communicate if there's an emergency?" Jasmine asked.

"I'm sure everything will be fine," Karl said. "There's no need to be dramatic. Also, there are these things called cellphones. You've heard of them, haven't you?"

The mage glared at him. "We'll be at the metal show. If we can hear your ringtone it means the night is sucking."

"Yes, we should be able to signal each other," Tanya said. "Sam, you'll be in the middle, geographically speaking. You might need to relay between us."

"Sure," he agreed.

Jasmine nodded, appeased. Ky wasn't quite as sure. Wasn't breaking the rules by going off alone something she was expected to do? What was going on with Tanya? But her friend seemed fine—more amused than distraught. Maybe she'd ask her about it later.

"We'll meet at south Congress when it's time to go?" she asked the group.

"It sounds good to us," Karl said and took his dragon form. Jasmine levitated herself onto his back and snuggled in a little closer than was strictly necessary for an easy flight over the city, and they departed.

"Shall we?" Sam asked.

Kylara nodded, excited about a great meal to end an awesome day.

CHAPTER ELEVEN

If Kylara thought it was odd that Sam had already placed a to-go order and suggested that instead of eating at the restaurant, they go to a scenic overlook instead, she didn't show it.

"That sounds great, Sam. My mom and I used to picnic at sunset."

He didn't exactly want her to equate him with her mom right now, but he supposed a positive association was at least better than a negative one.

They flew from the skyscrapers of downtown Austin to a hill on the west side of town that overlooked the rivers. Tanya's silhouette could still barely be seen against the clouds glowing in reds, oranges, and purples. In a moment, though, she was gone and it was only the two of them gliding over the houses and trees below.

Sam thought back to the advice his dad had given him when he'd made the mistake of saying he might have a date tonight. "I met your mother on the wing, you know. Back in those days, we did things the dragon way. I know you kids think you're humans half the time, but what girl could resist it? It's in our blood."

He had not known how to explain that he would not dive-bomb Kylara, lock claws with her as they fell to earth, and attempt to conjoin in their dragon forms. Although the idea was…thrilling in a weird way. Maybe one day.

"Wow, it's so amazing how different the houses here look than they do in New Mexico," Kylara said and peered at the homes below. "Everything here is so big!"

The golden dragon swallowed hard and tried to focus on the moment. "This part of town is fairly wealthy, so the houses reflect that."

"Sure, but still, I love the architecture. Everything where I'm from either looks like it was built because of the desert or in spite of it." She laughed. Oh, how he loved the sound of her laugh, as hard as it could be to earn it.

"That's the place," he said and pointed to the top of the hill. The locals called it Mount Bonnell but a few semesters at the Lumos School—nestled as it was between mountains—had a way of making the mound of earth look less than imposing. Although, when seen from the other side, he could understand the moniker. The west side of Mount Bonnell was a cliff that looked over the river below and across rolling green hills. He could see why the locals liked it.

"Sam, it's beautiful," Kylara said and descended toward the structure at the top that had been built surprisingly close to the precipitous drop. He didn't know exactly what it was, but it was beautiful in a rustic kind of way. All the low walls were made of fieldstones pockmarked here and there with fossils and a pagoda covered it. Scrubby plants looked positively lush after their time in the desert, if still somewhat prickly.

They landed, transformed, and chose a point on the wall that was a good distance away from all the other couples. Sam had thought this would be a romantic location to take Kylara and finally make a move but now, it seemed painfully obvious what his intentions must be. Part of him wasn't sure if this was a good idea. He liked Kylara, there was no doubt about that, but this was not how dragons normally did things.

If he followed tradition, he'd graduate first and perhaps announce his attentions informally before they left school—but certainly during their final year, not their third—and enter a year of a formal engagement. At that point, the two would be seen together in public and their mages could work out the details of providing the couple with enough gold, treasure, and holdings to get them started.

But of course, all of that had always sounded painfully old-fashioned, dry, and plain unromantic to the young golden dragon. He had never looked forward to the courtship process of dragon high society and now that he had met Kylara, it seemed ridiculous.

It wasn't only that she was a mage. Sam tried so hard to disregard that outdated idea, but it still haunted him. It was that she was Kylara. She had grown up outside dragon society and didn't know the rules of courtship. Her mom had been a member of Dragon SWAT and—if the rumors could be believed—not a particularly kind one. She had seen last year's Homecoming Ball as a chance to sneak off campus to fight a wizard instead of as the social event of the year.

He loved all that about her, but how was he supposed to say it? There was no rulebook and no established protocol. He tried to base all this on human custom, but he had no idea if that was the right approach either. Despite her being a mage—there was that idea again—she had not grown up like a regular human. She had grown up on a ranch, sparring with her mom and hunting for her food. For all he knew, Hester Diamantine had taught her daughter that a boy was supposed to present her with a fresh kill if he wanted to court her.

"Sam, is there something wrong with the food?" Kylara asked.

"What? Oh, no, you don't like it?" Sam realized that he had been woolgathering. *Not a good start, Lumos.*

"I love it. I had no idea that pasta could be this good. The sauce is like cream or something? And the vegetables and seafood are great. You haven't eaten any, though."

He looked at his bowl of spaghetti, meatballs, and succulent mushrooms and asparagus. Pop culture seemed quite clear in this regard—the proper cultural cuisine for a human date was Italian and preferably pasta. "Right! Yes! The…uh, view is so good too."

Sam stuffed a forkful of spaghetti into his mouth. He had no idea if he was doing this right. The other couples on the hill all murmured quietly to each other as they ate. His keen dragon hearing could pick out snippets of their conversations, but none of them seemed especially…topical. Some spoke of the weather or what they'd done that day or traded snippets of gossip and he didn't understand the point of any of it.

He wanted to tell Kylara how he felt so she would know that he cared for her. More times than he could count, he told himself he didn't care if she didn't feel the same way. And he didn't. No matter what she said, he would still have her back. Them fighting for and alongside each other was more important than them being an item.

And yet, despite the truth of that, he wanted her to feel the same way. He wanted her hand to hold his the way Karl's had held Jasmine's and to feel her warm skin again. And he wanted to know if she could make her lips warm when she kissed, a thought that had intrigued him for what felt like forever.

Damn it, Lumos! He shoved another forkful of food in his mouth. If he was too dense to talk, he might as well eat. Kylara certainly was. While most of the other couples on the hilltop nibbled meekly at their food, she had already polished her bowl off and was currently wiping the alfredo sauce—she had never tasted alfredo sauce before and it was so cute he wanted to tease her for it—with what was left of the garlic bread.

Had that been a bad idea? The Internet seemed to think garlic was bad for the breath and yet it was a primary ingredient in Italian food. When they'd stopped at the restaurant and the server had asked them if they wanted fresh garlic bread with their meal, she had said yes. Was that some kind of an indication that she wasn't interested in him? Maybe she should have said no.

"Wow, that was great," she said and wiped her mouth with a napkin.

"Mhmmm," Sam said like an idiot, his mouth full of food.

"I guess I should have eaten more slowly and savored it," she said, sighed with pleasure, and gazed at the sunset. "My mom always treated food as fuel. She used to joke that she ate so fast she couldn't taste it half the time. I used to make fun of her for it but now, of course, I do the same thing." She sounded calm, happy, and at peace like she was having a great time.

Sam had to do this. He had to ask her out. Even her saying no would be better than him not knowing. She would say no and he could assure her that he'd still have her back in a fight, and they'd be fine.

Or she would say yes.

"I ordered dessert too," he said. "You like chocolate, right?"

"Who doesn't?" Kylara grinned.

He took the dessert out and opened the box. It was a chocolate cake cut into the shape of a heart and the icing was black and red and so delicate, it was almost like lace. Two strawberries rested on top with chocolate sauce drizzled on them.

"Oh, wow," she said and her eyes widened. Her gaze didn't linger there, however.

Instead, it drifted up to meet his. Her aura was as inscrutable as always but still, he could read her face as plain as day. This was it. The time was now. Her big, beautiful, dark-brown eyes were lightly hooded, her mouth slightly open, and her lips moist. He licked his lips. Her gaze flicked to his mouth but returned almost immediately to his. She didn't look grossed out or uncomfortable. Instead, she looked…eager.

"Kylara, I—"

Before he could say another word, a dragon lurched from the cliff and exhaled freezing cold breath that turned the air into ice around her.

CHAPTER TWELVE

Kylara didn't even have time to bring her hands up to protect her face before ice crystals froze around her, adhered to her skin, and grew on top of each other. One hand managed to reach her chest and the other still touched the container that held the cake.

The ice grew thicker. She struggled at first and cracked it, but the dragon continued to exhale and made it grow until it was impossible to do anything but shiver inside. The screams of the other couples—she realized in a surreal moment that everyone there was on a date—faded as the ice grew thicker and they ran down the hill to their cars parked below.

She was trapped inside the block of ice, completely immobile and able to hear nothing but her heartbeat or to feel nothing except the frigid ice all around her. The cold began to work into her chest and her heart to slow her and drain her of the warmth all living things needed to live.

The sunset was still visible—even more beautiful refracted through her prison—and she could see Sam. He was in the sky, a human no longer but a dream glowing with light as bright as the sun. She had been in enough fights with him to be able to tell that he was fighting another dragon above her, even if his movements did look bizarre as seen through the lens of the ice.

Kylara breathed deeply and pushed her panic aside. She knew it would not gain her anything. Besides, despite being completely immobilized, she was not powerless. She heated her skin until the water around her was almost boiling. An advantage of the heating power was that she was also impervious to being burned while she used it. She would not die from the boiling water although she might drown if she remained encased.

Her lungs burned but she willed her body to heat the water to even higher temperatures. The heat spread through the water and melted the ice little by little until the outer shell cracked and all the liquid water around her flowed out and left her in a kind of icy shell.

With space to move, she thrust a diamond fist forward in a punch powered by her dragon strength. The ice shattered outward in an explosion of crystals and boiling water droplets. Completely covered in scalding water, she was steaming.

She didn't know what fool of a dragon thought he could catch her in a block of ice but they were about to find out the hard way how egregious their mistake had been.

But when the steam cleared it wasn't bared fangs, claws, or more ice breath that faced her. Instead of attacking her, the dragon…bowed?

The thought seemed crazy but it was the only descriptor that fit the action. The dragon had long thin legs and claws like icicles that were stretched in supplication. Its snout was on the ground and its eyes closed, while its tail lay flat and its wings were open but folded earthward. The picture was more like an ostrich kneeling to protect its young than a creature ready to fight.

Sensing that this dragon was not a threat—or not immediately, anyway—Kylara turned her gaze to the sky, where Sam was battling another.

She frowned when she realized that one wasn't fighting any

more than this one was. It tried to avoid Sam, begged him to stop, and continually dodged the beams of light and glowing claws she had seen through the ice.

"Sam, I'm all right!" she shouted.

The golden dragon ceased his attack as soon as he heard her and flew closer to land at her side, but the other dragon was faster. Kylara summoned her shadow powers and readied herself to bind this new opponent when the inevitable attack came. She waited, tense and expectant, but nothing happened.

This dragon, its patterns the colors of a coral snake, landed next to the other and somehow bowed even deeper than the first.

"Are they…genuflecting?" Sam whispered to her out of the corner of his mouth.

"If it pleases Her Majesty, the Sum of All Dragons, then yes, we kneel," the dragon with the ice powers mumbled and made no effort to lift his gaze to look at her.

"What are you talking about?" Kylara demanded. She turned to Sam. "Do you know what the hell they're talking about?"

"No," He shook his head. "I've never heard of the…uh, Majestic Sum."

"The Sum of all Dragons!"

"Please, shut up and tell me what this is. First, you attack me and now, you bow to me? Is this some kind of a prank or something?"

"Did Midnight put you up to this?" Sam asked.

"Lord Midnight knows not of our gift today. His son has already honored her Majesty, yes? You were about to use them on Pakkenen, yes?" Both dragons had odd accents. They seemed to be from the same place, though—somewhere in northern Europe judging by the accent, maybe? Pakkenen was the name of the icy one, they assumed.

"Okay…tell me why you did that," Kylara said when she realized she had told the dragons to both shut up and explain, which possibly created confusion. "You're not hostile, so why attack me?"

"We understood that you did not have the cold power, yes?" Pakkenen asked.

"No. I don't have ice powers," she admitted cautiously.

"Pakkenen thought he would give them to you. He would give you the ice powers and bring honor to himself. I have no powers —forgive me, I am your humble servant Hammas—but I wished to aid Pakkenen in this. I could not earn honor for myself, but I believe in the Sleeper in the Deep as firmly as any. It honors me to be in the presence of she who will herald her return."

"She who will herald her return? You're not making any sense," Sam said.

Kylara clenched her jaw. These two were talking about her. It was she who had been blasted with ice, after all, not Sam. It was somewhat annoying that he constantly interjected.

"So you blasted me with ice because you wished to give me ice powers?" Kylara asked to confirm what she'd heard.

Pakkenen and Hammas both nodded and pressed themselves even more firmly into the dirt at the top of Mount Bonnell. "We will help bring back the first dragon."

"We are loyal believers."

"We would follow her into the deepest depths."

The two dragons spoke over each other in their eagerness

"Follow who?" Kylara asked.

The two dragons shared a look and something besides awe or supplication appeared on their faces for the first time. It was Pakkenen who spoke first. "Tiamat, of course."

"Wait, like in the myth?" she demanded. "She's the...uh..." She snapped her fingers to try to remember. "The dragon in the deep, right?"

"Her Majesty knows her legends well," Hammas responded approvingly.

"Although she is no myth," Pakkenen added.

"Tiamat is real—as real as any dragon. If she was not real, how could we be?"

"It is she whose sacrifice gave life to the first dragons."

"But the myths all say that she died," Sam said quickly and emphasized the word "myth" like a weapon. "She was slain and her blood spilled magic into the cosmos or whatever, right? But that's all nonsense. Humans have practically disproven all of it."

"Her blood was spilled but she was not slain." Pakkenen practically spat the words and ice crystals formed on the ground around him despite the warm, humid air.

"Tiamat cannot be slain. She can never be slain," Hammas added, as furious as his ally at Sam's apparent blasphemy.

"But her blood was spilled?" Kylara asked.

Both dragons nodded energetically.

"You can get up, by the way," she said.

They shared a look and both seemed as if they were about to cry. "You honor us, Your Majesty!"

"Deeply and truly and profoundly, you honor us!"

She motioned for them to hurry and get on their feet as they blabbered on. "Great, yeah, you're welcome. Now, tell me who Tiamat is and why she made you blast me with ice."

"Yeah, did she send you a text, or what?" Sam raised an eyebrow.

"Tiamat sleeps," Hammas said as if this fact were plain as day.

"Okay, but…who is Tiamat?" she asked impatiently.

"Tiamat is the first dragon," Pakkenen explained eagerly. "A goddess of enormous magical power."

"She was magic," Hammas added. "Her sacrifice is magic."

"She battled a usurper who was jealous of her power and was wounded. Her blood was spilled and it stained our world with magic. A drop of her blood made the first dragon and a speck made the first mage."

"Her wounds were grievous." He looked down as if Tiamat

had been injured only recently and he still missed her. "But she could not be killed."

"She can never be killed!"

"But she had to sleep and rest."

"One day, she will return," Pakkenen said firmly. "But before she can, the prophecies say that a dragon will arise who has the powers of all dragons."

"The Sum of all Dragons!" Hammas looked hungrily at Kylara.

"And you think that's me?" She was stunned. This was all completely crazy. The only explanation she could think of was that they had heard about her on the news or whatever and jumped to conclusions.

Sam laughed. "You guys have it all wrong, though. Kylara can't be your 'Sum of all Dragons' or whatever. She's not a dragon, she's a mage. She can't even read auras. She only has one because of her pendant."

That pissed Kylara off. She didn't like being told what she was, not even by a friend. "I am not inferior because I was born a mage and not a dragon, Sam. I've beat you in enough duels that you should know that by now."

"Ky, I know. I'm only saying—"

"I want to be known for who I am, not some half-baked societal crap."

"And I agree, but—"

"This is the problem with dragons. This is still the problem with dragons. You think that everyone who's not one of you isn't as strong. Even with mages like Amy Williams, or Mort, or Jasmine, you still act like mages aren't worth your time."

"Kylara, I'm only saying that these two cultists don't know what they're talking about."

"The first dragon was made by Tiamat herself," Hammas interrupted eagerly. "There could not have been a dragon before then. Exactly like you, they became one!"

"Lady Kylara Diamantine is much more than merely a human

mage. She is also a dragon and some say she even has a little pixie in her. She is one of the most magical creatures in the world. A true wonder!" Pakennen already spoke as if she was one of them and Sam was the one who had arrived uninvited instead of them.

"We believe that in time, you could become the Sum of All Dragons," Hammas said and bowed again. "You will complete the prophecy. It is our honor to help you on that road so the Sleeper in the Deep will awaken."

They both bowed and took a step back as if her holy radiance had grown brighter since they had begun to speak to her. She supposed that—in their eyes, anyway—it had.

"If you think I'm coming with you, you're insane," Kylara told them.

"We would not ask such things of you, mistress," Hammas said quickly.

"We do not speak for Tiamat. No one speaks for Tiamat. We only wished to help you become what you are to be."

The two dragons bowed again before they took to the skies and flew away, leaving her even more confused than when Sam had shown her dessert.

CHAPTER THIRTEEN

Sam and Kylara flew toward the exit point where Professor Sharra would meet them. They had a few hours before they were supposed to leave but neither of them thought it was a good idea to spend any more time out and about. Not with what might be an entire cult interested in Kylara. He had already used his aura to contact both Tanya and Karl. When he had pulsed danger, both dragons had responded immediately with a feeling of support. He had said that meant they were on their way.

Tanya caught up to them first. "What the hell happened? Is everyone all right?"

"We're fine," Kylara said.

The other girl darted a look at Sam, but he looked wilted. Aside from anything else that had happened to ruin his moment, he felt bad that he had put Kylara down for being a mage.

"What happened?" Tanya demanded.

"Some dragons…introduced themselves to us," the dragon mage said. "I'll explain everything to Professor Sharra. I don't want to go over it now, then again for Karl and a third time for her."

Her friend nodded. "All right, but if you think I'll leave your side until you tell me what the hell is going on, you're insane."

"Oh, not to worry. Our evening was already over," Sam said despondently.

Kylara did not have time to get into whatever he had planned.

Karl and Jasmine met them a few minutes later. He looked more annoyed than Tanya had, but he and Jasmine wanted to know what was wrong as well.

"I'll explain everything," Kylara said and pointed to Professor Sharra, who had already returned to the rendezvous point as well. She looked like she had enjoyed herself. Her hair was a mess, she was drenched in sweat, and she smelled faintly of cheap beer.

"Kylara, is everything all right?" she asked. She must have used a gate to get there and she was still breathless.

"Yes…I mean, I think so? I'm sorry, Professor, it looks like you were having a good time."

"Please tell me why Jasmine sent me a message that pulled me out of the show." The woman smiled but her eyes were daggers.

"Two Followers of Tiamat found Sam and me. One of them blasted me with ice."

"Are you all right?" her entire demeanor changed and she almost snapped to attention.

"I'm fine. I melted the ice and they didn't attack after that. They said they wanted to make me the 'Sum of all Dragons' or something. I'm sorry. I'm overreacting, aren't I?"

"No, Ky, not at all." Professor Sharra pointed to the air and launched a blast of golden sparks. "You did the right thing coming to me. I'm simply glad you're all right." She touched the inked spell on the back of her hand and suddenly, Kylara heard the professor's voice inside her head.

All students, return to where we arrived on South Congress for immediate extraction. You have five minutes or you will not join us on our next trip. I repeat, all students, return within five minutes.

Karl, Tanya, and Sam glanced at each other and shared an

uncomfortable look. Kylara had no doubt that they could already feel the disappointment, outrage, and dashed hopes of the other dragons' auras.

She didn't have time to see any of the returning dragons, however. Professor Sharra had already opened a portal to the Lumos School. "Lady Amythist will want to hear about this tonight, I would think," the woman said, her gaze fixed on the skies in search of the other students. "Quickly now. Get through and wait for me in the U. Mages should be there to meet you. They're in charge until the headmaster shows up. You five be ready to fight, okay? The shields around the Lumos School will be down until we get all the students back on campus. This could be one part of a multi-pronged attack."

The young dragon mage blinked in astonishment. She hadn't thought of that.

"Go now." Professor Sharra waved them through impatiently.

"Come on, Kylara," Tanya said and caught her by the wrist as if she were nothing but a child trying to linger at the zoo. She let herself be led through the portal. A second later, she stepped from the bustling evening of a trendy part of a trendy city into the abandoned center of the U. A security mage was there and looked surprised that the portal had opened and even more surprised that students stepped through it.

"Is anyone hurt?" he asked.

"No," she said, "we're fine. But Professor Sharra said that we should expect an attack until the portal closes."

The mage nodded and pointed up. Kylara noticed the remnants of sparks up above and Kor's silver scales—which earned him the moniker the Silver Bullet—gleamed in the last vestiges of the setting sun. No doubt other mages were already taking positions on the rooftops.

"I'll get airborne and help keep an eye out. Y'all stay close to Kylara," Sam said and before anyone could argue, transformed to his golden dragon and took to the sky.

"Is he all right?" Jasmine asked. "He seems—"

"He'll be fine," Tanya cut in. "You two didn't look exactly thrilled about being called away from your concert. Now imagine that feeling but you were doing something romantic."

Kylara blushed at the truth of that, but before she could protest or defend herself, Karl spoke.

"Cult of Tiamat, huh? They finally found you?"

She nodded when she remembered what the two dragons had said. Hadn't they mentioned Karl's dad, Lord Midnight?

"You know about them?" Kylara asked.

"Yeah, you could say that," he said, but he shook his head in annoyance, not agreement. "We're specials, after all, with shadow powers to boot. The Followers don't fail to notice that kind of thing."

"I thought they were called the Followers of Tiamat," Jasmine put in respectfully.

He snorted. "They are. Officially, that's the name, but they're a cult, for sure. They worship a long-dead dragon and are waiting for the rise of a prophet or whatever. The thing is, they've predicted a number of prophets over the years and guess what, not one of them has ever been this—"

"Sum of all Dragons?" Tanya asked and glanced at her roommate.

"And they think Kylara is?" Jasmine was incredulous.

Karl shrugged. "The power absorption thing is weird, you have to admit. When my dad found out that you took my power, he was furious, but once I told him that you had taken powers from other dragons too, he was proud. And he is not a man who enjoys being kind." He snorted again and shook his head at a bad memory. "He asks about you sometimes, especially after that whole pixie mess."

"These two dragons knew I had pixie magic," Kylara blurted.

His pale face reddened. "Dang. Sorry. That might've been me."

"Are there many of these…uh, Followers?" she asked, not sure which noun to use.

"I don't know, honestly," he said. "It's not the kind of thing my dad talks about openly."

"There are not many of them!" Tanya said firmly. "My family would never be caught dead with them."

He shrugged and looked like he didn't want to answer that.

"What?" Kylara asked.

"It's only…" He grimaced. "Well, it's a group for special dragons. I'm not surprised that a family of vanillas wouldn't be a part of them. No offense, Tanya. I honestly think you're a better person than my dad, seriously."

The girl nodded, not sure what to do with that.

"All right, everyone back to their rooms!" Professor Sharra shouted the second she stepped through the portal. "No argument and no dawdling! Not you four," she said and caught the friends by their collars in her telekinetic grip. "Where's Lumos?"

Kylara pointed up to Sam who was already coming in to land. The shield was back up, a thin blue shimmer hardly perceptible against the deepening color of the night sky.

"Very good," the professor said. "You five did well."

"You're proud that we stepped through a portal and stayed put?" Tanya asked sarcastically.

"Compared to your antics over the last few years, this is a huge improvement," the woman quipped, then pushed them in the direction of the headmaster's office.

They found Lady Amythist in a nightgown that covered her from chin to toe. There were already five cups of tea on the table in front of her. A sixth was clasped in her hand, her pinkie out. An inscrutable expression had settled on her face. "Thank you, Professor. I'll take it from here."

"Yes headmaster," Professor Sharra said and seemed to notice that she still smelled of beer for the first time. She left quickly and when the door clicked shut behind her, it sounded louder than any other time Kylara had heard it.

"Now, tell me what happened. Start with any collateral damage if you'd be so kind," Lady Amythist sipped her tea.

"There was no damage, ma'am," Sam said.

Tanya elbowed him in the ribs. "Let Kylara tell it."

She agreed with the sentiment until the headmaster's gaze fell squarely on her.

The young dragon mage told the headmaster everything that had happened and tried to not leave out any details about what the two dragons had said, done, or looked like. As she recounted the night's event, the expression on Amythist's face grew more and more troubled. When she finished, the headmaster's eyes were wide and her teacup still full. She'd stopped sipping at some point, which was a bad sign.

"I'm sorry, but there's still much I don't know," she said when she saw the old dragon's expression. "Who exactly are these people? It was a weird encounter, but giving me powers isn't exactly a bad thing." Kylara had discovered that she did have a new power inside her and while she doubted she could do much with it yet, the ability to make ice instead of fire breath was now hers.

"I'm surprised Mr. Midnight hasn't told you something about them," Lady Amythist commented.

"I told her they suck," Karl interjected.

That put a small smile on the headmaster's face, although it faded as quickly as it had arrived. "I agree with the sentiment but there is more to it than that, of course. They are fanatics, prone to interpreting events as 'signs' of the prophecies."

"What exactly is in this prophecy?" Kylara asked.

Amythist shook her head and looked irked. "There is nothing specific about any of it. Most dragons don't believe in the Tiamat legend. These do, however, and they believe she will return. They've chosen a few dragons over the years—and a mage once before, surprisingly—to be this Sum of All Dragons. Not all of them have survived the attempts of the cult to…strengthen them, for want of a better word. It's quite a relief that you are back on campus."

"And there are many of these Followers of Tiamat?" Jasmine asked.

The old dragon shrugged uncomfortably. "No one knows, to be honest. Publicly, the Followers of Tiamat are mostly laughed at and dismissed by dragon culture. There are exceptions, of course." She glanced at Karl. "But by and large, neither their specific beliefs nor their general belief in the existence of Tiamat is accepted by dragons. However, dragons are secretive creatures. There is no telling how many Followers are out there."

"Far more than you'd think," Karl said darkly. "Some of them recruit, too—dragons with odd powers, especially. Their powers are considered to be tiny parts of Tiamat."

"But who is Tiamat?" Kylara asked.

"She is not a who so much as a what," Amythist began slowly. "As I said, there is no real evidence of her existence outside dragon and human legends, but then there is no real existence of dragons in the fossil record of this planet either, yet we had to come from somewhere."

"And these cultists think we all came from Tiamat?"

"Indeed." The headmaster nodded. "But don't let them hear you call them that. They believe she will return one day and bring a 'flood' or a 'deluge' with her. Those who study these kinds of things debate what exactly that means, but almost everyone—except the Followers of Tiamat of course—believes it to be a very bad thing. In human legends, Tiamat is a monster whose defeat allowed humans to flourish. In dragon legend, her return signals the end of the human era and the restoration of dragons' rightful place in the world. Honestly, with everything Kristen Hall has done recently, I'm surprised we haven't heard from them sooner."

"But doesn't the Steel Dragon's new government protect people better than dragon laws did?" Tanya asked incredulously.

"You don't understand these people," Karl explained. "They

see dragons losing power as a precedent for her return. The only way they can be given their rightful place again is if they were to lose it."

"So they predicted the Steel Dragon's revolution?" Jasmine asked.

"Are you seriously asking if a cult's beliefs are internally consistent?" He laughed. "They didn't predict crap. They never do. It's all nonsense, I'm telling you."

"It very well may be, but that doesn't change the fact that they are out there," Amythist said shrewdly. "We will need to be very cautious going forward. Field trips will have to be canceled. We can't risk taking the shields down now that they've shown an interest in one of our students."

"It's not that bad though, is it?" Sam said good-naturedly. "If all they want to do is give Kylara more powers, that's a good thing, right? She will be the first student in school history to learn things on a field trip."

The old dragon shook her head and her expression wiped the forced smile off Sam's face. "I don't know much about their beliefs, but I know that the people they've chosen in the past to be this Sum of all Dragons were never meant to be conflated with Tiamat herself. The Sum of all Dragons is supposed to be a precursor for something greater. I for one don't intend to let them push their ideas any further than they already have. And what exactly do you think the point of field trips is if not to learn, young man?"

He turned crimson while the rest of them nodded.

"So what do we do, Headmaster?" Kylara asked.

"For now, you all go straight to bed. Kylara, we'll begin training your aura skills in earnest in the morning. It simply would not do for something to happen to your pendant and for you to be caught unawares. Now, finish your tea and off to bed with all of you!"

CHAPTER FOURTEEN

Kishar watched Hammas and Pakennen return to the temple. Their auras brimmed with pride and satisfaction and made their actions clear. Still, she was not one to jump to rash actions. She would let the two Followers land and explain themselves. Only then would she pass her judgment with the powers Tiamat had given her ancestors so many millennia before.

Despite her having no more of a direct relationship to the slumbering goddess than any other dragon, the Followers treated her reverently. Her parents—long may they rest with the Sleeper—had named her Kishar after an earth goddess of legend, a daughter of Tiamat, in fact. A lifetime of devotion had all but cemented her as the leader of the Followers. She was sometimes called She Who Walked First in the Path of Tiamat.

"Where is the First Walker?" Pakennen said and rushed his bow in his excitement. "I have done it."

She wore a hooded robe, of course, as all Followers did when they spent time in the temple. It served the movement better if one could not identify every other member. Her face was known, of course. One could not be the First Walker and remain anonymous, but few knew how deeply invested she was.

"It has begun! Pakennen gifted his powers to the Diamantine girl. She is one step closer to becoming the Sum of All Dragons."

Kishar did not fail to notice that Hammas had not bowed at all. Even though he didn't know who he disrespected, he was still supposed to bow to whoever was serving their duty at the temple. Such arrogance could not be allowed, of course, but she would give them their moment. Fools tended to tell more truth than lies when they thought they were behaving well instead of poorly.

"How did you give her your ice breath, Pakennen?" Kishar asked.

Hammas' confidence didn't slip an inch. "She did not expect it at all. She was dining, unaware, and Pakennen surprised her and completely enveloped her in ice. I do not see how she could not see it as a lethal attack."

"You believe the rumors, then, that she must be truly tested if she is to take her place as the Sum of all Dragons?" she asked.

"I do not doubt Lord Midnight's intelligence if that is what you mean." Hammas sneered.

She wanted to slap the grin off his face right then and there. It was forbidden to speak the names of other Followers, even if it was an open secret that Lord Midnight was almost as prominent a member of the Followers of Tiamat as she was.

"You are certain she has ice powers, then?" Kishar asked, still hidden by her robe.

"I am." Pakennen bowed. "We spoke and while we did, I tried to freeze the ground around her but nothing happened. She has the power."

"Interesting." She nodded.

"Interesting?" Hammas snorted. "Pakennen and I have brought the girl one step closer to becoming the Sum of All Dragons. We are the first Followers of Tiamat to do so. Tiamat will honor us and laud us when she returns. We will be rewarded as true Followers."

Kishar had heard quite enough. She pulled her hood back to reveal her identity to the two brash idiots.

Pakennen recognized her and paled immediately. Even Hammas, as dense as he was, could not fail to know who she was.

She was beautiful. On this, everyone agreed. She had full, dark hair that tumbled past a perfect neck and shoulders. Her skin was brown and as rich as chocolate. The single golden ring in her nose was the only thing about her that was not perfection, and the asymmetry of it only added to her beauty.

Beneath her robe, she wore an orange saree embroidered with gold thread around the edges and the under-blouse had a plunging neckline. A long piece of fabric hung from one arm. Her other hand rose to point accusingly at the two dragons. "Do not think to know the heart of Tiamat. If I, the First Walker, cannot interpret her messages, there is no way that you two could possibly comprehend her wishes."

"First Walker!" Pakennen bowed furiously and began to take his human form as a swirling cloud of snow and ice emerged to eclipse his body while he shifted.

"Remain as dragons, you cowards!" she snapped and took her dragon form.

Kishar was no less beautiful in her dragon form. Her scales were a deep bronze and her features graceful. Kings—both dragon and human—had begged her for her hand, but she had always been devoted to another.

"We asked for you," Pakennen said. "When we arrived, we asked for you."

"You did, Pakennen, but Hammas showed no honor to the watcher and for that, he must be punished."

"No, Lady Kishar, please—" He screamed in pain as she blasted him with her breath.

It was not fire that engulfed Hammas but a cloud of dark smoke that wreathed around him like a hungry fog. The hapless dragon screamed until he could scream no more.

The mist cleared and in his place was a black statue of a dragon wrought in perfect detail. It even captured the expression of fear and pain he had worn during his final moment.

"Your ladyship—" Pekannen gasped.

"Do not worry. He is not dead, merely frozen in stone. As long as no one breaks him, he will stand here in the temple until Tiamat awakens."

"But your ladyship…the signs are already here."

"You make a fair point," she said and walked past the petrified Hammas. She flicked her tail as she passed him and struck the glass-like statue with the glassy tip of her tail. Fractures spread across the surface of the statue before it shattered into a thousand pieces.

Pekannen gasped in terror.

"Oh, hush, Pekannen. He was a vanilla and a braggart besides."

"He was proud of the work we—he—was doing for Tiamat," he stammered.

"Following Tiamat is something that all dragons should do. It is nothing to brag about. It is the way things should be."

"Yes, your ladyship First Walker. You honor me with your knowledge. I am nothing—"

"Shut up, Pekannen. You'd be gone too if I wished it. Are you so dense that you have not realized you have a purpose to me?"

"So dense, Lady Kishar. That is Pekannen. Tell me what you wish and I will make it so."

"I do not approve of your methods but perhaps there is something to your theory."

"You honor me, First Walker."

"This girl—if she is the one—will not simply become the Sum of all Dragons without help. Perhaps it would be useful to…expedite things."

"Of course, First Walker. Anything you say."

"There will need to be careful direction of course. It will not do for other dragons to go about this without a plan. That will be your task, Pekkanen. You will ensure that the followers of Tiamat understand the consequences for such recklessness."

Pekannen's gaze settled on the shattered rubble that was all that was left of Hammas. He bowed again, practically clawing to escape, but he controlled himself until she dismissed him with a nod.

He flew away faster than she had ever seen him move.

A moment later, Kishar took to the air. Tiamat would rise and she would be the one to make it so.

CHAPTER FIFTEEN

Kylara tried not to feel overwhelmed by Amythist's office, but it was difficult. There was so much stuff everywhere—potted plants in various levels of health, dried herbs hanging from the ceiling, and jars of who knew what everywhere.

She found the smell overwhelming as well. The fragrances of the wide variety of dried herbs fought for dominance, but there was also the fresher aroma that came from the ever-present pot of tea. Add a clock that ticked far more loudly than was strictly necessary in the twenty-first century, and it seemed like a room designed for the single purpose of assaulting the senses.

"Kylara, child, everything will be all right. You don't need to be overwhelmed by these lessons," Amythist said after she'd offered her a cup of tea.

"Thank you, Headmaster," she said and took the cup.

"May I ask why?" the old dragon enquired. That was interesting. She could detect what she was feeling but not why she felt it. That might be useful if Kylara had managed to resist an aural pulse from anyone.

She didn't much see the point of lying, even if the truth made her uncomfortable. There simply didn't seem to be any other option. "Honestly, headmaster…it's your office."

"What about it?"

The young dragon mage cleared her throat and tried to keep her tone as level as she could. "It's cluttered and disorganized. It always smells like a herb garden and your clock is almost pounding it's so loud."

Amythist nodded. "Ah, I see. And are you sure you don't find it comfortable?"

Oddly, now that she thought about it, she found that she did find it comfortable. Or she was comfortable there, at least. All the clutter made it feel like she could sink in and the smell of herbs was pleasant once she got used to it. She nodded. "It's nice."

The headmaster grimaced. "I was influencing your aura, Kylara. I made you completely change your opinion. That simply won't do, child. When facing a dragon, you must always keep your first impression in mind."

"You mean always trust your first impression?"

The old dragon clicked her tongue and shook her head. "Ah, but I wish it were that simple. Many dragons use their auras as a matter of course. What you need to think about is how you feel about them compared to how you feel about them when they're not around. You might not believe this, but that is one of the reasons why so many dragons have a lair. It is a place far enough removed from our kind that we can trust our own emotions."

Kylara sighed. "So even dragons have to worry about auras? How will I ever stand a chance?"

"There will always be those with powers greater than yours. I very much doubt there is a soul alive—dragon, mage, or human— who could resist Heartsbane if she wished to change how they felt about something."

"But then what's the point of even trying?" She tried to not lose hope but between the claustrophobic office and being told that she would never master this, it was not exactly easy.

"The point is to get you to a basic level of proficiency. Hearts-bane might be able to sway the opinion of any other, but it would take her days, weeks, and even months to wear down those dragons with the strongest auras. You cannot simply blast away at someone's emotional state. Even if it worked, the moment they left your range, they'd know they were duped. That's why subtlety is key. You must develop your skills to a point where your enemy at least has to work a little to control you. That will give you the time to try to change their mind or—in your mother's case, at least—pick a fight with them."

"Can we please do that?" she pleaded, only half-joking.

"If you liked me a little more that might work but as it is, I'm afraid not. Now, I'll try again and this time, you need to think about your emotions and if they are consistent with how you feel when you're not in my presence."

Kylara nodded and drew a deep breath, once more inhaling the delicious aroma of a hundred herbs and teas. The clock on the wall ticked loudly. Too loudly. But why didn't she feel like that?

The aura! It was the first time she'd felt it working on her. Hopeful, she focused on the tick of the clock and the smells in the room, but that didn't change how she felt. She still felt comfortable as if nothing was wrong.

"Fight it, child. Should you feel relaxed right now?" Amythist whispered.

No. No, she most certainly should not. She did not like being in this overstuffed office with this woman who had shackled her for no good reason. She only felt like she did because—

And then she felt it. It was a new sense—the awareness of a part of her awakening, almost like gaining a new dragon power but not quite. It was odd, almost like moving through a cool body of water and reaching a warm spot. Somehow, her brain knew that wasn't quite right.

"You're...calming me?"

"I am doing no such thing," Amythist said and Kylara leaned back and relaxed.

She was overreacting and honestly, she liked it there. It was nice and cozy and the ancient dragon was like a grandma.

She had never known her grandma so that was unfamiliar. Before she could think about this, she felt it again—the sensation that should not be. She always felt uncomfortable there. Why did she feel calm?

And then, like a slap across the face, she could feel that the calming sensation came from Amythist.

She gasped and the sensation was gone. The discomfort of the room poured in. It was too loud, too stinky, and too cluttered. "I could feel you trying to calm me!"

"Very good, yes." The headmaster nodded.

"But how is that possible? At first, all I felt was comfort, but when I fought it, I could tell it was you."

"Exactly," Amythist agreed. "Dragons can identify each other from our auras. This makes manipulating each other even more difficult because if we manage to determine who the alien emotions are coming from, the aura is effectively useless. You've never been able to tell it was my aura before?"

"No. Never. And all dragons are like this?"

"Yes. Some, like Heartsbane, can make others feel things while they keep their identity hidden. But if they push too hard, it becomes clear who is doing the manipulating. Most of us simply have to accept that if we do anything with our aura besides express how we feel, another dragon will know."

"Can we practice more?" she asked.

They spent the next hour practicing. Kylara wasn't always able to stop Amythist from making her feel something, but she discovered that once she knew where the emotions were coming from, it was at least possible to claw out of the feelings she had begun to accept as her own. By the time they were finished, she was able to recognize and stop when the old dragon tried to make her like her—most times, anyway.

"I thought it would be...I don't know, more direct," she confessed when the headmaster finally called an end to their practice.

"I suppose that makes sense. Humans tend to think of dragons as manipulative creatures and assume our auras are the center of our nature, but that's not quite true."

"What do you mean?"

"Our auras are primarily for sharing how we feel with others —that's my guess, at least. It is an interesting cultural adaptation that we use them to try to manipulate each other and the humans around us. I sometimes wonder if we would have done it if we'd never met human beings."

"We do share a planet and dragons can transform into human bodies, so I can't see how that would work."

"Forgive an old woman her thought experiment, then." Amythist chuckled. "I simply mean that humans are always in the business of manipulating each other. They're not as robust as us dragons so have had to rely on other means far longer than we have. That is why people dress a certain way, speak a certain way, or associate with certain people, is it not? Humans—and for millennia, dragons as well—have been obsessed with influencing others. It's only natural that we've put our ability to read and influence the emotions of others to this task."

Kylara chewed her lip. She'd never thought of that.

"Ah, but I can sense I made you nervous, child. Worry not about an old woman's ramblings. Here, take your pendant and put it on. I'd still wear it in class and while you sleep but try to make some time every day to practice reading the emotions of your friends. You can tell them this at first. Have one try to sway you one way and the other sway you another and see if you can tell which aura is coming from which. Always try to resist—

always. We'll work toward you going a day without your pendant but there is time before we get to that point."

She nodded. "Thank you, Headmaster," she said and took it.

"And Kylara, I'm sorry you don't trust me but I'm honored that you don't feel quite as strongly as you once did about it."

Kylara left her office and accidentally slammed the door in her haste. She put the pendant on hurriedly, not ready for her tutor, let alone the school at large, to know what was in her heart.

CHAPTER SIXTEEN

A month later, the weather in the high desert readied itself for winter's icy chill. Snow hadn't fallen yet, although precipitation there was a rare thing. That didn't stop Kylara from crunching across the frost covering the grass in the U most mornings. The cold had never particularly bothered her and was even less of an issue once she had absorbed Ruby's heat powers but now, it felt like something completely different.

It was her new ice powers. She could feel them exactly like she could feel her weather powers. When she breathed, she could practically taste the moisture in the air and feel the crystalline patterns of snowflakes, frost, or crystals she could turn them into with a simple exhalation. At first, she had only felt this new sensation in her dragon form, but as she had become more familiar with the power—and as the air had chilled—she had sensed it more acutely and had learned to use her human breath to make ice crystals.

She only wished her aura powers were improving as easily as this power over ice that she had never asked for.

Her ability to resist other dragons' emotions was improving, though. Lady Amythist had been quite clear and even complimentary in that regard. Still, it did not feel nearly enough for her. She could tell when the headmaster—or her friends as she'd practiced with them a little—tried to make her feel an extremely strong emotion.

Karl had been more than happy to test her resolve when it came to hate and fear, and Tanya had attempted to make her feel excited about dresses that she wouldn't be caught dead in.

She'd even had success deflecting love—albeit in an extremely awkward way because Sam had been the one to use the emotion on her. She didn't think he meant anything by it. They had been talking about how the positive emotions could be even more dangerous than the negative ones. It simply would not do for her to suddenly feel camaraderie with an enemy dragon in the middle of a battle. And yet the experience had still been odd. Feeling afraid of Karl's shadow powers or interest in Tanya's clothing choices ran against her normal feelings. Thinking about Sam in that way…well, suffice it to say it was more complicated.

Kylara still didn't like to go without her pendant on, though. Rumor had got out that the field trips to cities had been canceled because two cultists had found Kylara. Her classmates didn't razz her for this. She was far too powerful to tease, even by the fourth-years, but they certainly felt things about it. It was too much for her to enter another dull lecture and feel twenty students' auras of disappointment directed at her.

Fortunately, there was good news on that front. There had been no more hints of cult activity in the world so the headmaster was considering opening the field trips again. Lady Amythist had spoken to the Steel Guard about the incident and she'd gathered intelligence. From what they knew, Pakennen—the ice dragon, if Kylarla's memory served—had been seen in public only a tiny handful of times. Each time the Steel Guard's ears had managed to pick up anything relevant, it had always been him telling another Follower of Tiamat how foolish he had been for attacking her and that he did not think anyone else should do anything so reckless.

Of Hammas, there had been no sign at all.

Something about that didn't sit quite right with her. Dragons did not exactly disappear. They were too powerful and too accustomed to having human servants to tend to their needs and whims. She knew that—legally, anyway—it was a different world than it had been only a few years before, but those kinds of changes did not happen in everyone overnight.

Pakennen telling everyone to keep away was odd too. He had been so passionate about what he'd done to her. Plus, there was the fact that he had managed to give her ice powers. She did not know if he knew that for certain, but she thought that if he even suspected he had been successful, he would brag about what he had done for 'the Sum of all Dragons' or whatever.

Still, these were not opinions she wished to express aloud to anyone but her friends. There had been no attacks or developments, so the student body might get to go on more field trips. She didn't want to ruin that for everyone because a dragon who had given her a new power was now having doubts about waking his sleeping goddess.

These thoughts captured her mind as she moved from one class to another. It was only when Professor Sharra snapped, "Miss Diamantine!" that she realized how much she had been zoned out.

"Yes, Professor?"

"Why do we need to be on our best behavior today?"

Kylara reached for an answer and found nothing. They were not going on field trips yet, she knew that much. So why was Professor Sharra asking about today? She had no idea so there was nothing to be done except try a safe answer. "Because the reason we're at the Lumos School is so mages and dragons can learn to work together? And we need to focus on that today and every other day."

To her surprise, Professor Sharra didn't look upset. If anything, she looked impressed. "A very cosmopolitan attitude, Miss Diamantine, and one I would love to see more of our students pick up whether we are having class visitors or not."

"Er...thank you, Professor."

Professor Sharra began to go over the expectations again. This time, Kylara wasn't distracted by her thoughts but by Tanya poking her with her foot under the table. "Nice one, Ky! I thought she would murder you but your little butt-kissing routine worked!" she whispered.

"That wasn't butt-kissing!" she retorted with mock offense on her face.

"Oh, it was so butt-kissing, you grade—" Tanya's gaze flicked up and she froze in mid-sentence. The visitors had arrived.

"Ah, welcome. You must be Lady Kishar. Please, have a look..."

Kylara turned as the professor trailed off.

Standing in the doorway at the top of the stairs that descended into the classroom were two dragons in human form and a mage tour guide she recognized from around campus. She had her pendant on so couldn't tell they were dragons by their aura, but it was clear in their demeanor, the woman especially. She seemed so self-assured that if she had been a regular human, she would have assumed she was a member of royalty.

Her dark skin gleamed with vitality and her hair was full and perfect. She wore a beautiful green-and-yellow dress although the young dragon mage didn't recognize the style. Then again, she did not recognize very many so that was moot. She was almost breathtakingly beautiful, and the gold ring in one nostril only emphasized this. When she descended the stairs—no, a woman like this did not descend, she floated—each step was the very definition of grace despite her walking down a fairly rickety metal staircase.

The man who trailed behind her had the same proud posture of a dragon, but his physical appearance was at odds with the typical way dragons looked in human form. He was very thin—in Kylara's estimation almost dangerously so—a fact only heightened by his gray suit with subtle pinstripes. His eyes were wide and focused on the classroom before him as if he did not want a single detail to escape his notice. Oddly, he wore two wristwatches on one hand, a third on the other, and a chain that vanished into a pocket that she could not help but assume was connected to a fourth timekeeping device.

As the two descended, the class watched in rapt silence. She could understand why. Even without her dragon aura, she could sense magic pouring off them, or one of them anyway. As they came closer, she realized it was the man with the watches. He was doing something he shouldn't.

Kylara pushed up from her chair and knocked it back in her haste, but she didn't care. "Karl, shadows," she snapped. "Shields up, Jasmine." Sam and Tanya's powers wouldn't be effective down there but hopefully, they wouldn't be needed.

"Karl?" She glanced at him but realized he hadn't moved. In fact, he didn't even seem to breathe. Tanya was completely frozen as well. She had the same smirk on her face that had been there when she'd teased her friend about her answer.

"Professor, something's wrong!"

But Professor Sharra was also frozen. Her expression was blandly welcoming, her arm extended to the top of the stairs to greet the two dragons. It was odd, given that they were already at the bottom—walking easily while no one else could even move— yet the professor's gaze was locked on the doorway.

The two stepped onto the floor of the classroom. Kylara turned her fists to diamonds and prepared to fight. Whatever was going on here must be happening because of the dragon with the watches. His eyes were closed, his hands were raised in front of him, and his fingers twitched slightly as if he listened to distant music…or the faint ticking of clocks.

"Who the hell are you?" she demanded.

The woman—the breathtakingly beautiful woman with her kind, brown eyes—curtsied deeply. "I am Kishar, and I have gone through a great deal of trouble to meet you, Kylara Diamantine."

CHAPTER SEVENTEEN

Kylara didn't know what to make of this woman, but freezing all her classmates was not exactly a good place to start if the visitor had hoped to make a good impression. She made tendrils of shadow sprout from her feet and spread across the floor toward Kishar. Her eyes ignited with light, ready to blast the woman in the face if she came any closer.

"Not another step," she ordered. Her ice powers reminded her that there was more than enough moisture in this classroom to freeze this woman in her tracks.

"Whatever you wish," the woman said and bowed again.

"Why are you here?" she demanded.

"I am not here to start a fight if that is what you are thinking, and I certainly do not wish to hurt you. Not at all. The opposite, in fact." She beamed beatifically.

"I'll go ahead and assume that you're not here to enroll a student either," she said when Professor Sharra's explanation of this visit came to her.

"That is only partially correct. There is, in fact, a young dragon I would like to enroll here, but you are correct in assuming that my interest in their education is a secondary reason for this visit. The truth is that I wish to speak to you."

"About what?"

"I would like to help you understand what's going on around you. I value knowledge, perhaps even more than some of the staff here. I believe that if someone such as yourself has questions, they should be answered." Kishar spread her hands as if this should be obvious.

"Answers would be nice," Kylara said dryly. "For starters, what did you do to all my friends?"

"I didn't do anything to them."

"I'd appreciate straight answers, thanks," she snapped.

"Ah, I should have been more clear." The woman bowed in apology. "My associate is the dragon who is creating a spatial anomaly in this room, not I. A room like this takes all his concentration, you see, and leaves him quite unable to converse. It is my job—as the humans say—to do the talking."

"What kind of spatial anomaly?" she demanded. Tanya's face still hadn't twitched at all and neither had the professor's. For some reason, the fact that this power worked on both mages and dragons unsettled her deeply.

Kishar waved her fingers as if it were the most common, boring thing in the world. Something besides serene beauty tinged her face for only a moment. Kylara wished she could read the woman's aura although she also didn't trust herself enough around her to think she'd be unaffected. Come to think of it, she couldn't help but notice how strongly she felt about her beauty. Could this dragon have somehow penetrated the protection her pendant gave her?

"Temporus is able to distort the flow of space and time around himself and other individuals."

"Meaning..."

"It feels like time froze for everyone else, but we're in a kind of bubble outside their spacetime. When he releases the magic, it will be as if no time passed at all for them. There will be no issues with the flow of time inside this room and out of it, for that matter. The effect is isolated to only Temporus, you, and myself. Perhaps the way to think of it is that he pulled us out of time and will put us back when our conversation finishes. Does that answer your question?"

"Yes…thank you," Kylara said. She wouldn't trust this woman, not with this bizarre entrance, but that wasn't the same thing as not listening to what she had to say. Lady Amythist could be overprotective. If Kishar had told the headmaster that she wanted to speak to Kylara Diamantine, she felt almost certain that the headmaster would have tried to slap a cuff on her simply for asking.

"So if he's here because of his power, why are you here?"

"I am a Follower of Tiamat," the woman said simply and made no secret of the fact that she was gauging her reaction.

"I've heard of them," she responded. There was no point in hiding it. She was sure her annoyance was plain on her face.

"First off, I must apologize for the actions of two of our… lesser Followers. Our religion is not a regimented one. We believe this freedom is important but it can be dangerous. Sometimes, the liberty this gives our Followers is taken advantage of and beliefs are acted upon without thinking. Forgive us." She bowed even more deeply than before. "It will not happen again."

Kylara intended to ask why exactly she wouldn't hear from the other two dragons, but Kishar spoke first. "You must have questions about our belief that you are the awaited Sum of All Dragons."

"So it wasn't only them who thought that?" The knowledge surprised her.

"No, they were not alone in their belief." The visitor's eyes twinkled as if she wanted to say more.

"Well, I'm sorry to say you're all barking up the wrong tree. I wasn't born a dragon so don't see how I can be the sum of all of them or whatever."

"Before Tiamat, there were no dragons. After her sacrifice, there were. The creation of dragons is at the very core of our beliefs."

"And what do the Followers of Tiamat believe?" She was hoping that Kishar would explain that the being sleeping in the pixie realm couldn't possibly be their goddess.

"We believe that Tiamat spilled her blood—many quibble over the details of that, whether it was personal sacrifice or blood spilled in noble combat—and that her blood brought magic to the cosmos. With her last breath, she prophesied that one day, another like her would arise, someone with the myriad of dragon powers at their disposal. When the Sum of All Dragons appears, they will herald the return of Tiamat herself. She cannot awaken until there is one like her."

"And it's fine that I'm not a dragon?" she pressed.

The woman raised an eyebrow suggestively. "There are some Followers of Tiamat who believe that the prophesied one had to be male. Some thought she was speaking of the pixies. I believe I might be speaking to the Sum of all Dragons right now."

"And what if you're wrong? What if I'm merely an unusual mage girl raised by a dragon?" Kylara asked.

Kishar chuckled, the sound sweet like windchimes. "That is possible, Lady Diamantine. Prophecies are never clear until after they come true."

She snorted because she agreed with that, anyway. "But you still came here. Why?"

"I might be wrong, but the things you can do are certainly… unique. I've never heard of another dragon absorbing powers before," the woman all but purred.

"You should have talked to the Steel Dragon or my headmaster. Both of them have done it," she pointed out snappishly.

Kishar bowed but less deeply this time. "You are wise beyond your years, Lady Diamantine. Followers of Tiamat have explored both these women as potential Sums. However, even you must admit that what you can do is far beyond what either of them is capable of."

"I suppose," she said guardedly.

"I apologize. I didn't answer the question." She smiled and bowed again, the action always so ready. "You asked why I came here even though I knew I could be wrong about who you are. I came, first, to apologize. I have some amount of sway in the Followers of Tiamat and I should have used that sway to make sure none of our Followers harassed a young girl while on a field trip with her friends. I wanted you to know that their actions were unacceptable and will not happen again."

"And the other reason?"

"If you truly are the Sum of All Dragons, I wished to meet you myself." Kishar's eyes twinkled even more brightly. "It is not every day that a prophecy comes to life. I had hoped to discover if you were a person of merit, someone who would listen before speaking."

"And?"

"That you are even asking honors me." She bowed yet again. Kylara began to wonder if this woman truly was there because she thought she was a…a what? A prophet? No, a prophecy. She was either bowing because of that or because she was trying to hide her face.

"What happens now?" she asked.

"Now, I must depart." Kishar glanced at Temporus. He was shaking and his wide eyes were bloodshot. "Temporus won't be able to hold the temporal shift much longer. When it drops, we will all return to the moment we left. Come, Temporus, to the top of the stairs."

He nodded hurriedly and seemed to be in discomfort as he hurried up the stairs to where the mage tour guide was frozen in place.

The woman looked over her shoulder. "You might want to return to your seat or your friends will notice. I would not wish to draw any undue attention to you."

Kylara paused. This couldn't be the least obtrusive way for the woman to have talked to her, could it? She didn't know, but she was sure that any attempts to talk to the headmaster would not have worked. Finally, she nodded and sat.

"Grubber," Tanya blurted as time returned to normal.

"What?" she asked and struggled to remember what her friend had been talking about.

"Oh, dang it, I always get human phrases wrong. You're a rankings rat, then? A marks monkey?"

The dragon mage smiled. "Oh, yeah. A grade grubber."

"Ah, welcome. You must be Lady Kishar. Please, have a look around." Professor Sharra gestured to the classroom. "If you have any questions, please ask me rather than the students. Some of what they're doing will require all their concentration."

"I wouldn't dream of causing a scene," the visitor said and bowed to the professor once she reached the bottom of the stairs.

"Wow, talk about grade grubbers," Tanya whispered. "I've never seen a dragon treat a mage with so much respect."

Kylara nodded and watched the woman for a sign or some acknowledgment of the conversation they'd had but it didn't come. The two visitors let themselves be taken on the tour, asked their guide questions, and paused to watch the teams of mages and dragons work together. If it weren't for Temporus' bloodshot eyes, she might have wondered if she'd imagined the entire conversation.

Finally, Kishar thanked Professor Sharra with another bow, thanked the students, and left with nothing to show for the visit except the ideas in Kylara's head that she couldn't stop thinking about.

CHAPTER EIGHTEEN

Sam threaded through the crowded dining hall and tried to not bump anyone with his tray that was laden with food for both him and Kylara. They'd arrived together and hadn't seen their friends. He had begun to wonder if today would be the day he could finally ask her out but that would only happen if he could get to her.

The dining hall was packed for a Thursday night, but he had no idea why. Normally, Thursdays were fairly empty. Fridays were often used by professors for quizzes, exams, and turning projects in. That meant meals went neglected as students crammed but it seemed grades were not the order of the day.

Finally, he pushed through the crowd to Kylara, who was seated where he'd left her to hold a table. He put the tray down—miraculously, nothing had spilled—and went about dividing their food.

"Thanks, Sam," she said absently. She had been a little off, lately. He couldn't quite say how but he had noticed that she was distracted. Of course, he had been distracted too, thinking about her. He couldn't help but wonder if she had been thinking about him the same way.

"Hey, now that it's only the two of us, I've been meaning to talk to you." He grimaced inwardly at the overly wordy start to their conversation. Thankfully, she still wore her pendant most of the time and always in crowds like this. It meant that she couldn't feel his competing emotions of nervousness, excitement, anxiety, and terror. If she could sense those emotions, she wouldn't necessarily know that they were there because he was worried about asking her out. But at the same time, he didn't think a girl—especially a girl as amazing, strong, and confident as she was—would think that anxiety and nervousness were attractive.

"Oh, yeah?" she asked.

"Yeah, well, I've been thinking about what happened in Austin."

"Me too," she added morosely. Not a good sign, he decided.

Still, now was his moment. If Karl and Tanya were there, he would never be able to pull this off. "I wondered if you'd like to go with me. Out, that is."

"The school's locked down," Kylara said bluntly. "Where do you want to go?"

"No...uh... What I mean is..." *Why is this so difficult?* Sam had fought dragons, mages, and the undead, and asking his friend if she felt the same way as he did about her was too much? There was nothing to be done for it but ask her. He squared his shoulders and took a deep breath.

The sound of a silver fork clinking on a goblet rang out across the dining hall. Students jostled to find a space at the crowded tables. Those who were already seated shushed the rest. After a chaotic minute, the room fell silent and every gaze was focused on the front of the room, where the headmaster held a goblet and a fork. He realized that there would be an announcement, which was why the dining hall was so crowded. How had he missed that? He had hung around outside Ky's last class, hoping to find her. The message must have gone out then.

Kylara didn't seem to have any idea what it was about either. Her gaze was as focused on the headmaster as everyone else's.

Sam sighed. Yet again, he'd missed his moment.

"I am certain that all of you are quite curious as to why we're here," Amythist began, which of course sent a ripple of murmurs through the students. "As many of you know, the last time some of our upperclassmen left campus, there was an incident."

A few pointed stares were directed at Sam and Kylara. Even seated beside her, he could tell that most of the looks were for her, not him. He wondered what it would feel like to be singled out constantly as different. It was odd that so many people could look at her as something strange because he saw only beauty in her differences—well, beauty and general awesomeness.

"Since then, we have had no indications that the individuals involved in this incident are still active in any way," Amythist explained. "We appreciate your patience as we investigated what happened but have determined that there is no longer a pressing threat. I ordered the lockdown out of an abundance of caution, and your compliance made it work. So, in thanks, we are authorizing field trips again."

A great cheer rang out from all the third- and fourth-year students. The first- and second-years cheered too, carried along by the excitement in the room and likely the auras of all the older dragons. In all the celebration, Sam kept his gaze on Kylara. She chewed a lip as if something was still bothering her. He wished he could read her aura.

But before the room quieted, a few third-years approached and slapped her on the back in congratulation. By the time the fourth classmate had told her the equivalent of, "no hard feelings," she had brightened.

Sam grinned. He felt like such an idiot! Of course Ky had been stressed. The field trips being canceled was not her fault but he could see how other students would construe it to be at least somewhat because of her. And knowing her, if people even looked at her, she would take it personally. For all her strength, she was still on shaky ground when it came to maneuvering in dragon culture.

Amythist spoke again and the students quieted. "There will be additional precautions in place and we will not vote on a new destination this time. The next trip will again be to Austin, Texas. We feel we can maintain security for you there."

Whispered conversation followed this, but based on everyone's aura, no one seemed particularly upset about it. After all, Austin was a big city. There was more than enough to do there for everyone to enjoy another visit. Sam grinned. This was his chance.

He bided his time as the headmaster took a few minutes to talk about safety procedures. Kylara watched with rapt attention. She had a look about her like she wanted to say something, or maybe she was wondering if she should say something? It was so hard to tell without reading her aura for a clue.

Still, she seemed palpably relieved when Amythist finished her safety speech and let the students resume their meals.

Sam took a deep breath. There was still no sign of Karl or Tanya. It was now or never. "Do you want to go back to Austin?" he asked.

"I don't know. I want to." Kylara bit her cheek. "But I'm not sure if it's smart."

"What do you mean? Lady Amythist said they looked into it and it's fine." He was confused. Why didn't she simply say yes?

"I'm not sure she has…all the information." She looked at her food and avoided his gaze.

This was so frustrating. Something was bothering her, but why wouldn't she simply say what it was?

"I'm sure she talked to the Steel Guard. If she says it's fine, it must be fine. We should go together. I heard about this amazing pizza place. We could pick up a pie and try to watch the sunset without interruption this time. I think we should start dinner at six and see where that takes us?" He had to play it cool. Sam knew that. Girls didn't like boys who seemed desperate, or so he thought.

"Dammit, Sam, now is not the time to talk about pizza!"

He recoiled at her response. What had he said? "If you don't want pizza, we can do something else. Austinites think they invented breakfast tacos. We could do a taste test maybe?"

"I don't care about dinner with you, Sam! I have bigger issues to worry about than what we're going to eat!" She pushed her tray away from her. "You don't know what it's like to have nightmares every night, to have to hide behind a necklace that could break at any moment. Those cultists were after me, Sam! Me. If Amythist is wrong—"

"She's not wrong!"

"You can't know that, Sam! You don't know what she doesn't know!"

"And you do?"

Kylara met his glare and clenched her teeth. Sam didn't think he'd ever seen a human face look more ferocious than that of a dragon until now. "No...I think it'll be fine. I...I think those cultists acted out, is all."

"Then why can't we go out for dinner?" he pleaded. He hadn't meant it to sound like begging, but there it was. At least he wasn't on his knees.

"Who is going out for dinner?" Jasmine asked as she reached the table and put her tray down. "Dang it, I forgot a fork. I had to sit with a group of first-years. They looked like they thought I was a dragon." She laughed and raised a hand. A fork drifted from the other side of the dining hall into her hand.

"Dang, who rained on the sunshine boy?" Karl grinned and sat next to Jasmine. "Are you all right, buddy? Your aura feels like something died and it rolled in it."

Sam looked from one to the other in frustration. Both grinned like they had the world's best secret between them. He looked at Kylara, who still seemed like she couldn't decide if she wanted to be pissed at him or depressed that he had shown interest in her.

Tanya appeared and sat. "Sam, are you all right? Didn't you hear the news? We get to go back to Austin this weekend."

It was too much for him. He couldn't pretend to be happy when Kylara was pissed at him for asking if she wanted to go out with him. Not even that, he realized. He hadn't asked her that at all.

"Well, if anyone wants me there, let me know." Sam stood, dumped his tray in the trash, and stormed away.

He strode across the U, disappointed in himself, frustrated with Kylara, but also convinced that he didn't have the whole picture. Something was bothering her, he knew it. Yet he could not help but feel hurt that she was effectively leaving him out of whatever it was when all he wanted to do was have dinner with her and listen to her talk about whatever was on her mind.

CHAPTER NINETEEN

The wind blew gently from the south, slightly warmer after it had crossed the Chihuahuan Desert. Plus, it smelled of cinnamon and sugar. The aroma was so real that she looked around and finally noticed a dragon ahead carrying a cart filled with churros.

Kylara grinned and flew toward them. She reached out for one but realized she was not carrying her wallet and slid her hand into her pocket instead. While she did not recall when her dragon body had begun to come with pockets, she didn't question it for some reason and merely retrieved her wallet. She opened it but the wind ripped her money away and scattered it to the winds.

"Wait! Can I still have a churro?" she asked. But the dragon was much higher than it had been.

When she tried to fly after it, clouds of shadow had gathered all around her. Dark, twisting mists emanated from a dragon she couldn't see yet knew was beautiful—Kishar.

Suddenly, Boneclaw burst from the dark cloud and shredded her wings to leave them in tatters.

She lashed out immediately and struck him in the chest with her diamond-tipped tail. He exploded into a loose mess of bones.

Only his skull stayed together and the jaw moved up and down like a cheap animatronic model at a museum and laughed as it fell into the clouds below.

Kylara plunged into the dark clouds. Her healing powers weren't working. As she fell, her wings became even more ragged. She burst from the heavy underbelly of the vaporous mass and plummeted toward the pond in the swamp.

Unable to stop herself, she splashed into it and suddenly, she was awake.

Frantic, she pushed to the surface and shoved the dream away as she swam toward the edge of the pond. She didn't know if she wanted to still be dreaming or not, but she did not think she was. In her dreams, Boneclaw almost always tried to pull her into the muck and she could make no decisions.

Currently, there seemed to be far too many choices as she heaved herself onto the mossy tangles of roots that surrounded the water. Should she open a gate and go back to the dorm? Should she trudge through the swamp in hopes of finding a pixie? Should she sit there and try to finally do something about this…entity hiding in the pond?

In a dream, she would already be doing one of them.

But this was not a dream. She was sure of that and so, for a moment, she sat on the edge of the pond and tried to catch her breath and take control of her mind.

She had no sooner pushed the confusing dream images away when she felt it.

The aura was emanating from the pond again.

Instinctively, Kylara clutched the pendant around her neck. It was warm and growing warmer. Should it be hot already? Was it still working at its full power or was it weakening? She had no idea and it worried her.

Paralyzed by fear, she sat motionless, unsure of what to do but feeling like maybe she should get into the pond again. There must be something at the bottom. She felt that if she could only find out what it was, she might finally feel safe.

But that was not right.

The young dragon mage had never wanted to go into the water. Every time she'd been there, she had been quite clear about this. She usually felt repelled by the pond but at that moment, she felt like she wanted to go into it.

What did Amythist keep saying about their lessons? To trust her emotions and her first impressions, to compare how she felt about things in different situations. This was the first time she'd ever felt this way toward the pond. That could only mean that an aura was, in fact, affecting her. Something was getting past her pendant but for the first time in her life, she thought that might be a good thing.

She could tell what the aura wanted her to feel. It pulsed with both fear and security—fear of the outside world, fear of the unknown, and fear of being powerless. The sense of safety came only from one place—the pond. Whatever was down there wanted her to get into the water. Knowing this made it easier to resist.

Kylara had never wanted to enter this water before and would not do so now.

Instead, she stood, planted her feet firmly in the moss, and faced the pool. She did not need to be afraid there. She was the Big Pixie. While she still didn't know exactly what that meant—and doubted she ever would—she knew she had power there. She would not be bullied out of the pixie realm, not when it was her place as much as it was any other pixie's.

"Whoever is down there, I know what you're doing!" Kylara yelled at the water. "You're trying to make me scared so I go to you. Well, guess what? It's not going to happen. You might as well drop the aura crap and leave me alone."

Suddenly, the emotional press of the aura was gone. It didn't fade or shift or change. One moment it was there, as strong as any she had felt during her practice, and in the next moment, it was gone. That wasn't easy. It took Amythist and Tanya at least a few seconds to change their emotional state. This being had done it in a moment. She didn't know what that meant but she firmly believed that control often meant power and that this entity seemed to have tremendous control.

And it had heard her. Without a doubt, it had heard her. What did that mean? She could speak to it and it could understand. That much was obvious. But was that all it could do? Could it communicate?

"What are you?" Kylara asked. "What do you want from me?"

The emotional push to get into the pond returned. There was a sensation of…belonging? She couldn't quite tell as her pendant still blocked much of the aura. Still, the sensation was similar to how she felt when she returned to her mom's house. Again, she wanted to swim toward the bottom of the pool. She would be safe there, she was sure of it.

"Enough of that!" she snapped.

Again, the aura stopped.

"If you can, answer me in words," she said slowly and dearly hoped she wouldn't regret it. No answer came, but she had not asked a question.

"Are you…" She drew a deep breath and thought she already knew the answer to the question she wanted to ask. It fit too well with what the pixies had said, with what Kishar had alluded to, and with the legends Tanya had found in the old book. "Are you Tiamat?"

At first, there was nothing but then a voice spoke into her mind, as clear as a bell. It was a woman's voice and it brimmed with power—the confident voice of a dragon whose tone said it knew all and feared nothing. "Yes, my child."

She knew it was the voice of Tiamat.

Her emotions overwhelmed her. Stricken with terror, she opened a portal and fled to the safety of her dorm.

CHAPTER TWENTY

Kylara tumbled out of the portal, landed on her bed in a tangle of blankets, and slid heavily onto the floor. She pushed herself back until she struck Tanya's bed with the back of her head. The pain should have been insignificant to someone with her powers, but it was unexpected and sharp enough to force tears from her eyes. Her vision blurry, she closed the portal that was still open above her bed.

Surprisingly, there was no pain from bypassing the school's shields this time. Did that mean the shield was down? Or that Tiamat had somehow managed to bypass it? That would explain why she'd been able to gate out during her dreams without waking up from the pain.

"Ky?" Tanya's voice was thick with sleep. "Is that you?"

She tried to speak but her voice caught in her throat. Instead of an affirmative, all that came out of her mouth was a yelp. Her tears began to fall in earnest.

"Ky, are you all right?" The sleep vanished instantly from Tanya's voice. "Was that a portal to the pixie realm? I thought those wouldn't work with the wards on campus. Ky, what is going on?"

For about a tenth of a second, she considered trying to hide what had happened but the ball of anxiety her heart had become over the past month threatened to explode, the tears increased in intensity, and she began to tell Tanya everything.

"No, Tanya, I'm not all right! I've been having nightmares about Boneclaw."

"I know—"

"No, you don't! It's so much more than that. In some of my nightmares, he takes me to that pond in the pixie realm where…where…"

"Where Galen learned to control skeletons and I learned plant powers?"

Kylara nodded as her friend slid out of her bed and sat beside her, pulled her in for a hug, and wrapped a blanket around them both.

"And where he almost killed me. I first thought they were only nightmares, but they're more than that. Sometimes…sometimes I wake up there on the bank of that pond."

"How?"

"The mage defenses don't stop me from gating. They never have. They merely tie my stomach in knots and make me want to puke. It's a great way to wake up after having terrifying encounters with Tiamat, by the way." She choked out a laugh.

With her head on Tanya's shoulder, she could feel the other girl swallow. "What do you mean, encounters?"

"She's at the bottom of the pond."

"Tiamat is only a legend."

"No, Tanya, she's not. The pixies have kept her asleep there. I saw them go to sing to her once and I didn't think a damn thing about it. Boneclaw knew too…he knew he was resurrected because of the magic in that pond. He knew it was her."

"Are you sure it's not him?" Tanya asked.

Kylara nodded into her friend's shoulder. "Oh, Tanya, I wish it was only him. I've felt her aura, though, and it… I don't even know how to describe it. Have you ever been around Heartsbane in a bad mood?"

"Sure. Yeah. She wasn't exactly pleased with us when she debriefed us about the wizard who had been stealing pixies."

"Right. Okay. So I worked for her all summer. She was pissed with me every single day. Not once did I feel her aura through my pendant. Do you understand what I'm telling you, Tanya? Not once!"

"And you felt something in the pond?"

She took her roommate's hand and put it against the pendant, which was still almost scalding hot around her neck. The girl gasped.

"And it's not like it even completely blocked it," she continued, aware that probably was rambling now. "I could still feel her, Tanya. She's so powerful, so much more powerful than Boneclaw. He never got through the pendant either, and she…I think if I had stayed any longer, she would have broken it. She wanted me to go to her—to be afraid of everything but her. I…I almost did it, Tanya."

"Okay, but Ky…that doesn't mean it's Tiamat down there. I've studied the origin of magic. There are rumors of other things with aura abilities. Nothing is confirmed, of course, but we're talking about the pixie realm. How do you know it wasn't a giant turtle or something?"

"She spoke to me," Kylara said, her voice hollow. "I asked if it was her and she said yes."

Kylara broke down in a fresh flood of tears.

"Oh, Ky… You know I have to call our friends now, right?"

She merely wept as the girl called Jasmine, who said she would call Karl while Tanya called Sam.

The mage arrived first, which wasn't surprising except that she had managed to stop at the dining hall and fetch a pot of coffee and mugs for everyone. Kylara had never understood why snacks, coffee, and tea were available at all hours of the night but it made sense now. Being a dragon-mage-pixie was not always easy. It was nice to have a human comfort available when magic powers failed.

"What the hell is going on?" Karl asked as he entered with Sam moments after Jasmine had poured coffee for the girls. "No, wait—give me some of that first."

Jasmine snorted at his discourtesy but filled a cup and levitated it to him.

"What's going on?" Sam asked. His gaze had not left Kylara since he'd appeared in her doorway—escorted by Ruby Firedrake—and she appreciated his very obvious concern.

She took a deep breath and tried to calm herself enough to go through it all again, but Tanya patted her on the shoulder and told her to hush so she could explain instead. A few minutes later, Karl, Jasmine, and Sam all had looks of complete and utter shock on their faces.

"I knew you were having nightmares but this…this is an entirely different level," Karl said.

"I'm so sorry I wasn't able to tell you were hurting so badly," Sam apologized. "And I pushed you so hard the other day…I'm so sorry, Ky, truly. I feel like an idiot." He snorted in what appeared to be disgust at his insensitivity.

"Is there anything else we should know?" Jasmine asked, ever the pragmatist.

Tanya slid an arm around Kylara. "Yeah, Ky. If there's anything else at all, even if you think it's unimportant or whatever, you must tell us."

"Well, I was visited by a dragon named uh…Kishar? She said she was a Follower of Tiamat."

Karl spat his coffee out. "That *was* her! I thought it was Kishar but God, I didn't dare say anything." He pronounced the name "kee-shar." "She's, like, stupidly attractive and has a gold nose ring? She came to Professor Sharra's class for a tour, right?"

Kylara nodded.

Karl—already pasty—paled even further.

"Who is Kishar?" Tanya asked.

He took a deep breath. "She's a big deal in the Cult," he explained. "Or...more like the biggest deal. The Followers of Tiamat all believe they're walking this path, right? Everyone is on their own path to enlightenment or whatever, but Kishar is known as the First Walker. She's supposed to follow directly in the path of Tiamat herself."

"Isn't that inconsistent?" Tanya pointed out. "How is everyone supposed to follow their own path and follow this lady?"

"They're a cult." Karl sneered. "Logical consistency isn't exactly their forte. For that matter, the Followers of Tiamat are supposed to be secret. Even my father—who is something of a big deal to these people—wouldn't be caught dead talking about any of it in the open. He won't even talk about it at our house. Kishar, though? It's an open secret that she's the First Walker. How did you end up talking to her, Ky?"

"Yeah, good question," her roommate agreed. "When she came through, you two didn't talk. I was with you the entire time."

"We did talk, though." She told them about Temporus and how he had frozen time so the woman could talk to her. This, of course, opened a whole new box of questions. Karl was especially ardent and asked her about the exact particulars of what she had said and if she had made promises or threats.

He wasn't able to dig out whatever details he tried to find, however. Everyone else joined the conversation and couldn't stop talking once she revealed that Kishar thought she was the Sum of All Dragons.

Sam's voice was loudest and cut through the din. "So those dragons who attacked you were working for her?"

"No. She said they acted on their own and that that would not happen again."

"She said that? Are you sure?" Karl asked.

She nodded and frowned as she thought back to the conversation. "Yeah…yeah, she said they acted on their own and she thought it was reckless or something like that. I believed her. I know I don't have access to auras but I think she was genuine."

Midnight shook his head. "Not to be rude but it wouldn't matter if you had access to your aura with her. She can manipulate my dad into giving the Followers money. That's not easy."

"Okay." Tanya took a deep breath "So a manipulative secret cult leader thinks you're a goddess—"

"More like a prophet—" Karl corrected

"Prophet, then. Whatever," she snapped. "On top of this, you've had nightmares that make you go to a super-secret spooky pond in a swamp that we know gave Galen skeleton powers."

"Your plant powers came from there too, right?" Sam asked.

"Don't remind me." The girl sighed. "So I guess my first question is how much of this does the headmaster know? Bonus points if the answer is 'all of it.'"

Kylara grimaced.

"Are you serious, Kylara Diamantine?" Tanya demanded. "You've gone to tutoring lessons with her every day and she doesn't know?"

She stiffened. "I didn't want her to put another cuff on me."

"That is hardly a reason—"

"Hey, cut Ky some slack," Sam interjected. "She was able to tell what…this entity wanted because she's been practicing with her aura. If she had gone and told the headmaster everything, I don't think it's unrealistic to think she would have overreacted."

"Sam's right," Karl added. "If Lady Amythist knew about this, she probably would not have let Kishar onto campus at all, which means you wouldn't have got to talk to her."

"It's not like Ky talking to her was a good thing," Tanya protested.

The two men shared a look. Jasmine seemed out of her depth.

Sam spoke first. "I don't know. I think it's a good thing in one way. It sounds like the Followers of Tiamat have known about Kylara for a while. Now, we know more about them, too."

"It's not like we've tried to keep ourselves a secret," the mage pointed out. "And besides, magic battles in the heart of Detroit will always be recorded on smartphones no matter how much we might try to keep them out of sight of the general populace."

It turned out that despite the various magical protections and shields around their recent hijinks, some enterprising humans had managed to capture a fair amount of it on camera. Videos of their battle had trended on YouTube for weeks afterward.

"Right, which means this whole cult must know about Kylara," Sam continued. "They would probably all have come to the same conclusion—right, Karl? Didn't you say your dad had suspicions or something?"

Karl nodded slowly. "When he found out that Ky took my powers, he was pissed, but when he found out she could take multiple powers, that changed everything."

"But that doesn't mean the headmaster shouldn't know," Tanya protested weakly, but she could see the tides shifting against her.

"All she'll do is ground Kylara," Jasmine said. "That's what dragons do to 'dangerous' mages. They did exactly that for thousands of years, and Amythist Skyjewel—you know she was called the mage eater?"

"That was a long time ago," the other girl said.

"But we don't need to worry about any of that," Sam said. "Kishar told Kylara that those two acted out of turn and that it won't happen again. The question is whether we can trust her on that."

All eyes turned to Karl. He shrugged. "If she tells the Followers of Tiamat not to attack Kylara, they won't. Period."

"Are you sure?" Kylara asked.

"Kishar's a big deal," he explained. "Even my father doesn't go against her. If we were attacked in Austin again by one of their peons, I'm sure any other Followers—and there are always other Followers around—would step in to stop them."

"Wait, so you honestly think Kylara should still go on the trip to Austin?" Tanya was appalled.

"I don't see why that would be dangerous," Jasmine said.

"Not dangerous?" The other girl's eyes blazed.

"Why would it be?" the mage asked. "She's ported in her dreams. It's not like we'll all take a nap on the trip."

"Do you want to go, Ky?" Sam asked.

Kylara shrugged. "It sounds better than being stuck on campus. And I want y'all to go but it might be more fun for you if you ditched me."

"We will not ditch you, Kylara! Don't be ridiculous!" Tanya was flustered now. "If you want to go, we'll go with you even if we all know it's a terrible idea."

"I don't think it is," Karl said. "If Kishar told the Followers to not attack, they won't. But at the same time, they might try to talk to her. It could be a great opportunity to learn more about whatever they want from her. It's not like this will go away, not if they think she's the Sum of All Dragons."

"Can't you simply ask your dad for more intelligence?" Jasmine asked.

He laughed. "Yeah, right! Like my dad will believe me for a second if I start asking questions about his religion when I've spent the last ten years mercilessly ridiculing it. Sorry, y'all, but that bridge is burned."

"It's something to pursue later, maybe," Sam said. "But I'm with Karl on this. If Kylara wants to go, let's go. It won't affect what's been happening at night, and if we meet a Follower of Tiamat, we might learn something."

"For the record, I think this is utterly insane," Tanya stated crossly.

"It'll be fine," Jasmine said. "It's not like it could be any worse than Mort or Boneclaw."

With their minds made up, they all returned to their rooms. Kylara didn't want to sleep, but Tanya insisted and promised to stay up and watch over her. It was the best night of sleep she'd had in months.

CHAPTER TWENTY-ONE

It had been a long time since a convocation of the Followers of Tiamat had been called. Centuries, in fact, and even then, it had felt different. A few Followers had thought the newly invented pixies might be the Sum of All Dragons, but most of the Followers—Kishar included—did not think an experiment turned quasi-sentient would prove to be the being that ushered in the return of their goddess.

It felt very different this time. Kishar—who stood atop a stepped Aztec pyramid that had been swallowed by the jungle and lost to human maps long before—could practically taste the excitement. The air around the temple at the top of the pyramid was filled with dragons. That in itself was unusual. Normally, what meetings she did hold were tiny, secretive affairs conducted in human form and human places. But with a proper convocation called, many dragons had thrown caution to the wind and came to the Temple with their heads held high and their wings spread wide.

She could feel their excitement as much as her own. A hundred auras all hoped that now was their time. After so many years of waiting, the shards of Tiamat would fill the Sum of All Dragons and she would usher in the reawakening of the Sleeper in the Deep.

Already, the jungle around the hidden pyramid had been cleared. Fire breath had played its part, of course, but almost every Follower of Tiamat had powers far beyond the vanilla variety. Acid had been used to melt some of the plants. Water in the shape of a dragon had carried away much of that filth. Stones had been made to walk of their own accord and form low pedestals on the land that only days before had been covered by the thick undergrowth of the forest.

Clouds hung low overhead to hide the convocation from the Steel Guard. Parts of the temple had even been transformed from stone to gems. All these changes were effected without mages. Dragons of wondrous powers worked together to make this place a fitting throne for when Tiamat returned.

When, Kishar thought and chuckled. *Not if.* She had given up on if when she had met Kylara Diamantine. The girl was strong-willed and fierce. She was brave and reached for her powers with ease. Without a doubt, she must be the Sum of All Dragons. The prophecies would soon be fulfilled.

But that was no reason to rush. The first vote of the convocation had been about the proposed invasion of the Lumos School.

Kishar had argued forcefully against such a rash action and had barely managed to use her position as First Walker to push the vote in her favor. It might not have had intelligence not come in that this very weekend, Kylara would leave the grounds again. It was an opportunity—perhaps a holy, preordained one—to give the girl more powers and most of the dragons wanted to rush out to do exactly that. She could not let this come to pass.

"Dragons, please, find a place so we may begin the debate," a dragon with the ability to greatly augment his voice said. If anyone disobeyed, he could launch sonic booms that would not only deafen them but knock them from the air.

The dragons obeyed and spiraled closer to the ziggurat before they landed either on its stepped sides or the huge stone pedestals readied for them below. Despite not having a formal hierarchy, the Followers of Tiamat knew there was a pattern to the way influence worked. Those who were most powerful found places near the top of the pyramid with little more than a gesture needed to scatter inferior dragons.

As these landed farther down the steps, they scuffled more and more. On the fields surrounding the ziggurat, disputes for proximity were settled with lashes of flame, searing pieces of melted metal, blinding dust, or a hundred other unusual powers. Every dragon there wished to give Kylara their exceptional powers so she could usher in the return of Tiamat herself.

After a few moments of infighting, they all settled and turned to listen to Kishar. She had deliberately let the fighting reach its natural conclusion. It was best if everyone feared the person above them. That way, all of them would fear her, the dragon at the top.

"We are here because we believe the Sum of All Dragons has returned!" she bellowed and a mighty cheer rose in response.

"I believe that our time of trying to interpret prophecies has come to an end. I believe that Kylara Diamantine is the Sum of All Dragons and that once she has collected all the shards of Tiamat, she will awaken She Who Sleeps in the Depths."

Raucous cheers told her she was not at all alone in this belief.

"I know many of you wish to hasten the arrival of the First Dragon, but I must urge caution."

"And who gives you the right, First Walker?" a dragon shouted from halfway up the pyramid. A grumble of agreement followed this, which was no issue for her. She had told the dragon to ask the question, after all, and had told him to include her title in his words so that her preeminence would be clear even before she spoke.

"No one gives me this except experience," she responded. "As some of you know, I have spoken to the Sum of All Dragons. Temporus gave us a precious moment together in private. She is a strong-willed young woman, powerful and fierce. I am quite certain that if all of us come at her with our powers, she will not react kindly. I tried to explain what she is but she does not yet believe it. We cannot drive her away from the Path. It would be unacceptable if she turned her back on us and Tiamat."

"You would have us sit here and do nothing, then?" a dragon—and another plant—yelled.

"Not at all." Kishar smiled and pulsed her aura subtly with interest. A hundred dragons leaned in, eager to hear what she said. Truthfully, she didn't need to do much with her aura. Most of the dragons already wanted to hear what she was planning.

"The girl needs to be convinced of her powers," she continued. "Until now, she has absorbed only a few. Some are unusual, yes, but they are all things she is familiar with. If we simply bombard her with breath attacks, I do not think we will inspire the kind of confidence she will need if she is to summon Tiamat. I suggest a more cautious approach. Let us test both skills and that she is the Sum of All Dragons. If she truly is, she will be able to absorb all dragon powers."

"Even mine?" Bull asked.

She turned and smiled at the massive, hulking dragon. He was her third and final plant. He did not always cooperate, which made sense to her. After all, his power was practically the physical embodiment of stubbornness. Once moving, he became unstoppable. His momentum intensified as he moved and he could drive through walls, blast boulders apart, and run over any dragon he ever collided with. One could not have such a power and not let it affect their personality. She had known that winning Bull over would be a difficult thing, so she had made sure to do it long before this convocation.

"Yes, Bull," Kishar said slowly as if this had occurred to her for the first time and she had not planned this entire exchange. "In fact, your power could serve as a test. We know she can absorb breath weapons but she has yet to demonstrate anything that mages and pixies cannot do." That was not strictly true as she had never heard of a mage or a pixie with shadow powers, but if someone wanted to point that out, they could do so after she put her plan in motion.

"I ask for a vote!" she yelled to the assembled dragons. "I say we send Bull to test young Kylara. Let him engage her in combat and see if she can absorb any of Tiamat's powers. All in favor?"

The vote was almost unanimous. A hundred blasts of fire, ice, acid, and the movements of stone, water, and air erupted to proclaim support for the plan.

The response was perfect.

"The Followers have spoken. Bull, do you accept this will of this convocation?"

"I do." He grinned.

"Very well. Engage her in combat and be sure to strike her with all your momentum. She is a powerful dragon—powerful in combat and capable of healing like all dragons—but still, I must advise caution. If you were to kill her—"

"It would prove she's not the Sum of All Dragons," Bull cut in.

Curse that lummox. That had not been part of the script but she was nothing if not alacritous with her tongue. "Which means you would have killed the most famous student from the most prestigious school in the Americas. That is not something the Steel Dragon and her guard would be able to ignore."

Bull nodded at this.

Kishar had to be careful. She also didn't want it to go too far the other way. If she was wrong and Kylara was not the Sum of All Dragons, they needed to find out sooner rather than later.

"Do not reveal yourself to be a Follower of Tiamat and end the battle if you sense she has absorbed your power. If all goes well, and she can carry your…momentum, we will enact the next step in our plan. Patience now, dragons. Very soon, we will arrive at the world we have walked toward for so long."

A great cheer rose, louder than any of the others, as Bull took to the air to give Kylara Diamantine exactly what she deserved— a reckoning with what she truly was.

CHAPTER TWENTY-TWO

The third-years clustered together in the blustery cold of late fall in the New Mexican desert. Despite the cold, Kylara could practically feel the excitement in the air, even with her pendant blocking their auras.

"Under no circumstances are any of you to go anywhere alone." Professor Sharra's hands rested on her hips, her expression firm. "I realize this was a rule last time but it's even more important now. We're taking a risk by allowing this, and I need you all to understand that."

No one said anything, not even Karl. That seemed to mollify the professor somewhat.

"You will all stay within ten miles of where we port in. As before, you will hear my voice if there is anything wrong. We did all right on the evacuation last time. I don't want it to happen again but if it does, I want everyone back in less than three minutes. Any longer risks the security of the campus. Is that clear?"

"Yes, ma'am!" the students responded.

"Very well. Now…I don't know how quickly the rumor mill churns these days, but there is one more piece of information I need all of you to heed." She paused to let every gaze settle on the stern expression on her face. "If anyone claiming to be a Follower —or more specifically a Follower of Tiamat—approaches you, exit the situation as quickly as you can and report to me immediately."

"Shouldn't we kick their butts or whatever?" Karl asked.

"No." The professor's voice was as hard as stone. "Don't answer any questions but don't give them a reason to attack you either. Remember, you're all still young. Any dragon you face out there will likely have centuries of experience on you. Engaging is a recipe for disaster. Questions?"

There were none.

Professor Sharra nodded once as if this was to be expected, then opened a portal to the capital of Texas.

Kylara and her friends waited their turn, then—one by one— they stepped through the gate. One moment, they were in the high desert, trying to shiver to stay warm against the biting wind, and in the next, they were in the still cool but much less windy weather of Austin in November.

Her friends began to shed their jackets and hats. She had used her heat power against the cold so didn't have to do this and simply turned it off.

"All right, where to first?" Karl asked.

"Are you sure that you all want to stick together?" Kylara asked. They had been over this already but it still seemed extremely generous of her friends to spend their entire field trip with her when they could be gallivanting.

"Yeah. Being friends with you for two years has all been an elaborate ploy." The sarcasm was so thick in Jasmine's voice that she could almost taste it.

"Don't be such a drama queen, Ky," Tanya said briskly. "You're our friend. We want to spend time with you."

"Plus, it makes sense," Sam added. "If the cult does try something, we should all be together to face whatever it is."

"Yeah. If someone attacks, we don't want you to take all the credit," Karl joked.

"You are all the best," Kylara said.

"So? What does our little goddess want to do anyway?" Tanya asked. "I feel like all we've talked about is how to stay safe. We haven't talked about what to do."

All eyes turned to the dragon mage. She smiled and tried to not look embarrassed. "I…well, I'm down for whatever."

"Oh, hush, Kylara Diamantine!" her roommate chided. "You're the least traveled of all of us. You've been in more fights than you have cities. We've all seen cities like this numerous times. Most of us live in cities like this. You're the country bumpkin. So dish. What do you want to do?"

Kylara couldn't help but smile. Tanya was right of course. There were things she wanted to do there. "Well, I know this might not be the most exciting thing, but I've always wanted to go on a tour of the Capitol building! Did you know it's made of pink granite and that it's the biggest one in the country?"

Everyone groaned strongly at that.

"What?" she asked. "There's no way you've all already done that."

"Of course we haven't done that!" Karl snapped. "I haven't watched paint dry either, but it's not exactly on my bucket list."

"I think it sounds…informative," Sam said although he seemed to grasp for words. "I've never been on a tour of a building before, even though I've given dozens at the Lumos School."

"It's fine by me," Jasmine said. "I don't have any money for shopping anyway."

"Oh, if you want money for more old clothes, you know all you have to do is ask," Karl said to her. Shockingly, there did not seem to be any sarcasm in his voice at all.

Tanya had noticed as well. One eyebrow raised high on her forehead. "And why is that, Midnight?"

"Yeah, you hate my vintage stuff," Jasmine replied before his face could turn too red. "Besides, I'm hungry. I'm all for the boring tour but let's get food first. Cool?"

"Of course," Kylara agreed quickly before anyone else argued against the boring tour.

"There's supposed to be a great breakfast place here," Karl said.

A half-hour later, the dragons and mages were crowded together around a table on an outdoor patio that was wrapped in fabric to keep the temperature stable. At the center of the table was one of the most delicious things Kylara had eaten.

"And that's it? Only cheese?" Tanya asked the server, who grinned through her collection of lip rings.

"It's called queso. You've truly never heard of it? It's a blend of melted cheeses."

"It's fantastic," Sam enthused. He had some on his chin.

"Would you all like another bowl? Or are we ready to order?"

They ended up ordering three bowls of it—dragon metabolism with a little magic involved made short work of calories—plus platters of pancakes, French toast, omelets, and tacos by the dozen. While the waitress went to put in their massive order, they chatted easily.

When they'd first arrived, they'd asked for this table as it was far enough away from the building to give them all good eyelines to the street out front and the alley in the back. They had even looked at the menu in shifts. Despite Professor Sharra saying the cult would probably not be an issue, Kylara and her friends were determined to not let anyone get the jump on them.

After a while, it began to seem like their paranoia was unnecessary. No one stared at them, no tourists jostled and encroached on their space—November seemed to be off-season, anyway—and no other dragons were visible either. Kylara took this to mean that Kishar had been serious about her promise to call the Followers of Tiamat off, and she gradually relaxed and tried to enjoy herself. That was, after all, why they were there—to attempt to have a good time. As her tension eased, the others' did too. She was their de facto leader and them following her lead was another reminder of this.

"Check it out," Karl said, brought Kylara back to the moment, and stopped her from scanning the street for the umpteenth time.

He was balancing a spoon on his nose.

"Big deal. Humans can do that," Jasmine said and giggled.

The dragon mage was not the only one who noticed that. Tanya and Sam shared a look about the giggle too.

Jasmine levitated everyone's cutlery, then put it on her head. The illusion was excellent. She let it wobble a little so it seemed like it was all balancing there.

"Not bad," Karl said, plucked a fork from her head, and shattered the illusion. Despite the fact that the other silverware had appeared to balance on top of the fork, it continued to float as if the fork were still there.

"But my eye itches." Karl rubbed his eye with one hand, then jammed the fork directly into it. White puss shot out and dribbled through his knuckles onto the table.

Jasmine screamed and Sam bounded up, his eyes glowing with light as he searched for an enemy. Tanya was frozen, a look of horror and disgust on her face.

"Jasmine, see if there's a mage around who made him do that! Tanya, there were oaks out front. Use them. Sam, get ready to get airborne on my mark."

But Karl merely laughed. He opened the hand that had rubbed his eye to reveal a little package of creamer he had punctured with his fork to create the effect.

"Oh, my God. You jerk!" Jasmine punched him in the arm.

"Oh, were you worried I was hurt?" he asked innocently.

"I was worried that you messed up your big dark eyes and that would be a total dealbreaker for me."

"I thought you liked men with scars."

"Men with scars from battle are rad. Boys who stab themselves with forks are merely boys."

"Excuse me, I don't mean to interrupt, but your food's ready!" The server had returned with a tray of food in each hand. A busser carried another couple of trays as well.

"Oh, it's quite all right," Tanya responded, although her gaze remained on Karl and Jasmine. "These two were flirting but it didn't quite ruin my appetite, so we're happy to see you."

"Can I clean that?" the server asked, her tone deferential as she pointed at the mess. She knew they were dragons, then, and didn't wish to offend beings so powerful.

"No, it's fine," Karl said hurriedly, and Jasmine used her telekinesis to take a napkin and wipe the mess.

As the server went about matching plates with people and making sure everyone was happy and didn't need more salsa, syrup, or creamer—her tone was only slightly begrudging at the last one—Kylara thought about Karl and Jasmine.

They were flirting, weren't they? She hadn't noticed before because she'd been preoccupied with her nightmares and aura practice and everything else, but she realized that the two had been flirting for weeks now. Strangely, the thought filled her with giddy excitement. Stranger still, the idea of them flirting made her think about Sam.

She had known that he was…into her or whatever. That was why he'd gotten the heart-shaped dessert and found a place for them to watch the sunset. But in the chaos of what had followed, she hadn't been able to follow up with him, even though the idea sounded… Well, suffice it to say that it increased the giddy feeling in her stomach.

He had asked about the field trip too. Had he been asking her out? She felt like an idiot. He'd asked her to dinner and she had snapped at him because her mind was preoccupied, even though going to dinner with him—going on a date—sounded, well…pleasant.

Not that they could go on one now. But that didn't mean they couldn't flirt, right? She wasn't exactly sure how to do that, but if all it took was joking around and teasing, she could do it.

Although not at the moment. Her mom had trained her that when it came to food, it was time to eat, and the table was currently overladen with plates.

They all tucked in and each of them except Jasmine ate as much as three people could have. It was all delicious and better still because the omelets and pancakes were slightly different than the way the dining hall chefs prepared them. Not better, exactly, but distinct enough to make their visit well worth it. They didn't bother to wait for the check when it was time to leave. Instead, Sam and Karl argued over who left the server a gold coin and eventually decided they both would. They heard her scream of delight at finding their tip from the air.

"All right, Capitol tour, huh?" Tanya asked.

"Yeah, we should probably go early. It most likely closes at two pm since only senior citizens do this kind of thing," Sam joked.

Kylara was about to defend her choice but realized that maybe this was him flirting with her. "Senior citizens and country girls, I guess. We could go somewhere else but Sam probably can't keep up."

"Is that a reference to when you left me for dead in those cliffs?"

"They're called the Straits and I did not leave you for dead! I dug your pretty face out."

He chuckled at this and his gaze lingered on her a little longer than was strictly wise for a dragon in flight. Kylara returned the smile, which seemed to hold his attention.

The moment ended abruptly when he almost crashed into the spire that protruded from the top of a high rise.

"Easy, golden boy," Karl said between peals of laughter. "People don't like to wipe glowy bugs off their windows any more than they do moths."

Sam, for once, did not rise to the bait. Instead, the grin remained plastered on his face while he followed Kylara to the Capitol.

They landed on the immaculate grounds and proceeded to enter the buildings. The well-trimmed trees and neatly mowed lawn was a little tame for her taste, especially after a summer spent at the Steel Guard headquarters, where the landscaping focused on providing habitat for insects, birds, and pixies, but it was still beautiful.

They proceeded inside and through security without issue as dragons didn't carry weapons. The guards advised them to wait beneath a massive oil painting of the survivors of the Texas War of Independence for the next tour to start.

She was already amazed by the space. Even the entry hall was beautiful and historied. Ahead, the rotunda opened into a huge room that was large enough for smaller dragons to fly around inside it.

They signed up for the next tour and went to explore while they waited the fifteen minutes until it began.

Kylara went to admire the portraits of the governors of Texas —they had a portrait of every single governor on the walls of three floors of the Rotunda. Whenever a new one was elected, they had to move them all up a space to make room for the newest portrait on the bottom floor.

She had circled to a woman named Anne Richards when Tanya grasped her shoulder.

"Ky…something's wrong out there. I can feel it through the grass."

"What is it?"

Her roommate's eyes were closed as she concentrated on the unseen plant growth.

Her question was answered a moment later when the opposite entrance to the one they'd come through exploded inward. A massive dragon barreled down the hallway and shook oak trees off—not branches but entire trees—as he followed a direct trajectory toward Kylara.

Karl stepped forward and launched a huge web of shadows at him, but they snapped easily and didn't even slow the great brute.

"Kylara, take your dragon form," Sam snapped as Jasmine threw shield after shield up in front of the dragon. He bulldozed through these as effortlessly as he had Karl's shadows. "I'll try to hold him off."

The tourists had not failed to notice the massive dragon inside the building, so the rotunda was empty when Sam and Kylara took their dragon forms.

He put himself between her and the attacker, only to be knocked aside and through a wall.

She dug into the floor with her diamond claws and braced herself for impact.

The dragon pounded into her like a baseball bat hitting a ball. She catapulted away and through the front of the Capitol, leaving her friends inside with their seemingly unstoppable enemy.

CHAPTER TWENTY-THREE

The granite facade of the Texas Capitol building didn't slow Kylara in the least. She careened through and tried to get air in her wings but landed heavily before she was able to do so. She righted herself and shook to dislodge a few portraits of former governors from her spines. Thankfully, she had shifted to diamond before the impact so she was all right. Sam, though… she had to get to him.

The dragon did not give her a chance.

He exploded out of the building and thrust aside granite walls and pillars as if they were nothing but tissue paper.

"What do you want?" she demanded as he lowered his head and charged toward her. He had two huge, curling horns like those of a ram.

"The First Walker is wrong. You must learn this. Bull will teach you," he bellowed seconds before he drove into her chest. Again, she was hurled back as if she weighed only a fraction of what he did. She cracked an oak tree that must have been growing before the pink granite building had been constructed and wished she could have shattered its trunk as easily as this dragon seemed to be able to knock her about.

Kylara shook her head and stood slowly, ready to bring the attack to this cultist. And she had so hoped that they would leave her alone.

Bull snorted, pawed the earth like his bovine namesake, and charged a third time.

But before he could build momentum, he slipped and sprawled awkwardly. Karl Midnight emerged from the broken hole in the Capitol in his dragon form. He had sent tendrils of shadow under Bull's feet. Every time the aggressor tried to step forward, he moved the shadow so the dragon couldn't take a step.

Finally, Bull severed the connection with a flick of his tail. Despite Karl having increased the tensile strength of his shadow tendrils, the massive tail cut through them as if they truly were nothing but shadow. The darkness under the massive dragon evaporated, his feet dug into the earth, and he lurched toward Kylara.

He took only two paces before two oak trees bent forward and blocked his path. Their trunks crossed to make a barrier the dragon mage did not think she would be able to break through, even with her plethora of powers. The branches grasped Bull and tried to tether him in place.

None of it worked. He pushed through the trees as if they were not even there. They erupted into splinters, the strong oak behaving like balsa wood.

She had to get to Sam, but that meant going through Bull. Which, she decided, was fine with her.

Her decision made, she lowered her head and ran toward him. She hoped he would think her plan was to collide with him and that she was overconfident because of her diamond scales. In reality, she intended to go airborne and soar over his head to check on Sam. He didn't have any wings so taking to the air seemed like the obvious solution to defeating him.

But her plan changed as soon as she began to run toward him. Something new stirred inside her, a type of magic she had never felt before. She hadn't been able to sense it when she had sat still but now that she was in motion, she felt a force in her chest that wanted to keep moving. As she increased her speed, it began to build. She felt like a train gaining speed and very soon, she would be unstoppable.

She crashed into Bull and his round horns met her diamond ones. A concussive shockwave blasted out from where they made impact with each other, and the two dragons were both flung aside by the force.

Kylara careened into the top of a hill, tumbled down it, and crushed a statue of a man riding a bronco on the way. She pushed to her feet and tried to blink away the fuzziness that came to her brain after the powerful collision. Her head spun and her eyes begged to stay closed.

After a moment, she managed to locate Bull. He had been knocked back as well but while she had been stunned, he simply looked angry. She understood that she had absorbed some of his powers but did not have the mastery he did. While she might be able to crash into him and hurl him away, she would suffer from such a collision far more than he would.

"Ky!" It was Sam!

The golden dragon dropped from the sky and landed next to her. He put a claw on her shoulder and warm light suffused her to clear her head and give her focus.

"You're all right," she said.

He smiled. "I was about to say the same about you."

The moment was interrupted by a roaring Bull who initiated another charge toward her. If she were a train, she was a steam engine with a few passenger cars compared to his diesel loaded with fifty cars heavy with ore.

"Get out of here, Sam!" she said, pawed the ground, and ran toward the other dragon.

Sam cursed—he didn't like being told to get out of the way— but he obeyed. He understood that this was not his fight.

Kylara ran toward Bull and again felt the sense of momentum building inside her. It was a dragon power unlike any she had felt before and came from her movement. She did not feel like she could will it to be stronger or weaker. It simply was and her adversary surely understood this far better than she did.

They raced toward each other, but she sensed her disadvantage, turned at the last minute, and destroyed a statue of a soldier. Of course, she felt terrible about it. Bull rocketed past her but he lurched to the side and swung his massive tail. He caught her rump with only the tip of it and it hurled her forward. He had somehow been able to redirect his momentum from his body to his tail, then add it to hers.

The result was that she collided face-first with the wall of the Capitol building and created a massive hole that she plunged through until she stopped at the oil painting of the aftermath of the Texas Revolution. *Okay, so there is more to this power than simply charging forward.*

She did not have time to learn it now, however. Then again, she had learned it. Didn't that mean he should go away?

"You have given the Sum of All Dragons your power!" she yelled as she stepped out of the Capitol building and onto the grounds. "You can leave. You...uh, proved that the First Walker was wrong."

Bull—who stood about fifty feet away from her, a distance he seemed to favor for his challenges—only snorted. "You do have my power but now, Bull wants to have fun."

With a roar that sounded like the horn of a diesel engine, he lowered his curved horns and surged into motion again.

Unsure what else to do, Kylara lowered her diamond horns and returned the charge.

She almost didn't notice Jasmine out of the corner of her eye. The mage was spinning up a massive shield. Based on her body movements, her pale face, and the speck of red that rimmed one of her nostrils, it would be a big one.

"Jasmine, no! It won't work!" she shouted. She had yet to fully understand what all these powers could do but she felt certain that the mage would not be able to stop this behemoth of a dragon with her barriers. Bull shattering her shields wouldn't be a walk in the park either. Professor Sharra had devoted a recent lesson to what happened when mages overextended themselves. A brain aneurysm was a common cause of death.

The girl didn't listen. A shield ten feet wide and fifty feet tall erupted from the ground between the two combatants. It was hard to tell because it appeared so insubstantial, but it looked as if her side was smooth while the side that faced Bull was pockmarked. Kylara had no idea what the texture was supposed to do until the high wall collapsed toward her.

The base of it stayed in the middle of the two dragons, but the top teetered, fell, and stopped a few feet up. Instead of a wall, Jasmine had made a ramp.

"Foolish mage!" Bull laughed as his front claws stepped on her shield and pulled him forward faster.

"Foolish dragon," the mage muttered as she extended the shield upward.

The aggressive dragon's eyes widened as he raced over Kylara's head. He rose continually, neither stopping nor slowing, and had no idea what to do with this turn of events. The girl gave him no time to come up with any solutions, either. She made the shield move under his feet to increase his speed, double it, and triple it. A moment later, she collapsed.

Her work was done, though. Like a train, Bull had far too much momentum to simply stop. He launched over the Austin skyline like an errant rocket.

"Jasmine!" Karl's tendrils of shadow caught her and instead of falling onto the concrete beneath her feet, she fell into his tender embrace and onto a bed of shadow.

"If my trigonometry is any good, he should splash into the

river about now." The mage smiled through the blood that trickled from her nose.

Sam landed and approached her. He looked at Karl, who nodded quickly. The golden dragon changed to his human form, put a hand on her body, and suffused her with light. She perked up slightly and a little color returned, but she was no dragon. She didn't have healing power.

"So, this was much more exciting than I thought a tour of the Capitol could be," Tanya said and winged closer to land beside them. Kylara saw over the dragon's shoulder that she had taken a moment to grow a few oak trees to replace those that had been destroyed. "It was so exciting, in fact, that I think we should get back to campus now and have a chill night at home."

"Agreed!" Karl and Sam blurted together.

Kylara helped support Jasmine—"I'm fine, you're all overre-acting," she complained—while Karl transformed and she helped the mage climb onto his back. The five of them returned to the rendezvous point.

Before they even landed, Professor Sharra began the move-ments needed to open a portal. "What happened?" she demanded as the portal to school started to coalesce.

"Long story short? Kylara was attacked by a freaking cultist who Jasmine dumped in the river." Karl grinned.

"He said he was acting alone," Sam added.

"Of course, we don't believe him," Tanya interjected.

"Ky did get a new power, though, right?" Jasmine asked. "She's unstoppable now. Or something."

"Okay. I'm sorry I asked. Back to school, all of you," Professor Sharra ordered as the portal opened fully. "Report to the head-master and tell her the rest of us will be back before she's done with you five."

"I don't think you have to do that, Professor," Kylara protested. "He was after me, not anyone else."

"And what if someone else was attacked by an unstoppable

dragon?" the woman snapped. From the way she said it, she got the sense that the idea of an unstoppable dragon was not entirely alien to her. Still, her point was a good one. Her diamond skin and the power itself had protected her. If Bull turned that ability on some of her classmates, she didn't want to imagine the result.

"I understand." She sighed.

It seemed her brief moment of being forgiven would prove to be exactly that—extremely brief.

CHAPTER TWENTY-FOUR

"This is quite troubling, indeed," Lady Amythist said before she took a long, slow sip of her tea. The beverage always grounded her, even when receiving such terrible news. With more poise than she had demonstrated when getting the play-by-play of what had happened, she addressed Kylara's friends. "If you would all please excuse us, I would like to have a few words in private with Miss Diamantine."

Jasmine Patel—bless the mage's heart—stood and bowed to the headmaster, but the other dragons all glanced at the dragon mage before obeying. She clenched her teeth—during their aura lessons, Amythist had learned that this tic betrayed distress in the young mage—and shook her head.

"Ma'am, with all due respect, there's no point in sending them away."

The old dragon detested the human phrase, "with all due respect," simply because humans used it as a preamble to say disrespectful things. She kept a stern expression on her face and gestured for her to continue.

"I'll tell them everything you say to me," Kylara confessed and at least had the decency to look slightly embarrassed. "We're a team, ma'am. I can't be expected to protect myself without them. And if this school has taught me anything, it's that knowledge is power. I wouldn't want them to be powerless."

Well, that was perhaps too much groveling for her, but if the girl thought flattery would work, who was the headmaster to disagree? Besides, friendships and alliances like this were one of the most important things to emerge at the Lumos School. She noted that Miss Patel was still quicker to obey a dragon than the others but at the same time, the girl had not left the room or taken another step when she had seen that her friends hadn't hastened to obey.

"Very well," Amythist agreed. "Although in truth, Miss Diamantine, I didn't wish your friends to leave to protect my privacy but yours."

The girl paled a little at that, which the headmaster considered a small victory. "Right. Of course," she mumbled.

"Kylara, I will be quite blunt with you. In our lessons, I have had the sense that you are holding something back from me. Do you know why the Followers of Tiamat are paying so much attention to you?"

She bit her lip and hesitated, but—exactly as Amythist had predicted—one of her friends gave her away.

"Miss Fastwing, you look as if you will either vomit or claw your best friend's hair out. Why do I get the sense that she has told you something she has neglected to tell me?"

All of them squirmed at this which was, of course, a good sign. They were loyal to their friend but not so loyal as to lie to their headmaster's face.

As expected, Tanya broke first. "Tell her, Ky! We need help."

Kylara gritted her teeth.

Sam put a hand on her shoulder. Amythist made a note of that and what the boy's aura betrayed. "We tried going to the city and it didn't work out. I'm with Tanya on this." That did not come as a surprise either. Sam Lumos had always been a rules-follower.

The dragon mage took a deep breath, then sighed and nodded. What followed was a flood of information told not only by her but also by her friends in a mad, overlapping confession of secret events that had taken place since the beginning of the school year.

The headmaster sipped her tea and kept her aura firmly under control and her face impassive while they told her of Kylara's dreams, a secret visit from that snake Kishar, the adulation of the Followers of Tiamat, her being named 'the Sum of All Dragons,' and—most distressingly—about a being trapped deep within a pond in the pixie realm. A being the girl had communicated with and who claimed to be Tiamat herself.

It was that last part that distressed the old dragon most. She had been to the pixie realm far more times than any other dragon and in fact, had been the only dragon to go there for centuries. As such, she knew of the entity Kylara spoke of. She had sensed it herself on more than one occasion. The pixies had no name for it, but that was hardly surprising. Naming was a human habit, not a pixie one.

Besides, they had discovered the realm, not created it. When they went there in a pique of rage after being created by mages, they had found that it wasn't completely empty. Sensing the animosity that haunted the entity—even in its dreams—the pixies had set to work doing what they did best—using life itself to solve their problems.

Over the intervening centuries, they had introduced trees, vines, aquatic plants, ferns, and even mosses, all in an attempt to create a living cage above the entity deep in the pond. Even with all that, they still had to lull whatever was down there to sleep every so often.

Amythist had known that the being there was rife with magic and that it was dangerous, but she had never thought it might be Tiamat. The pixies knew nothing of the old legend, of course, and she had never put much stock in it.

Kylara communicating with it changed all that, though.

"Is this entity the reason you became more interested in learning aura powers?" she asked when the flood of explanations was over.

The girl nodded. "Yes, ma'am."

She sighed. "Developing your aura is a worthwhile skill and one we should have focused on earlier. However, I wish you had come forward with this information sooner."

A small nod was the only response. She looked like she felt guilty about not doing exactly that and also…Amythist wasn't entirely sure. Not being able to read the girl's aura continued to be frustrating but she thought she looked frightened.

"Is there a reason you did not tell me all this?" she asked.

Kylara met her gaze and nodded. "Since you asked, ma'am…I was worried that you would put a magic-blocking cuff on me to try to prevent me from opening the pixie gates in my sleep."

"I would never—"

Jasmine coughed and looked pointedly at the headmaster. Amythist blanched. The mage was right, of course. She had put a magic dampening cuff on Kylara. And if Jasmine Patel was willing to point this out to her—albeit in a culturally accepted way for mages to historically address dragons—she knew she had messed up.

"We talked about that, Kylara. I had hoped to make it clear that I view the choice to put that device on you as a mistake."

"Yes, ma'am. I should have trusted you more fully but it was hard. You put a dampener on me last time as a precaution. The gates that opened at the time were not even my doing. I couldn't help but think that if you knew it was my fault this time, you would do it again."

"Kylara—"

"I couldn't risk that, ma'am," Kylara said, her tone slightly less subservient although—bless the child—she still tried to be polite for once. "Not with this cult interested in me and not when I found out the full extent of what auras could do to me. I know you care about me and only want me to be safe, but you could still use my emotions when we started. I couldn't risk someone else having that kind of power."

The old dragon did not bother to point out that her command of her aura powers was still lacking. The girl was right. She would need her full faculties to face this threat. She only hoped that she had not damaged their relationship so severely that Kylara would be unable to trust her fully.

Nothing could be done about it now except apologize and make it clear that she had nothing to fear in the future. Amythist put her cup of tea down, stood, stepped to the side of her desk so she was in full view of the girl, and curtsied deeply.

Sam gasped at the show of respect. Such things were usually not done by someone of a higher position for someone of lower rank, and never when such an age difference existed. "Lady Kylara Diamantine, I swear to you I will never restrain your magical abilities again, be it with a magic dampening cuff or any other method. My intention was to keep you safe but I see now that I still caused you—and your trust in me—harm. I apologize."

Kylara uttered a vaguely surprised, 'Um...' before Tanya elbowed her in the ribs and told her that she needed to formally accept the headmaster's apology so she could stand and not offend her further.

"Oh, sure. I er...accept your apology, Lady Amythist. I appreciate your promise and despite my um...earlier...misgivings, would very much like your help."

The old dragon returned to her seat as if nothing had happened. "Of course, child. You are still one of my students. It is my duty to protect all of you."

"What do you think we should do, ma'am?" Sam asked.

"For the moment? I think we should do nothing at all."

All five of the students' brows furrowed.

"If there are more attacks on your classmates before they can return to campus, that will change things but for now, it seems we can assume you are their target."

"So you don't think Bull was working alone like he said?" Kylara asked.

"Not for a moment," Amythist stated. "I have met Kishar once or twice over the centuries—despite her looks, she is of an age with me—and have always known her to be an accomplished schemer. That she came to school for an alleged student visit and used the opportunity to privately communicate with Kylara only proves that she excels in deception. If I were her and truly did believe that she was the Sum of All Dragons—"

"But you don't—right, ma'am?" Karl forced a chuckle.

The headmaster eyed him so coolly that frost could have formed on his greasy black hair. "There is much I do not understand, Mr. Midnight. Kylara and her abilities are at the very top of that list. Divinity aside, we know there is something in that pond. I have sensed it myself. And—as little as I do not like having not been told the entire truth—I am inclined to believe that all of you are being honest with me now. Although your father might not appreciate you working against his…associates."

Karl made a face. "My dad versus my friends. Hmm, tough call. Not." He smiled at Kylara and stretched a hand to Jasmine, who took it.

"If that's your call and it's good enough for your friends, it's good enough for me," Amythist said.

Five curt head nods and a quick check of the three dragons' aura put any doubts in their story to rest.

"So, the presence of that being in the pool means that my beliefs are irrelevant," she continued. "We know the Followers of Tiamat are interested in Kylara and that Kishar is invested as well. If I were in her position, I would tell my Followers to do exactly as Bull did. I would tell them to attack and claim they acted of their volition. That way, they can test whatever they wish to test."

"I think they want me to get more dragon powers," Kylara said quietly.

She nodded in agreement. "All of this means we must act as if there is coordinated effort to give Kylara these powers."

"Is that necessarily a bad thing?" Sam asked. "More powers make her more powerful, right?"

The dragon mage also looked curious. "I was only able to stop Bull because I absorbed his power, ma'am. Sam might have a point."

"Perhaps…" Amythist admitted reluctantly. "But they are not doing this to simply make you more powerful, Kylara. They believe you will usher their goddess in. It seems that they wish this to happen by any means necessary. If they truly wished for you to simply become more powerful, why not contact the Lumos School and ask if the Followers could duel with Kylara one by one to grant her powers?"

"Why not?" Tanya asked.

"Because that would put them under scrutiny," the headmaster snapped and her gentle tone slipped at the stupid question. "And under the scrutiny of the Steel Guard as well, for that matter. They obviously do not wish their actions to be known, which makes me believe they do not have the best interests of young Miss Diamantine at heart. Tell me, Kylara, did Kishar give you any indication of what would happen to you when Tiamat returned—or indeed how your powers are supposed to bring her back?"

"I…I don't know what you mean," Kylara admitted.

"That is a problem," Amythist said. "And an indication that whatever your place in all this is, it is not one of leadership."

The five students nodded and seemed to grasp the import of that.

"What do you recommend we do, Headmaster?" the dragon mage asked.

"For now? I think it would be best if we wait and see what the cult does next. I do not think any of you should leave campus for any reason and especially not Kylara." She expected protests so it was a pleasant surprise when none came. "Can you all agree to this?"

The friends shared a look that said they'd already considered being grounded. It was Kylara who spoke for them. "Yes, ma'am. If dragons with crazy powers attack, I'd rather have teachers around to help to protect me."

"Yeah, a little extra help sounds like a good idea," Karl added, completely ignorant as to how arrogant and full of himself he sounded. At least he was bragging about the group and not only himself.

"Well, it's nice to know the defensive barriers and guardian statues we put up to protect you children will be appreciated this year, Mr. Midnight. In fact, it might do you good to spend time scrubbing them. They work best when free of dust."

"What? No way! What if I step past them and they activate?" he whined.

"Mind your step and that won't happen," Amythist snapped.

Karl snorted and threw his shoulders up in a pouty shrug. While he avoided the old dragon's eyes, she winked at the others. She needed them to know she was still in charge and powerful enough to protect them, but also that she cared about them and would not let them come to harm. She hoped Midnight cleaning the statues would serve as a reminder of both things.

"If anything else suspicious happens—and I mean anything at all—please tell me right away."

"Define suspicious," Karl said in an attempt to regain some of the face he had lost.

"We are speaking about a cult of dragons who worship unusual dragon powers as shards of the divine," Amythist explained. "If you think a bug is behaving oddly, it could be a shrunken dragon. A dark cloud on an otherwise clear day could be the work of one of these cultists. I want you on campus but I want you alert. Are we clear?"

"Yes, ma'am," the five assented.

"Very well. Then you are dismissed. Try to get some rest. Kylara, we'll continue your aura training in earnest tomorrow."

<h1 style="text-align:center">CHAPTER TWENTY-FIVE</h1>

Kishar knew she was dreaming. After millennia on this planet, she had come to know the feeling of her dreams. There was an inevitability to them that did not exist in the waking world. She spent much of her time in various attempts to make her hopes and aspirations become a reality. In dreams, she did not feel that pressure. It was as if everything was already preordained. She hoped that with the rise of Tiamat, life might finally start to take on a more dreamlike quality in that regard.

So when she realized that she soared high above an endless swamp hidden beneath a thick canopy of trees, she did not question it but followed the current of air that propelled her through her dream sky.

Before long, she felt a strong, almost overwhelming desire to look at the forest far below. Instead of an endless, unbroken canopy, she saw an almost perfect circle hollowed out of the forest. The pond was hidden so deep in the swamp that nothing could be seen on any horizon. Curious, she descended.

She spiraled into a slow descent, fanned her wings to cut her speed, and landed on the edge of the placid water. Remarkably, the wind from her wings did not send so much as a ripple across the surface. Now that her gaze had rested on the pool, she did not want to move it away. She did not fight this feeling at all. Instead, she embraced it, assuming this was part of the path she must walk as a Follower of Tiamat and that it might be even more important since she was the First Walker.

As she stared at the surface of the water, ripples formed from nowhere. When they resolved, Kishar could see a reflection in the pond. A beautiful dragon, hidden in shadow but with scales that sparkled from the darkness in a rainbow of color, sat on the far edge of the pond. The First Walker looked up, startled—she had not seen or heard anyone approach—to see if someone had come through the swamp, but there was no one there. The reflection existed only in the pond. It was strange magic, even to someone like her who had made a life of studying and recruiting dragons with unusual powers.

"Who has summoned me here?" she asked and bowed respectfully. Her dreams often had answers for her and they were more easily deciphered when accepted, not fought against. In the real world, she hadn't bowed to another dragon for millennia but societal norms did not apply in the world of dreams. Whatever was in the pond was only a reflection of her, after all, odd powers or not.

"Kishar. You walk a path of honor." The voice was one of strength, ancient yet still brimming with power. It was that of a mother who knew better than her children yet was proud of them all the same. She had never heard the voice before, either in real life or in the world of dreams, and yet she recognized instantly who it must belong to.

She lowered her snout to the moss-covered roots in front of her and prostrated herself before her goddess. "Tiamat. You wake!" She gasped as tears trickled unbidden from her eyes. A lifetime—hundreds of human lifetimes—had been spent in preparation for this very moment and now, it was there. Tiamat, the Sleeper, was speaking to her. She even knew her name. If she were to die now, it would be with pride.

Although she hoped the goddess had more for her to do than that.

"Rise, my daughter. I have felt you laboring, even from within my dreams. You bring honor to my Followers, First Walker."

Kishar pushed out of the muck—the smell had not been terribly pleasant—and looked across the pond. Tiamat was still not there, of course. She existed only in the reflection. A quirk of this type of existence meant that she had to permanently keep her snout pointed toward the pond if she wanted to see her goddess at all. Although she no longer prostrated herself, her head was still bowed in respect.

"I believe we have found the Sum of All Dragons, Your Eminence."

"You speak of Kylara Diamantine," Tiamat responded.

"You know of her? Is she indeed who we believe her to be?"

"She is."

"How can you be sure?"

An incredible wave of rage rose from the pond and it filled her with terror, dread, and inescapable fear. "Never question me, Kishar. You have followed my path for thousands of years without question. Do not think because I have presented myself to you that you may now question me like an old and withered wisdom."

"Yes, Your Eminence. Of course, Your Eminence." She bowed repeatedly and barely noticed that she dirtied her snout with mud and muck from the pond. She would do anything to escape the feeling of dread and terror that overwhelmed her ability to think.

"I have drawn the girl here and spoken to her," Tiamat explained as if Kishar were but a mewling dragonling. "She has resisted me, which is unfortunate but to be expected. I have tasted her dreams and she was raised far off the path."

"I humbly beg your forgiveness. If I had known sooner—"

"You have done well enough," Tiamat acknowledged.

For the briefest of moments, she felt that well enough was not adequate. She had spoken to the girl, cataloged her powers, and even sent a dragon with particularly unusual powers to test her. Not only that, she had been successful on all fronts. She certainly deserved more praise than "well enough!" In a moment, however, those feelings were gone, washed away like a child's sandcastle in the wake of a tidal wave.

Her disappointment was swallowed by a deep well of gratitude at being praised by her goddess. While she had done well enough, she would strive to do better. She would do anything she could—anything at all—to please Tiamat and bring her out of her sunken prison, out of this dream, and into the material world.

"What can I do for you, my goddess?" she asked and bowed deeply.

"You will bring the girl to me," Tiamat all but purred and her aura radiated praise and pleasure. Kishar basked in it like a cat in a patch of sunshine.

"Forgive my impertinence, Your Godhood"—referring to Tiamat's divinity felt right—"but shall we give her more powers before we bring her to you? There are still a great many shards of your essence that she does not have. Do you require more before you take her?"

The being paused at this, seemingly pleased that the First Walker attempted to find different ways to please her. The resulting approval made Kishar very happy.

"More powers would be better. However, she already has a great many. Simply bringing her to me might be enough. You must capture her and bring her to this pond."

"Yes, of course."

"It is not in the world you live in but the one where I am imprisoned. The girl can already come here. You may need to use her power to come to me. I leave the particulars of how to do that up to you. If, in doing this, you give her more shards of my divinity, that would please me."

"Consider it done. We have followed your path for millennia and will follow you longer still, oh dreamer of amazing dreams."

"Very good. Now wake."

Kishar felt a thousand needles stab between each and every one of her scales. Her eyes opened to the sound of her screams and when she looked around her, she was in bed and the pain was fading.

She dragged herself from her down bed and dressed in a colorful wrap of dark-blue fabric with shards of silver stitched into it. She would address the other Followers of Tiamat in her dragon form, of course, but she had found that centuries of dressing as a human, doing her hair as one, and using their architectural structures had left an imprint on her.

For some reason, she felt more comfortable when clothed in beautiful garments, even if the other dragons would not see them. In fact, if she didn't dress and simply took her dragon form while she was still naked in her human form, she still felt naked in her dragon form. It was a habit that would likely be broken when Tiamat returned and made the human form irrelevant to dragons. But until then, she would do as she had done for centuries.

Dressed and with her make-up applied and her golden nose ring inserted, she strode out of the room at the top of the temple. The other dragons except those on watch slept on the steps of the Aztec pyramid or on the slabs of stone positioned around its base.

She approached Sonic—the dragon who could augment his voice—and prodded him awake. He resisted at first but as soon as his eyes flicked open and he realized who tried to wake him, he sat bolt upright as quickly as she had when awakened by Tiamat.

"How may I serve the First Walker?" Sonic bowed.

"Wake them. Wake them all. The time of waiting has come to an end."

"You mean—"

"She who Sleeps came to me in a dream. The path we follow approaches its destination. Now, wake them!"

He nodded, excitement plain in his body language. He puffed the sack of skin on his throat. Once full, he released a great bellow that shattered the birdsong of the jungle at dawn. In an instant, the dozens of dragons who remained woke, complained loudly, or took to the air to fight. It was not often that a dragon was wakened from its slumber. They were accustomed to controlling the high place in society. It was something they had better get used to. Tiamat would be above them all, as was her right. Dragons would rule the lesser species as intended but She Who Has Spilled Her Blood For Us All would rule above them.

They all fell silent as their gazes turned to Kishar. She could hardly see them. The light of the rising sun was in her eyes, a necessary sacrifice for the effect she wanted. She knew that at this hour, the rays of light only reached the temple at the very top of the pyramid. The jungle, the dragons, and indeed the pyramid itself were all in darkness, but she was illuminated, a beacon in the gloom.

"Our time of waiting is over!" she roared to the still half-awake dragons.

Many cheered but more only stared at her, dumbfounded, likely wondering if this was a dream.

"The Sleeper in the Deep summoned me to the place where she has been confined and has waited for us to come far enough down the path to her. She is pleased with the work we have done."

A cheer followed this, louder than the first, although she could still feel disbelief emanating from the auras of the dragons below.

"She told me—in a voice richer and more truthful than any I

have ever heard—that Kylara Diamantine is the one. She is The Sum of All Dragons as we had dared to hope!"

The gathering erupted in cheers. A key tenet of the Followers of Tiamat was that everyone walked their own path. This meant everyone had to make their interpretations of the best way to serve their long-absent goddess.

Naturally, mistakes had been made in trying to bring her back over the centuries. This made the Followers a naturally cautious group. Those who had put their faith in the pixies, for example, were either no longer part of the Followers or were held in such low esteem that even the newly initiated outranked them. Everyone knew that despite Kylara Diamantine's considerable promise to be the Sum of All Dragons, there was still a chance they were wrong.

The First Walker speaking to Tiamat changed all that, though. No one had ever claimed to speak to the goddess, not even Boneclaw. It would be too big a lie to maintain to potentially hundreds of dragons who would always read the emotional state of the liar. Kishar had never so much as considered making such a thing up and the Followers knew it. As a result, they believed her now.

"She is proud of the work we have done!"

The dragons cheered even more loudly as they warmed up to the idea that their goddess was closer to them than she had ever been before. None cheered louder than Bull or Pakennen.

Kishar waited for them to fall silent before she continued. "She is ready for the girl to be brought to her."

Gasps followed and one dragon even fainted. All their auras evidenced astonishment.

"We have done far better than we could have imagined," she continued. "I had hoped to give the girl more shards of her divinity but, despite her not leaving the fortress of the Lumos School since Bull gifted her his ability a few weeks ago, our goddess has deemed that the time is now.

"She has enough powers to fulfill her role as the Sum of All Dragons. Tiamat has ordered that we bring the girl to her place of resting." Saying her name aloud sent a shudder through the crowd. Anticipation and eagerness were thick in the air.

"But how, First Walker? How do we travel to the place where she is imprisoned?"

Kishar could not see who spoke with the sun glaring in her eyes but—despite the impertinence of the comment—it did not matter. It was something that needed to be addressed although she wished they had not ruined the pace of her speech.

"There will be a struggle, this is true, but now that we have been shown the True Path, we know what we must do. We will attack this school and the splinters of the divine we have at our disposal will overwhelm their defenses. I have spoken to the girl and she may not wish to go. That is as it will be. But do not worry, she can be convinced."

"How?"

"That will be my mission," she said. "The responsibility will be mine, as will the shame or the glory."

A general mumble of assent followed this, not that they had a choice.

"Your role will be twofold. For those of you who have not yet given the girl your ability, you must do so if given the opportunity. We do not yet fully understand how much of your power must be wielded against her for her to take the ability, but I wish each of you to strike her at least once. Your other mission will be to keep all others away from the girl. Her friends will doubtlessly try to fight, as will the staff and likely some of the students. Although if any of your children stand against us, they betray themselves as those who have gone astray and left the path."

She looked for Lord Midnight—she knew his son was friends with the girl—but she could not see him in the glare. Still, she knew he could hear her and that he understood who she was talking about.

"The girl is the key to the door at the end of the path we have followed for centuries. She is almost certainly the Sum of All Dragons prophesied in legend, the being whose arrival is the harbinger of Tiamat's return. Yet we must still endeavor to do all that we can to make the prophecies come to fruition. If we fail to bring her to the place where the Sleeper sleeps, or if she does not have enough splinters when she arrives there, it could be another millennium before one comes who is the Sum of All Dragons. It will not be easy but together, we will be successful!

"Together, we will follow Tiamat to our destiny!"

CHAPTER TWENTY-SIX

Weeks passed and Kylara almost wished for the excitement of when Bull had attacked her. She liked school and had made progress in her aura abilities—at least according to Amythist, although she still felt she had much to learn. Yet it was hard to focus on any of that when a cult of insane dragons lurked out there, seemingly biding their time. She wished one of them had attacked and given her a dragon version of patience because she honestly felt like she was going stir-crazy.

The headmaster had allowed the field trips to continue—albeit without her and her friends—and every time the other students went out, the young dragon mage waited for another attack to come but none did. Amythist said this was a good thing and that it meant it was Kylara who had their attention. As long as they kept her on the school grounds, she would be safe. The Steel Guard was actively searching for Kishar and although nothing had turned up, she was convinced that something would.

The girl sometimes wished that the cult would attack. Then, at least, there would be some progress instead of the endless waiting.

These thoughts ran through her head—like they did every day

—while she was in Professor Sharra's class. Their latest challenge was to move ten gallons of water from one vessel to another. The only thing was they were not allowed to touch either vessel or get any part of their bodies wet. Sam, Karl, Jasmine, and Tanya thought the challenge was an interesting one and had come up with a few ways to try to solve it, but she simply couldn't focus.

The result of this was that despite waiting for an attack to come, it was not she who first noticed it, but Jasmine.

"Did you see that?" the mage asked and pointed at the water.

"See what?" Sam asked absently. He tried to use a complex pattern of light to make the water evaporate and condense in the other vessel. Thus far, it hadn't worked.

"Something made it ripple."

"There's another one," Karl said.

Kylara looked up. She had felt that one and dust drifted from the ceiling as if something had struck the building hard enough to shake its magical foundation.

Their group was not the only one to notice the interruption.

"Professor?" A student from another group raised her hand tentatively.

Professor Sharra was already clutching a glass sphere and muttered into it as she received messages from other mages around campus.

Another rumble followed, this one hard enough that it knocked a piece of plaster off the ceiling. It fell into one of the group's vessels of water with a splash that made half the class almost jump through the roof.

Professor Sharra looked up from the sphere and addressed the class. "Students, it seems that someone is attempting to trespass onto school grounds. Usually, I would send everyone to their dorms but we should be fine in here. Let's try to get back to work—"

The wall behind her exploded inward.

Brick, mortar, and dust filled the room, although none of it reached the students. The mages had all thrown shields up against the blast. There were certainly advantages to going to a school that spent much of its curriculum focusing on self-defense.

Kylara did not move. She watched the opening in the wall as the dust settled. It was odd to look out of the magically enlarged room into the more pedestrian hallway. Somehow, it created a kind of optical illusion that caused the corridor to look bigger than it was. She had begun to wonder if that meant this room perhaps shrank the people inside instead of growing larger to accommodate them when she saw what had made the hole.

It was Bull.

And—thanks to the magic of the room—he looked twice as large as he had the last time she had seen him.

"Bull is here for the Sum of All Dragons," the massive, ram-horned, wingless dragon bellowed. "Everyone else, get out of my way."

"I'll need to see your visitor's pass," Professor Sharra snapped and wound the dragon in a sphere of shimmering blue energy. Unfortunately, she wasn't fast enough. She had only lifted three of his four feet off the ground but he pushed himself into motion with the toe of one of his back legs. Kylara knew from her practice with this particular power that one toe was more than enough.

His momentum built and he pushed through the professor's shields like a cow walking over a chain-link fence. It might not have been a quick—or a particularly graceful—process, but the end result was inevitable.

Bull broke through the shield and crashed into the room. Kylara's brain had to try to work around how the dragon appeared to shrink for a moment, but by the time he had righted himself ungracefully and upended a wall of shelves in the process, she was in her dragon form and the two were of a size.

"Bull doesn't want to fight," he said. "Come with me."

"You have no right to be here!" Professor Sharra attacked once more, this time with spears of sparks.

He deflected them with his scaly hide and roared in displeasure. Mindless of the students between him and his target, he surged toward the professor. Most of the mages either jumped clear of his charge or threw shields up and were knocked back by his one-dragon stampede but to Kylara's horror, a few fell.

That was enough for her.

She roared and her breath transformed into ice crystals that encapsulated Bull. Unfortunately, it wasn't fast enough. Before she could completely immobilize him in a block of ice, he flicked his tail and shattered most of it.

"Professor, get the class out of here!" the young dragon mage shouted.

"I will not abandon you!" the woman retorted.

"We've fought this cow before," she replied. "We can handle him. Get the class to safety!"

"Cow?" Bull bellowed. "You dare to insult Bull?"

"Hey, what do you call a bull with no legs?" Karl asked, still in his human form. "Ground beef!" Shadows that had worked under the massive dragon yanked suddenly and he fell heavily with such force that another shelf toppled.

"Professor, go!" Kylara shouted again.

"Very well," the woman said as if a coworker had asked her to chaperone a field trip and nothing more. "This way, class!" She made a staircase of shimmering blue magic and directed the students up it.

A few remained behind. "We want to help!" one of the dragons said.

"You need to get to safety!" Sam ordered.

"We are going to help!" the student responded.

"Fine," Kylara agreed, her gaze still on Bull. Karl was doing well with his shadow powers. He was using them to make the dragon overcompensate so he stumbled and constantly collided with things. It wouldn't work for long and was hell on the building, but it had bought them some time. "He won't be here alone, though. Get to the U and help drive back any other dragons you see."

The student didn't look pleased to be sent away, but he looked at the group he was with and they all nodded. "Yes, ma'am. We'll see you there."

Kylara only had time to nod before Bull regained his feet and charged toward her. She lowered her head, lurched forward, and felt the now-familiar sensation of the momentum growing inside her until it felt like nothing could sway her from her path.

She collided with Bull and both of them were hurled back. She was not nearly as dazed as she had been when she had first run headlong into him, but the uncomfortable fact remained that she was still dazed. He stood without any sign of weakness, lowered his horns at her, and charged.

The dragon mage shook her head. She couldn't beat him in a contest of strength. He was too familiar with his powers and too thickheaded…but maybe she wouldn't have to.

"Jasmine, no!" she shouted as the mage stepped into Bull's path. Her hair whipped wildly as she layered wall after wall of paper-thin shields between her and the advancing dragon. A brilliant flare of light accompanied by an ear-splitting boom flung everyone and everything away, even Bull.

Kylara was knocked into the final wall of shelves. It collapsed around her but she was uninjured. Her diamond scales had protected her. Her friend could not have been so lucky.

"Jasmine!" she shouted and looked frantically for the mage.

She found her wrapped in a cocoon of Karl's shadows. He brought her to him and cradled her in his arms. She was conscious although woozy and bleeding from both nostrils. That shield must have taken everything she had.

"Rest now, Jasmine. That was seriously badass. I'll take it from here so I can at least get some of the credit."

"I guess we now know…what happens when an unstoppable force…meets an immovable object." Jasmine smiled at her attempt to make a joke.

"Immovable object?" Karl asked. "He threw you across the room like a doll."

"I was talking about the Patel stubborn streak." The girl laughed so hard Kylara thought she might choke herself to death.

"I find your stubbornness adorable," Midnight said and kissed her on the forehead. "But immovable, you are not. Professor Sharra!" he called and used his shadow powers to transport her to the top of the stairs. "Get her to safety. We'll hold this cow off."

"Very well," the professor said grimly.

"Are you ready to come with Bull?" the dragon asked Kylara.

"Over my dead body."

"Kishar wants you alive. But she also didn't want me to damage you too much. Oh, well." He lowered his head and initiated another attack.

CHAPTER TWENTY-SEVEN

Kylara managed to gain enough momentum to catapult both her and Bull away but it was clear this would not work. She couldn't beat him like this, not one on one.

"We need to get out of this room!" Tanya shouted. "I can't do anything here. There's no water."

"Sure there is," Sam said and used a blast of light to shatter all the vessels the students had used. The girl's eyes gleamed as she slid her hand into a pocket of her dress— Kylara had no idea when she had those stitched in—and tossed a handful of seeds out. The moment they touched the moisture, they exploded into life and grew a thick mat of grass that turned green and threw seed heads out before they turned brown and died.

For a moment, the dragon mage thought the attack had failed before it had even begun but a moment later, all the seed heads exploded into more growth to create a tangle of long grasses that was a hundred times thicker than the first had been.

The aggressive dragon plowed through it like it was nothing.

Karl sent tendrils of shadow through the grass, but once Bull was in motion, the shadow dragon's powers did nothing to the beast.

"My turn to help," Sam said and blasted a beam of light at their adversary's eyes. The dragon screamed and stumbled but he knew his power well enough to not stop moving. Instead, he barreled past Kylara and into a wall. Before the building had even stopped shaking from the impact, he pawed the ground and attacked again. He bulldozed into the opposite wall, cracked it, and brought down a large piece of the roof with it.

Bull backed away from the wreckage, snorted, and jerked his head about as he looked for Kylara. He got only the briefest of glances before Sam blasted his eyes with another flash of light.

Undeterred, the dragon lunged into another run toward where he had seen his quarry.

She dodged easily and let him rocket past her and into a broken part of the wall. More of the roof came down.

"Let me try something!" Tanya shouted as the dragon bellowed in rage.

An agave plant grew in the middle of the room, unlike any in the natural world. Normally, the blueish-gray plants had spines at the tips of their fleshy, modified leaves that were perhaps an inch long. Those on the plant Tanya had made had spines that were at least a foot long. They were slightly twisted, too, which Kylara had a feeling would make them even stronger.

The dragon mage positioned herself on the other side of the plant and raised her voice. "Can't you see where you're going?"

Bull, blinded by Sam and rage, launched forward.

Unbelievably, he plowed completely over the agave plant. It didn't so much as slow him. He ran through it and didn't seem to notice until he pounded into the opposite wall. When he turned, Kylara saw that despite him destroying the plant, the thorns had punctured his scales. Like a curious dog that had tried to attack a porcupine, spines protruded from his face and front legs. They bled freely and his dragon power was unable to force them out. He pulled some of them from his face with his claws, but he was not a dragon of fine motor skills and succeeded only in agitating the spines further.

"Forget Tiamat. Bull will kill you, little girl. You will wish you were a thousand miles from here when he is through with you!"

That gave Kylara an idea.

"Sam, blind this moron!" she ordered. "I have a plan."

The golden dragon obeyed, launched a tight beam of light at Bull's eyes, and held it firmly to shine in his face.

"Hey, bozo, over here!" she yelled.

"How is that any different from what we've been doing?" Tanya said, her voice tight with fear.

The dragon—predictably—lowered his head and raced toward her. He seemed unconcerned that the impact with her would likely drive the spines deeper into his face. She had no intention to rely on the stubborn dragon's wounds to stop him, nor would she use her version of his power. Instead, she opened a gate to the pixie realm and another a millimeter away from the first. A cold wind blew out of the second one.

Bull—blind and furious—rushed into the open portals and she snapped them shut behind him. All that was left of him was a few snowflakes that melted quickly in the heat of the classroom.

"Where did you send him?" Sam asked and looked genuinely impressed.

"I sent him home." She chuckled.

"You mean to Diamantine's house?" Tanya asked.

"Your mom's tough but she's not mountain-cracking tough," Karl added.

"No, no. My first home. The lodge at the bottom of a lake in northern Canada. It was his idea. He said I would wish we were a thousand miles apart. He was right. I thought he wouldn't cause us too much trouble from there."

Sam laughed and agreed. "That was amazing, Kylara. Truly. Instead of simply bruting the brute, you outsmarted him."

"Ky, your horn," Tanya said.

Kylara felt her horn and realized it was indeed broken. Despite being made of diamond, Bull's momentum magic had cracked it.

Sam touched her face. Light infused her and the horn was healed.

"Thank you." She smiled and thought of when she had first met Sam, of how—even in his dragon form—she had always found him handsome. Getting to know him only made her trust that first impression all the more. He was brave, kind, and always had her back. He was great…exceedingly great. She leaned closer to him.

"Yeah, sorry to interrupt, but I don't think this is exactly the time." A tendril of shadow touched the backs of both their heads and pushed them together so they bumped horns.

"Right, the attack." Sam straightened.

Kylara looked out of the classroom through the hole Bull had made when he entered. What she saw outside was a scene of magic-induced chaos. Dragons flew across the small window into the outside world with fireballs in pursuit. Whirlwinds of ice tried to push back dragons with unusual body shapes and powers that she could only guess at.

"I've always preferred to fight outdoors," Tanya said.

"What are we waiting for?" Karl said, took his dragon form, and launched into the air. He flew not only on his natural wings but another pair made of pure shadow.

"Sam—" Kylara said.

"Come on. Professor Sharra probably needs cover to get the kids to the dorm," he pointed out.

She nodded and followed her friends into the fray.

They stepped into the U and a fight the likes of which she had never imagined was possible. She had never seen so many dragons all in one place. There must have been a hundred, at the very least. A couple of dozen of them were on or near the ground and had engaged the school's security and staff but at least twice as many were still in the air and soared around the campus in enormous circles.

The team of security mages fought with methods now familiar to her. They used shields to protect themselves as they tried to drive the dragons back with blasts of air, fire, and telekinetic force. The few who had the ability to augment their strength and speed tried to engage the dragons in close-quarters combat, but even with supernatural abilities, the human form was simply at a disadvantage when facing a massive, winged, lizard with four talons and a long whiplike tail. She would have included fire breath in that assessment, but it seemed none of the dragons relied on such pedestrian powers.

One sprayed acid from his mouth that the mages tried desperately to block with shields. Anything it touched—even brick—melted like butter on top of a stove.

Another inflated its throat and released shrieks that seemed to vibrate things to pieces.

Yet another was surrounded by lumps of what appeared to be metal. It used them for both defense and offense, blocked mage blasts by making the metal flatten into discs, and attacked by creating and launching spikes.

Kylara pointed to the metal one. "We start with him."

Her friends didn't bother to agree. They simply leapt into action. Sam streaked beams of light at the dragon. The first hit its eyes, which made it divert its attention from the mage and follow the beam of light he held focused on it. A disadvantage of light powers was that they became a literal beacon to anyone he used them against.

In the blink of an eye, metal spikes rocketed toward him.

Kylara and Karl had his back, though. Both fired tendrils of shadow that lifted off the ground and intertwined into a web between their friend and the metal spikes. The shadow was not dense enough to stop the organic bullets, but it did manage to disrupt their trajectories. Instead of a half-dozen puncturing the golden dragon in as many places, he was pelted with the sides and butts of the metal projectiles. It must still have hurt but there was a difference between being whacked and being shot.

She rushed forward to engage the metal dragon. It immediately launched metal spikes at her and she and Karl managed to stop some, but not all. Those that streaked through did not hurt her any more than the deflected ones had hurt Sam, though. Her diamond scales blocked them.

The dragon mage had expected the metal dragon to become angry at being stopped but instead, it bowed to her. She shook her head at the strange behavior but before she could even choose another target, the dragon launched every scrap of metal it had at her. Kylara blocked the first few with her diamond scales but one spike lodged between her scales. A ball of metal followed it and pounded into the back of the spike. Like a hammer to a nail, the force of the blow sank it deep into her forearm.

She cried out in pain and the metal dragon smiled. It bowed but before it could do anything else, grasses reached out and bound it to the ground.

"The dude was a creep. You never asked for a piercing," Tanya said as her friend ripped the piece of metal from her flesh. Oddly enough, as soon as she thought about pulling the spike out, it came free despite being deeply lodged inside her. Did it mean she'd absorbed that power?

Kylara did not have time to make sure. Suddenly, her ears rang and she felt like she was being vibrated to nothing. The sound increased in pitch until she felt a sharp pain in one of her ears and heard nothing more on that side.

"Ky!" Sam landed next to her—having taken a moment from his battle, no doubt—and put a claw to her ear, healed her, and returned her sense of hearing. "Are you all right?"

"Yeah, I'm fine."

"They know it's you, Ky," Tanya shouted as she flew over

them. Indeed, the dragons had stopped attacking the mages and now spiraled around the dragon mage. Her friends drew closer.

"I don't want to sound like a quitter, but I don't think we can defeat them all," Karl said.

"We don't have to," she said. "We only need to hold them off until the Steel Guard gets here."

Reflexively, all four of them looked to the sky, hoping to see a portal open and a team of dragon-mounted mages pour through, but no such help seemed to be coming.

"In that case, I could use some water," Tanya said.

Kylara nodded and summoned moisture and wind. A wisp of cloud high in the atmosphere descended, then grew from ice crystals to a puff of white and into a thunderhead, while other dragons attacked with more fury than any storm.

She prepared to fend them all off at once but a coordinated attack did not come. Instead, the acid dragon swooped and spewed the foul stuff as she raced toward her, while the others tried to distract her friends. She had no doubt what was happening. The dragons fighting her friends did so only to keep them busy. The acid spitter wanted to force her to absorb her power.

The annoying thing was that she didn't know how to stop her. She exhaled ice and created a wall between her and the other dragon. The glob spattered when it met the barrier, but it melted the ice even faster than it had melted the brick buildings. She summoned a gust of wind to blow the next spray of acid back at the attacker. It worked and speckled her with the substance, but she merely grinned.

"It will only hurt for a moment, Sum of All Dragons. Once you have my power, you can no longer be scalded by your own acid."

"Yeah, no thanks," she replied and summoned thick cords of shadow to bind her adversary. It did not even vaguely work. A drop of acid was enough to burn through even the thickest of cords and in moments, the dragon was free.

Kylara was ready, though, and used her ability to be unstoppable combined with her diamond scales to surge into the dragon and hurl her away. The beast careened over the building Bull had broken a massive hole into. She tried to flap her wings to catch herself in the air, but from the way her limbs refused to function, it was clear that the bones had snapped. That dragon would be out of the fight for a few minutes, at least.

Unfortunately, when Kylara had struck her, she'd knocked the breath from her opponent and a splash of acid with it. This now burned her shoulder and worked slowly through the diamond scales. As soon as it found the cracks between them, it seared her skin.

She winced in pain and tried to blow ice breath on the wound to cool the painful sensation. The ice froze the acid into globs which no longer scorched her scales. She wiped the chunks off with another claw, knowing as she did so that she'd probably absorbed yet another new power. Honestly, she didn't know how to feel about that. It seemed a good thing to have access to more magic but did each new power pull her deeper into Tiamat's clutches? Was there a threshold that she might cross, after which point there would be no way to escape the dragon who'd already sunk her claws into her nightmares?

"Last chance to retreat!" Sam shouted and dragged Kylara's attention to the battle. For a moment, she thought Sam was talking about their group. The problem with that was she had no idea where to retreat to. But when she saw the headmaster fly into the fray, her scales sparkling like amethysts, she realized that Sam wasn't talking about them but the cultists.

The ancient dragon attacked without warning or hesitation, an army of one in the body of a dragon.

Kylara knew that Lady Amythist had a multitude of powers. After all, she was the first dragon to go to the pixie realm and was the first dragon to acquire a power besides those which she had been born with. She had seen her use these many times in the office. The headmaster could heat a pot of tea without touching it. She had seen her lift that same teapot and pour it into cups without touching them, or make balls of light to help her read.

But she'd never seen anything like this.

Amythist streaked relentlessly into battle and hurled rubble from the damaged buildings. Bricks, desks, and the debris of an all but demolished school building rocketed forward into the attacking dragons. When one of them withstood being pummeled with bricks, she would superheat the materials so instead of merely being bludgeoned, they were burned as well.

Beams of light shot from her eyes to blind any dragon foolish enough to look at her. One managed to make it through her perimeter of molten bricks and she surged into them with her teeth and claws as if she were the attacker, rather than playing defense. Blood spurted and the dragon's wing was torn away. It fell to the earth, a piteous heap that no longer had a place in the battle.

The acid spitter might have been able to do something had her wing still functioned. As it was, the headmaster blocked her spurts of acid with a shield of telekinesis and simply buried her in a great pile of brick.

The metal dragon fared no better. His ability to control metal did not seem to be as powerful as her telekinesis. She ripped his spheres away from him and pummeled him with them. While she couldn't make them change shape like he could, the shape of an object hardly mattered when it was whacked repeatedly against one's skull.

Another tried to attack and she simply seared them with fire. They plummeted, many of their scales burned away.

It looked like the fight was as good as over until a dragon appeared at Amythist's back. It was Kishar, Kylara was sure of that, but she had no idea where she came from. A moment later, she saw the figure on the new dragon's back, concentrating as the watches on his arms ticked away. He leapt away and turned into a dragon to flee the battle.

Temporus had frozen time long enough to let Kishar get past Amythist's defenses.

At such close quarters, the ancient dragon was forced to brawl with her attacker. The two scratched and clawed relentlessly, each trying to find purchase on the other's throat with their jaws. They plunged to the earth and continued to kick and scratch each other.

"Come on!" Kylara told her friends. The cultists had not fought fair, so there was no reason for them to. Kishar might be skilled at close-quarters combat, but she couldn't stop Amythist, Kylara, and her three friends.

They formed up and together, they ran toward their headmaster.

Before they could get close enough to help, the invader exhaled a cloud of dark mist that surrounded both her and Amythist.

It was gone before Kylara could blow it away with her storm powers, but she soon wished that the obscuring cloud was still there.

Where the ancient dragon had been a black stone statue stood —the same color as the dark mist—that was a perfect replica of the headmaster. She was frozen in stone, locked in combat with an expression of shock on her dragon face.

CHAPTER TWENTY-EIGHT

Even though only Amythist was turned to stone, the entire battle froze. The dragons who had attacked either nursed their wounds after being defeated by the old dragon or maintained a perimeter and kept their distance from Kishar.

Kylara wasn't able to move any more than they were. She had never seen or heard of such a thing. To think she'd had had a conversation with this woman and all the while, she could have done this to her and the other students in the room at any moment. Her friends were also frozen. She knew they were all thinking the same thing. Their headmaster was dead.

Before she could attack the newcomer—before she even knew if she should engage her—the dragon stepped between her and Amythist.

The young dragon mage stared, frozen and seemingly as petrified as the ancient dragon was. How could this be a power? How could Kishar live with herself knowing that she could simply do this to anyone who so much as looked at her wrong? She had a feeling she knew what had happened to Hammas, the missing vanilla dragon. He was dead, his body turned into black stone and tucked away where he would never be seen.

The invader moved toward her, which broke the stillness of the moment. Kylara called on all her powers. She called on the thundercloud above to churn more tightly and charge itself with static electricity so she could call down bolts of lightning. While she sent tendrils of shadow across the ground, her eyes glowed with white light. She heated her diamond scales to scalding hot. Of course, she didn't know which—or indeed if any—of these powers would do a damn thing to Kishar, but she was not about to become a damn funeral statue without a fight.

Sam, Karl, and Tanya also looked more than ready to avenge their headmaster. Every scale of the golden dragon's body glowed, and Karl had wrapped himself in armor made of shadow itself. Tanya was in her human form, and her fingers twitched as she called on the roots of the plants beneath the U and readied them to attack at the right moment.

"No," Kylara said to her friends and swished her tail in front of them before they could take up their typical square formation.

"Ky, what are you talking about?" Sam snapped.

"We already lost…the headmaster." She choked on the words. It was too hard to think that Lady Amythist was gone. With her gone, who would train her or fly to the students' defense? Who would take residence in her office and kindly push tea on everyone who walked through the door? "I can't lose you too."

"She's right!" Kishar said, her tone as cool as a teacher praising the correct answer of a student.

"Go back to your cult," Tanya snapped.

"We are not a cult," the dragon snapped, her voice like venom. "But if that is how you feel, why not attack me and see what happens? Plants don't usually turn to stone when I use my power on them. Perhaps you'd have a chance."

"Tanya, don't," Kylara said.

"You are the culty-ist cult there ever was," Karl all but snarled.

"Oh, and you think arguing with your father about things you know nothing about makes you an expert?" Kishar growled.

"My father's an idiot," he retorted and took a step toward the enemy.

"Finally, something we can agree on. I warned him to not let you stand against us. He will pay for this. Tell me, do you think he'd prefer a statue of his son in your dragon form or human one?"

"Kylara will not go with you. Your plan failed," Sam said and took a step forward to match Karl.

"Oh, really?" Kishar all but purred. "And why not?"

"Because if she's truly the Sum of All Dragons like you think she is, the second you try to attack her with that wispy power of yours, she'll simply absorb it and use it on you."

Kishar—to Kylara's surprise—threw her head back and laughed. "Do you think I came here to force the Sum of All Dragons to do my bidding? You really are as dimwitted as your grandfather was. No, when I leave, Kylara will come with me willingly—won't you Kylara? In fact, it will be she who makes our escape possible."

"You're crazy," Sam remarked coldly.

"Delusional," Tanya added.

"Dumber than you look, which is not easy," Karl said.

Kishar's gaze settled on Kylara and she smiled. "And yet I'm right, aren't I, Miss Diamantine?"

"Why on earth do you think I would go with you?" the dragon mage demanded.

The First Walker tsked and shook her head in disappointment. "I guess there is no dragon ability that grants extra intelligence. A pity, that. You will come with me because you must."

"Sam's right. You can't hurt me with that power of yours."

"I don't wish to hurt you. Not when I can hurt them." Kishar exhaled and wisps of black mist poured from her nostrils and crept across the ground toward the young dragon mage. "So now you understand. You will come willingly with me now because if you do not, I will turn all your friends to stone and your only hope to ever save them will rest with me."

Kylara frowned. What did that mean? Was there a way to save the headmaster? Could Kishar's power have more than one way it worked like the acid dragon's?

"We can take her," Sam muttered. "I know we can."

"Hit that mist with your wind," Karl murmured.

"Wind?" The First Walker laughed. "Do you think a dragon has never tried to simply blow my attack away with their wings?"

Kylara brought up a gentle breeze. It tugged at the mist but not the way it did normal air.

"Maybe you can save one of them," Kishar continued. "Perhaps two. But do you wish to risk it? Wind is unpredictable at best. What if you miscalculate and some of my power drifts into the dorms? Are you willing to sacrifice so many when all I wish is to make you into what you were meant to be?"

"Fine," she agreed roughly.

"Ky, no!" Tanya said.

"I have to do this, Tanya. It's the only way." Was it? What if she let Kishar attack, took her power, and used it to save her friends? Although that was assuming far too much, namely that Kishar had told them the truth and hadn't simply given them false hope. She didn't think it had been a trick. It had seemed like a slip of the tongue, nothing more. But could she risk her friends on such a half-baked hunch? Could she risk Sam?

She knew the answer because it wasn't a choice at all.

"I'll cooperate as long as you don't hurt any of my friends or anyone else at the Lumos School," she declared.

Kishar bowed. "Of course, Kylara. Now, open a portal to the pixie realm and take us from here."

"I will do no such thing," she said. "We'll fly to wherever you want to go. But I won't let you hurt any pixies."

"The pixies are mere insects, girl. They mean nothing to me. If you wish me to swear it, I'll swear it. No harm will come to them or any of the students of this school. I'll even throw your mother in for good faith, but if you think we will leave on the wing, you are even dumber than I thought possible."

"That's how it is—" Kylara tried to stand firm.

"Do you think I want Kristen Hall and her Steel Guard to catch up to us? I know they're trying already. The only reason they can't is because one of my dragons has the ability to stifle mage magic."

That made her swallow despite herself. That was troubling and it explained why Amy hadn't opened a gate yet.

"Hurry, girl. One group of guards or another will be here in minutes, of that I have no doubt. I will not extend my promise of protection to anyone who tries to stop us from taking you to her. What do you think happens to a dragon who turns to stone in the air? Do you think there is blood when they shatter? I assure you there is not. Only pieces."

"Fine!" she snapped and opened a portal to the meadow where Professor Sharra had taken them on field trips. With luck, they'd all go through, the professor could tell Kristen where they had gone, and—with help from the pixies—they would follow.

"No, no, no. That will not do," Kishar said and peered through the portal. "You seemed so sharp, Kylara. Are you trying to be intentionally dense now or were those earlier indications false?"

"I don't know what you're talking about," she replied.

The First Walker smiled indulgently. "Take us to the place we both know, Kylara. The place where this path must end. The place where a new path—our new path—will begin."

"Tell me where, and I'll take you there," she said. "Do you mean Professor Sharra's classroom? We were both there."

"I am speaking of the place of your nightmares. The pond without ripples. The place from which Tiamat has summoned you from your dreams."

"You are truly crazy if you think I would ever go there," Kylara said.

"This conversation is over," Sam said and his eyes glowed brighter.

"Is it?" Kishar asked and exhaled puffs of dark clouds that crept across the ground. It was not like fire breath or acid but more like Karl's shadow powers. She could control where the petrifying clouds she created went. Right now, she made them creep toward the golden dragon. They stopped a few feet away from him and began to move around his sides.

"That's enough!" Kylara said and buckled under the silent threat. "I'll take you there but don't hurt him,"

"I wouldn't dream of it," the First Walker said, inhaled, and pulled the rolling clouds inside her. "The portal."

The dragon mage clenched her teeth but she did as she was told. She opened a portal to the shore of the pond.

"Take your human form and follow me through. Close it when I say so after the rest of the Followers have come through," Kishar said. Her voice had grown imperious.

She saw no choice but to obey. All that mattered was that she could not lose Sam—she couldn't, not with everything that had happened between them these last few months and not ever. She took her human form and walked through the portal as the boy she was doing it for choked out a loud, "No!" and had to be restrained by Karl's shadows and Tanya's plants before he got himself killed.

"Kylara, no—it's a trick!"

Of course, she knew it was. But what choice did she have? And besides, if she was the Sum of All Dragons, didn't that mean she would have power? What could they do to her? She had absorbed many of their powers.

All her confidence evaporated when she stepped through the portal and onto the shore of the pond. The sense of terror was palpable. It seeped into her and made her heart hammer and her breath catch as the other Followers of Tiamat stepped through. Kishar told her to close the portal behind her. She complied and was immediately overcome with how alone she was, even though she could feel the other dragon's talon on her shoulder.

CHAPTER TWENTY-NINE

The cult dragons formed an arc behind her and cut off any thought of a quick escape. On one side was the still pond and on the other, more than two dozen dragons, all towering over her as she was still in her human form.

Terror continued to pulse within her and pushed through the protection the pendant gave her. Or perhaps not pushed but rather circumvented. She did not want to know what it would feel like if she did not have the pendant her grandfather had made for her. As it was, she could use the terror to fuel her rage. She directed this at the cultists who had forced her to come to this horrible place.

The being at the bottom of the pond did not care about her feelings. She could feel its powers and the enormity of it and understood that compared to its will, she was nothing but an insect. The cultists, on the other hand, did not seem to know what to do with a teenage girl with diamond fists that glowed from within. She wondered if she should channel her plant powers and make the swamp simply swallow them. The vegetation was especially strong in the pixie realm.

But she was still alive, which meant Kishar probably didn't

want her dead. What did she want? "What next?" Kylara demanded as she summoned a thunderhead to this place in the swamp. "You might as well tell me what you want before I kick all your butts."

"Do you forget the power I possess so quickly?" the dragon retorted and more tendrils of the dark mist issued from her nostrils.

"Did you forget that before, I was worried about my friends and now, the only dragons around are you cultists?" A crack of thunder boomed in the distance and the wind kicked up. "I wonder how many of them I can get to turn into stone before I attack with my other powers?"

"How dare you speak to the First Walker this way!" a dragon she had seen on the periphery of the fight said. She realized with a start that it was Lord Midnight, Karl's father.

"She dares speak this way because she is friends with your impudent little brat of a son!" Kishar whirled on Lord Midnight, having seemingly forgotten about Kylara.

"My lady misunderstands—"

"I saw you in the attack, Midnight. That was a test and you failed. Approach the pond."

"Please, my lady—"

"Approach!"

He shuddered but he obeyed.

"How long can you hold your breath, Lord Midnight?" the First Walker asked.

"My lady?"

"Two minutes should be enough. Put your head in the water, Lord Midnight," Kishar snapped.

"Please, this is unbecoming of the girl's introduction to—"

"The girl is the Sum of All Dragons, not your son's best friend. Two minutes. If you count wrong, I will grant you the ability to survive for centuries without drawing a breath."

Lord Midnight dunked his head into the pond.

"If this is supposed to impress me, it's not working," Kylara said and tried to keep the bluster in her voice.

"That was not my intention." Her captor bowed. "Please, ignore him. He is beneath us both."

"You might have wanted him to help. You're about to find out that I won't be an easy person to take down. Some of them will fall before I do. He could have bought you a few minutes."

Despite Lord Midnight only being under the water for a few minutes, he had begun to thrash as if something attacked his face. Still, even with his tortured movements, the surface of the pond did not make a ripple.

Kylara tried to ignore him, even though his pain made her extremely uncomfortable. "Did you want to try to threaten me again?" she asked and summoned a great gust of wind. "I'll blow that mist of yours out of here and like Sam said, if you do use it on me, I'll simply absorb it. Face it, you cannot succeed with that trick here. The only people you'll be able to kill are your cultists."

Kishar chuckled, even though her face looked murderous at the word cultists. She assumed a fake smile. "Kylara, dear, I have no intention to hurt you at all. None of us have."

Lord Midnight twitched as if in agreement.

"No intention to hurt me? All your followers have done is attack me!"

"And yet, are you not stronger for it? Are you not more powerful than you were before these attacks? You have not suffered permanent injury. You have only grown stronger."

She scoffed. "How very convenient."

"Kylara, you are the prophesied one. Any one of us would die in your place if we had to."

Lord Midnight's motions grew more intense. Still, he did not pull his head out of the water.

"We have followed our path for centuries," the First Walker continued and ignored him. "We are so close to the end of our path. We do not wish to hurt you but rather to help you finish your journey and become the Sum of All Dragons."

Kishar flicked her tail sharply against Midnight's neck and he pulled his head out of the water and gasped for breath. Like his son, he had a mane of hair running down his neck. Soaking wet, it looked completely undignified. Despite his frantic movements, his face was not injured, only his pride. He limped to join the other dragons in the arc.

Kylara studied them all. She shook her head at how these dragons stood patiently and bowed every time their leader called her a prophet. It was insane, given that these same dragons had attacked the Lumos School.

Why were they there? Why did they believe in Tiamat, her divinity, and all the rest of it when so many dragons did not? Was it because they were ostracized by society?

But no, that wasn't it. Karl came from wealth and many of the dragons there seemed as distinguished as him. It was hard to tell from how they looked, of course, but there was something in the way they sat and the way they held themselves.

There was more to it, though. It dawned on her what the dragons who had attacked her had said. They had all talked about their powers as if they were more than quirks of whatever the equivalent for biology was that controlled the rules of dragons. All of these—with the exception of Lord Midnight—had powers she did not.

That was what united them. It was the same thing that had ruled Tanya's life when Kylara had first met her. Tanya had been a vanilla—a lesser dragon, someone who could never rise to the heights of those with more spectacular powers. Was there more to it than simple power, though? Were all the social benefits of extra powers a result of this religion? Had this hidden cult managed to influence dragon culture so much, even in secrecy?

And if so, what did that mean for her?

She looked at the ranks of dragons. What did they want from

her? Why was she there? Despite Kishar's pontificating, she had not said exactly how Kylara was supposed to…what? Usher in the rebirth of Tiamat?

"Are you ready to be completed?" the dragon asked.

Then, she understood. She transformed into her dragon body as the dragons all attacked her at once.

The pain was unlike anything she had ever experienced. She felt the crushing blows of animated stones, the cold slap of water given form, and the sting of hurricane-force winds in her eyes. She was pummeled, stabbed, burned, frozen, gored, and a hundred other things.

Her diamond scales only barely protected her. Her other powers refused to help her. Too much of her energy went to her dragon healing power. She could do nothing but stay alive. She fell and flailed and screamed in pain as the dragons tortured their prophet.

CHAPTER THIRTY

Kylara's eyelids felt like they were made of lead. That was the most pleasant thing she'd compare any sensation in her body to. She assumed she was alive since she could still feel, but she was not at all sure if that was a good thing. It certainly did not feel like a good thing. She felt like she had been attacked with every major element and every element of the periodic table and like she had been assaulted all the way to her constituent atoms.

And yet she was alive.

She opened her eyes, as heavy as they were, and realized that she was still in the swamp in the pixie realm and at the edge of the pond. Of course, she had no idea how much time had passed. Time was always slippery in this realm. Pain and a loss of consciousness were also notorious for affecting one's sense of time.

It could not have been that long, however, she realized as she raised her gaze from the tangle of roots and moss in front of her to the swamp. The Followers of Tiamat were still there, their focus locked on her. They wanted her to be strong enough to stand. She could feel the confidence in her and their hopes. She scowled. How could she feel what they were feeling?

Her hand flew to the pendant around her neck but it was no longer there. At her movement, the Followers of Tiamat's auras pulsed with excitement. Kishar had spoken honestly about them, at least. They did not want her to die—well, not most of them. She could tell one of them—Lord Midnight perhaps? It was hard to tell with so many auras—would be more than happy if she didn't manage to stand.

She pushed to her feet—not to spite that one Follower of Tiamat but because she knew that if she could read their auras, they could read hers. They knew she was conscious and if not what she was thinking, at least what she was feeling. She could not allow them to sense her fear. They could not know the pain they had put her through. If they could read her aura, they would read only the fire of fury they had ignited inside her.

"Oh, come now, Miss Diamantine, it's perfectly fine to feel tired and weakened after the onslaught you survived," Kishar said as she stood on shaky legs. "I do apologize for that. I had been led to believe that you were already capable of performing the task you were prophesied to accomplish, but that did not prove to be the case."

"Give me that pendant," Kylara demanded quietly.

The woman smiled. She was in her human form and wore a beautiful green-and-yellow dress that was completely free of mud, water, or any signs of distress at all. In her hand, she held the pendant, dangling by its thin chain. Seeing her made the girl realize that not only was she not dead but she was also not a statue. Did that mean she had absorbed Kishar's power? Or had the woman had more sense than to try to turn their prophesied sum of all yadda-yadda-yadda into stone? There seemed to be dozens of new sensations in her chest, fighting to be understood. She did not know what any of them were, much less if the petrifying shadow mist was one of them.

"Do you think this trinket of turquoise and silver might be the reason it has not yet worked?" the First Walker asked rhetorically.

"Please. My grandfather made that for my mom. It belongs to me."

"Yes, I've heard the stories, as hard as they are to pry out of the vaults of the Steel Guard. A pendant made to protect mages from the world of dragons—a curious thing. It would almost be commendable if it was not so cowardly."

"My grandfather was not a coward."

"You are when you hide behind it." Kishar let the chain of the necklace go but before it could fall into the pond and sink beneath its placid surface without a ripple, she caught the pendant itself and squeezed.

With a sound like broken glass, a puff of ethereal dust issued from between her fingers. She opened her hand to reveal the shattered pendant.

"Why?" Kylara roared and tears came unbidden to her eyes. She was painfully aware that all the dragons could feel her emotions right now. They could all feel how devastating it was to lose the last link to a family she had always wanted to know better and how conflicted she had felt about it since discovering its true maker. Her adopted mother had used it for years to protect her, but it was her family of mages that had made it and hoped it would prevent her from being discovered by the dragons who would have seen the threat she might pose to them. Now, it was gone.

"Oh, don't be so dramatic," Kishar said and tossed the broken amulet into the pond behind her. It sank beneath the surface and left no wake, and it was as if it had never been. "You no longer need such petty protections. The goddess Tiamat will protect you."

Kylara was crushed at losing the last link to her family, but she also knew that now was not the time to mourn. When the First Walker had tossed the pendant into the pond, nothing had happened on the surface, but it felt as if the being sleeping deep in the pool had finally awakened.

She had been able to sense something of the presence from the moment she had arrived. But before it had seemed…patient, perhaps expectant. Now, it felt different—hungry maybe, or ravenous and not for food but power itself. It seemed to not grow stronger—it was already impossibly strong—but closer like it was rising from the depths of its prison.

And still, she did not have the answer she so desperately needed. "Why am I not dead?"

"I told you, we don't wish to kill you."

"But why not turn me to stone? Am I supposed to think that everyone else here used their power on me except the First Walker?"

Kishar smiled fondly at her. "I did turn you into stone, child. For a moment, I spared you your agony, but then I changed you back."

She had not misheard what she'd had said earlier and the petrification could be undone. That meant she could do so as well. She could save the headmaster. Although, given that a super-powerful goddess was rising from the depths for some unknown purpose, helping her headmaster suddenly seemed like a lesser priority.

"My power did, in fact, work on you, but it was simple enough to return you to flesh again as we were careful not to break off any of the important parts. I do hope it worked, but one way or the other, I had to return you to flesh. The goddess is not interested in a statue, after all." Kishar giggled at this, and the Followers of Tiamat joined her as if she had made the silliest sally over a cup of tea.

The First Walker's gaze shifted and her aura changed. Indeed, all the auras of the Followers changed from various degrees of interest, pity, and a dozen other different feelings about their captive to almost uniform awe and adulation.

Kylara whirled and looked at the pond. The surface was as placid as it had ever been but beneath it, a presence began to rise from the water. It was like a dark shadow—formless and distinguished only by the sheer magnitude of it. She wondered if this is what the first people to cross oceans felt when they saw whales.

As it ascended, its darkness fractured into color. All the hues of the rainbow flickered beneath the surface like the shades of an oil slick. It felt ancient and powerful beyond her imagining. She knew she was not alone in feeling this because some of the Followers in the arc behind her began to weep and fall to their knees.

She squared her shoulders, planted her feet, and thought about her training with Amythist. No matter what, she would not let this entity control her. She would not let its emotions control hers, no matter how powerful it was.

"I don't care what you think you are," she yelled at the surface of the pond, which remained placid even as the formless shadow bigger than any other moved ever closer and flickered constantly with the colors of a dark rainbow. "I'm not afraid of you.

"I've fought terrible things before, and I won. I'll fight you and I'll beat you, exactly like I did the wizard and like I did Boneclaw. You've been kept imprisoned by lullabies and you think you can hurt me? Your *Followers*"—she added as much vitriol and disgust to the word as she could—"gave me their powers. I have more abilities than I've ever had, and you…you're merely a shadow of an old story that a group of freaks has turned into a legend."

Kylara let the words empower her. She let them fill her with confidence and with power, even though much of what she said was bravado. The reality was that she was still exhausted and still in pain. Besides, she might have these new powers but she had never been able to control a new ability without practice. Even if she could beat Tiamat, there were still the other dragons, each with a power she had no practice in defending against. All of them were far more adept with their abilities than she would be even if she had practiced for months.

None of that needed to be in her aura, though. She knew that auras could be manipulated to go against the feeling one truly had in their gut. Tiamat had tried to make her afraid ever since she'd first arrived at this pond. There had to be a reason for that. She had to show the false goddess that it had not worked.

The shadowy form rose faster as Kylara spoke. She knew it could understand her because its aura twitched and shifted in response to her words. It wasn't angry that she wasn't afraid, though. If anything it seemed…impressed.

Seconds before the shadow form burst through the surface of the pond, it stopped. It was a formless shadow no longer but the graceful, aquiline shape of a dragon who could swim. Her scales were black—Kylara realized that she could not help but think of Tiamat as a she, much as she wanted to think of her as an it—although they sparkled in the same rainbow of colors that had displayed while she had been rising. Her claws splayed against the surface of the pond but created no ripples as if she were on the other side of a pane of glass instead of water.

"It is good you are not afraid," Tiamat said in an ancient, powerful voice. "Fear is for the weak. Beings like you and I are not weak. We cannot be, not if we are to accomplish so much together."

"I will do nothing to help you."

The goddess chuckled. "Oh, but you will. Like the pitcher holds water or the roof shelters the human, you will provide shape and usefulness in the era that is to come." She pulled back into the pond, then pumped her tails and wings and raced upwards toward the surface.

She drove into it but did about as much damage as an egg would do to a brick wall. With a roar, she thrashed and scratched at the still surface of the water but it did not move or make a single ripple.

Without warning, Kishar shoved Kylara from behind and she fell into the pond with a splash.

Whatever magic had kept Tiamat imprisoned failed. The shadowy dragon form coursed through the water and into the young dragon mage. She flowed into her like water into the soil. Her view of the pond went black as Tiamat slipped into her mind and filled her like water fills a pitcher.

CHAPTER THIRTY-ONE

Kylara regained her awareness in a round room with a light high overhead. Her first thought was that she had somehow returned to the cabin where she had been born and where Hester Diamantine had found a baby mage and given her sanctuary from a cruel world. Her aunt Cassandra had used her formidable abilities to remake that cabin and place it at the bottom of a frozen lake. The light there felt like it had when she had visited that place as if it were being filtered through a lake's worth of water.

But there were differences too. There was no cabin and no mementos of her childhood. And while the other place was cold, it was warm there and even humid, as if she were at the bottom of a swamp instead of a frozen lake…or a pond.

"Where are you, Tiamat?" she demanded. She understood where she was but not why her mind had refused to see that at first, as obvious as it now seemed.

"Above you, girl. And around you. Inside you."

Kylara took her dragon form and leapt skyward. "Show yourself!"

In the next moment, they were in the cabin on the lake. She

was in a crib and looked at her mother's face. It was so much like her aunt's. Why hadn't she gotten to know either of them better?

Fire ignited all around her. Her mom screamed as she tried to cast a spell to save her child. She put the pendant around her neck and put her in a crib built into a canoe.

The roof crumbled in the flames and smoke and she saw a lustrous black dragon whose scales sparkled in a thousand colors fly overhead, laughing.

"Weak from the start!" Tiamat laughed gleefully.

Kylara clenched her fists and got out of the canoe. She was no infant. No, she was the girl her mother had blessed at birth and who had won the heart of one of the hardest dragons on the planet. No matter what else might have happened, she was Kylara Diamantine!

She took her dragon form again, took flight, and augmented her speed with an extra pair of shadow wings like she had seen Karl make. She called on the wind to make her fly even faster.

In seconds, she was no longer above the frozen lake but above Detroit. Mort was there despite her knowing he had been turned into a tree in the pixie realm. She looked about for Tiamat, confident that this was an illusion. And yet, while she searched, she saw Mort systematically capture pixie after pixie and use their lifeblood to power himself. Every time he caught one was her failure.

"No!" she screamed and spat acid at the illusion.

It melted away and she was suddenly at home with her mom.

"Run, Kylara!" Hester screamed and together, they scrambled into her old beat-up jeep and tried to race over the mountains with a fire spirit in pursuit.

Her mom—a warrior and always so brave—turned back to fight while Kylara kept driving and crying, powerless and weak.

She pressed the gas pedal as far down as it would go and willed the vehicle to go as fast as it could and get her out of there —anywhere but there.

Moments later, she crashed through a wall and was in Lady Amythist's office. A magic dampening cuff was fitted to her wrist. She tried to fight, but her powers... She couldn't reach her powers.

Panicked, she ran from the headmaster and went outside, only to find Galen there. He was a monstrosity, trapped between his human and dragon forms. She was the only one who knew he was alive out there. No one knew how she had failed him.

"Galen, you're all right?"

"I have grown far more powerful than you," he snapped. His voice was Tiamat's and yet she couldn't force herself to attack him, even though there was no cuff preventing her from doing exactly that.

He raised his arms and a thousand skeletons of dragons rose from the dirt. Boneclaw, wielding the stolen black claw of an even longer dead dragon, stabbed her in the chest, and she fell back into a never-ending vacuum.

Kylara landed in the canoe that Cassandra had shown her and her crib.

She was in her normal body but she was so tired, exhausted, and overwhelmed.

Tiamat's voice sang to her, a gentle soothing song. "You fought well. You could never have won but you fought all the same. There is bravery in that, bravery and honor. Never forget that I am a goddess—*the* Goddess—and you are merely a girl."

She knew she should fight this and she should not accept the words of this dragon, but she couldn't. At this point, she was too cold and too weary.

Shadows wrapped her like blankets. She shivered against them until they were infused with warmth. Tiamat's voice was closer now as if the blankets were not shadow but the dragon goddess herself. She surrounded the girl and suffused her with comfort and warmth.

"You have failed before but together, we will not fail. Alone, you were weak but with me, we will be strong. I am the Mother of All Dragons, after all. You may not have been born as one of my children, but you are one of my children now and I love you. To resist me is to resist my love, to resist this song is to resist that which you feel to be right. Do not suffer needlessly, not when you can rest."

"But…my friends…"

"Will greet you with respect when you awaken, my daughter. Sleep now. Let your mother rock you. I will tend to your wounds. I will heal you and help you. As the Sum of All Dragons, this is your right. Hush now, child. Hush now, and sleep."

Kylara was so, *so* tired. And this was better than any of the other horrible places had been. Her mom—Tiamat—was right. She had failed so many times and did not want to do so again. She wanted to help…

She wanted to help her mom…

She wanted to help…Tiamat?

Was there a difference?

No…no there was not. There was only Tiamat and her song, a soothing melody gentler than any she had known before. She would share it with the world and would lead others… She would…

Tiamat's lullaby soothed her into unconsciousness.

CHAPTER THIRTY-TWO

Kylara might have thought that her only choice was to go with Kishar, but that did not mean that Sam couldn't try to rescue her. After all, she had rescued him. The least he could do was repay the favor. Although he also knew he couldn't do it alone.

"Midnight, see if Jasmine's doing well enough to go with us and meet me here in three minutes."

"I'll be back in two," Karl said and pulsed his aura to tell him he knew exactly what the plan was. He projected confidence, trust, and worry that was obviously for Kylara. The guy could be a real pain in the butt but Sam had long since stopped wondering if he could trust him. He vanished in a puff of shadow, which left Sam and Tanya in the U.

"Oh, my God, Lady Amythist!" Tanya screamed the moment the portal snapped shut. She was still beside the headmaster and touched her while she tried to listen for a heartbeat or feel for body heat or something that would indicate life.

"We can't save her, not only the two of us," he said.

She wiped her tears, but she nodded. "Do you have a plan to get Kylara?"

He forced a grin on his face, the perfect opposite of how he felt. "I'm more of the tactics guy. I hoped you could get the ball rolling."

Rather than teasing him for not having a clue—which would have been fair—she merely nodded and rubbed her chin in thought.

Sam tried not to rush her, but when Karl returned in his dragon form with Jasmine lashed to his back with his shadows, his patience ran out.

"Anything?"

"Yeah," Tanya said and snapped her finger as if the idea had just occurred to her. "They went to the pixie realm, right?"

"Right, which sucks because Kylara is the only dragon who can go there," Karl pointed out.

"But Kylara's not a dragon at all." The girl's eyes gleamed.

"So what? She's a mage. If you think I can get us there, you're crazy," Jasmine said.

"She's a mage, a dragon, but also the Big Pixie!" Tanya exclaimed.

"Oh, my God, you're a genius!" Sam exclaimed.

"So what? Kylara's a pixie. It won't help us," Karl said dourly.

"She won't get us there," Tanya said. "The pixies will."

Jasmine was the first to find one. Fortunately, it was Petalwing, who was at least slightly more familiar with human and dragon urgency than most pixies. She was flitting about Amythist's garden, but the mage brought her to the U after she'd sent up a shower of sparks to tell the rest of them that they had found her.

"Petalwing, can you—" Sam tried to ask but was cut off by the little pixie.

"I can and I will!"

"I already explained the problem," Jasmine said.

"You explained about the dark presence in the pond too?" he asked.

The pixie nodded. "We did not have a name for this being. It has existed much longer than us pixies and is powerful and fitful. We have kept it asleep for many years with our songs. If it wants Kylara, no good can come of it. We will help."

"What do you mean we?" Karl asked.

In response, pixies began to arrive atthe U. Sam recognized some of them. Rider and Hound came, no doubt indebted to the group after being rescued from the mad wizard the previous year. Lady Dragonfly, the pixie ambassador, also appeared although she offered a quick apology and said she would not be able to accompany them as she could not risk herself.

In no time, a dozen pixies had gathered. All of them asked about the Big Pixie while they sniffed flowers and generally seemed very relaxed given that the plan was to fight a dragon goddess and rescue their friend from a cult.

"Thank you all for coming," Sam said when new pixies stopped appearing.

"Anything for the Big Pixie!" Rider shouted from the back of an alligator. How the little being who normally lived in the Rocky Mountains had come across an alligator was a question for another day, as was how on earth he had managed to fit it with a bridle.

"I can smell her from here," Hound said and his wasp-like nose worked and twitched at the air. "But I can't tell where she went."

"That's because she went to our realm," Petalwing explained. "To the place with the sleeping behemoth."

Sam expected surprise or fear at this revelation but instead, the pixies took it as a matter of course as if they had their prophecies and this was simply something that had to happen. He certainly hoped he would look back on all this one day and see it as a good thing. Right now, it didn't seem like anything good could possibly come from it. He didn't even know what the Followers of Tiamat wanted with Kylara. Her life? To serve

Tiamat as a slave? As a ruler? He could only guess at options, none of which he liked.

"The plan is to take us to the pond, where Tanya will restrain Kishar—"

"By any means necessary," Tanya added.

"We'll fight the dragons and you pixies get Kylara back here," Sam said. "Petalwing, if you have to abandon us to take Kylara, do so, but if you can get us back home that would be appreciated."

He had not checked with Tanya, Jasmine, and Karl to see what they thought about offering themselves in exchange for their friend, but none of them even blinked at what he had said. They —like him—must have understood how important she was and how stopping a cult from using her was more important than any of them.

"It sounds fun!" Petalwing said, which he supposed was better than her being scared but was also not exactly comforting.

Before he could ask them to please take this seriously—he wasn't even sure that pixies knew what serious meant—they had opened a portal.

Sam had never been to the swampy part of the pixie realm before and he did not much want to go now. On the other side of the portal was a sunken landscape dominated by massive cypresses that looked like they would fall if leaned on the wrong way. Roots and moss battled mud for what dry ground there was. Vines and strange plants clung to the trees, fighting for space. In the middle of it all was a pond and on the opposite side was a group of dragons. And there, in the center, was Kylara.

"Let's go!" Sam said and led the team through the portal.

As soon as he stepped into the pixie realm, the dragon mage opened a portal on the opposite side of the pond.

"Ky, wait! It's us!" Sam said as Tanya, Karl, Jasmine, and the pixies hurried through behind him.

She didn't turn at first and instead, gestured for the other dragons to go. Astonishingly, they obeyed her.

He grinned. It was so like her. She'd been alone for five minutes and had managed to bully these cultists into obeying her. Not that he was surprised. She was nothing if not assertive.

Grinning like a fool, he ran around the edge of the pond. He couldn't believe it was all over. They had come ready to fight but she must have already seized power.

Sam catapulted back, struck by a wave of concussive force. He slid through the mud, startled but unhurt. "Kylara?" he asked as he pushed to his feet. "Ky, it's me."

She turned to him. It was her face, her dark hair, and her troubled brown eyes, but her aura was all wrong. The first indication was that she had an aura instead of the smudgy, unclear faux aura she usually presented. Her aura was unbelievably powerful and it radiated disdain for him.

"Ah, the golden trespasser," Kylara said, but her voice was not her own. It sounded like someone else was using her vocal cords.

"What's going on?" he asked.

"Don't think I meant to fool you," the person who looked like Kylara but wasn't said. "I have no reason to hide. I simply wanted to feel everything this body could do."

"Who are you?" he demanded and took his dragon form.

In response, she transformed as well, but not into the form he knew—and had fallen for. This dragon was bigger than Kylara and curvier. She had wide hips—as if she were about to lay a clutch of eggs—a narrower waist, and a broader chest and was a little plump for a dragon as if she had accumulated the fat needed to make eggs. Instead of diamond horns, she had a mane of dark hair that sparkled iridescently.

Her body was black, although Sam realized it also glinted with color. To call it a rainbow would be to oversell what a rainbow was. There was more color to this dragon's scales than he knew there were colors. She was undeniably beautiful and motherly as well. She looked as if she could bear clutch after clutch of eggs.

"You know damn well who I am, boy. I am your mother. The mother of you all."

"Tiamat." He choked the words her aura compelled him to speak. Her aura made him want to bow and prostrate himself to this vastly more powerful being, but he would not cave.

"You will bow the next time you see me, child. I promise you that. Go now. Tell the world of my return. You may be my herald if you wish it." She opened a portal to leave.

Sam wanted to bow—or, more accurately, Tiamat wanted him to want to—but he resisted. Instead, he managed to say only two words. "Ky, wait."

The dragon turned to him and answered in Kylara's voice. "She is gone, Sam. Only Tiamat remains."

A shockwave of aural power that made Heartsbane seem to have about as much power as a sparrow pounded into the young dragon. He felt terror and awe battle for supremacy inside him, and judging by the gasps and screams of his friends, they all felt the same thing as he did.

"Do not follow, my children. I do not wish you to be hurt. But do not worry. We will meet again—quite soon, in fact." She stepped through the portal. It closed and she was gone.

CHAPTER THIRTY-THREE

Sam pushed shakily to his feet and looked at where she had been. No, he thought bitterly. Not Kylara. Where Tiamat had masqueraded in the young dragon mage's body.

"Kylara." He choked, stumbled toward the spot, and felt in the moss and mud for some sign of her—some clue that everything Tiamat had said had not been the terrifying truth. Desperately, he wished he could believe that she had lied but he had felt the goddess's aura as his own. She knew the dragon mage was gone, a drop lost in an ocean and impossible to find once it had been lost.

He felt a human hand on his dragon hide before Tanya's sense of loss pushed into his own. Her pain did not make him feel any better.

"Sam, I'm so sorry," she said, her voice thick with emotion. She tried to keep it together despite how close the two girls had been.

Sam took his human form and embraced her. They hugged and she wept on his shoulder while the plants around them in the swamp wilted and dropped their leaves in solidarity with her misery. No tears came from the golden dragon's eyes. He was too angry and too distraught. Every tear that might have been shed was evaporated by the light that poured unbidden from his eyes.

"She's not gone, though, right?" Jasmine asked as she walked around the pond to join them.

"She's gone," Karl said from the other side. He had not moved an inch, nor had he wiped the tears from his eyes. He wore them with pride as if Kylara deserved every single one. "You couldn't feel it like we can. Tiamat…she's more powerful than anything I have ever even imagined. I…I understand why my father follows her now." It looked like it hurt him to admit that and that it shamed him.

"But…she's Kylara," the mage said and her voice became frantic. "She can't be…gone."

Sam clenched his teeth. "There's a monster in her body, Jasmine. We have to accept that." Even saying the words felt like a betrayal but at the same time, he knew Kylara would be thinking about the powerless, which was not Tiamat in this situation. He had to harden himself. Somehow, he had to, even if it felt like stabbing himself in the chest.

"Petalwing, tell them that they're wrong. Tell them it had to be a trick," Jasmine said and her voice rose in pitch.

The pixie fluttered closer and even her wings seemed to be despondent. The others looked like they felt no better than she did. "They are right," she said gently to Jasmine. "She is gone."

Tanya started to cry even harder and Sam held her tighter. She was the closest thing to Kylara left. Karl, still across the pond, finally moved. He sank down, sat in the mud, and lowered his head so his hair covered his face.

"No! No, it has to be a trick!" Jasmine shouted, angry at the three dragons. "It was an illusion. She couldn't simply take Kylara's body like that."

"But she did," Petalwing said. "The Sleeper was kept in that deep place below because she had no body. Now that she does, she is free. That is how it is. That is how we always knew it would be."

"Godammit," Karl cursed. "This is all our fault. She's dead and gone forever and it's all because we couldn't stop that stupid Kishar."

"Kylara isn't dead, though. Not yet anyway," the pixie said in a voice thick with emotion.

"Wait, what?" Sam straightened.

Tanya had heard it too. "What did you say?"

"She's not dead!" Petalwing mourned and tears poured from her too-large eyes. "I could sense Kylara's pixie essence still trapped inside. She's not dead. She's merely stuck…taken away from here." She flung herself on the earth and threw a bigger tantrum than any of the dragons had.

"But…if she's trapped, can we save her?" Karl asked.

The little creature bolted up with a smile on her face. "That's a great idea! Maybe we could free her."

Sam felt a grin break out on his face that was so broad it hurt. "Petalwing, why didn't you say you could sense her sooner?"

She looked confused. "Well, you were all so sad and sometimes, it's healthy to be sad and it is sad. So…um, wait. Are you all mad at me?"

"We're not mad!" Tanya beamed and flowers bloomed all around them.

"You aren't?" Petalwing buzzed around the pond and showered sparks on everyone.

"No!" Sam grinned.

"Well, we won't be if you can tell us how to free her," Karl said.

The pixie rubbed her chin in thought. The little creatures were so strange. Sam could not tell if she was thinking about how to free Kylara or if she was concerned about them being mad at her.

"I do not know how to free her," she said finally. "But I know she was still in there. It felt like she was…walled in? Like she was a captive inside her psyche—like a bug in a web, trapped but still alive."

"We have to save her," Sam said, already furious at himself for doubting that she was all right. How could he have dared to think that she might not come back? Friends couldn't abandon each other like that and he knew Kylara would never abandon any of them. Sam wondered where the thoughts had come from. Could Tiamat have influenced him?

"Yeah, well, obviously," Tanya said. "We won't leave her in there."

"She's so strong," he exclaimed. "If there's even a speck of her alive, we can bring her back."

"I don't know…" Karl shook his head dubiously.

"Karl!" Jasmine snapped.

"Come on. I want to save her," he snapped, "But can we? Yes, we've faced some tough opponents together but this one claims to be a goddess. And you all felt her aura as much as I did. I have never felt anything like that ever."

"That doesn't necessarily mean that she's a goddess," Jasmine pointed out.

"We can quibble about semantics, but even if she's lying about that, she is still in control of Kylara's body."

"And all Kylara's powers," Tanya added. "And I bet she got some new ones."

"Even before she got that momentum power and whatever else they hit her with before we arrived, we couldn't beat her in a duel."

Sam nodded. That was true. It had been months since either of the boys had come close to beating her in a duel. It was the combination of her powers and how Hester Diamantine had raised her. Kylara knew how to fight in a way that the rest of them did not. "But if she's trapped in her body, maybe Tiamat won't be as good at fighting as Kylara?"

Karl shook his head in disagreement. "I get what you're saying, but she kicks butt not because she knows how to use her claws but because she knows how to use her powers. We can't go into a fight thinking that Tiamat—the original creator of all these abilities—won't know how to use them."

"You don't believe that the pond ghost was a goddess, do you?" Sam asked.

The other boy shrugged. "Well…my dad does and he's not exactly unintelligent. If we try to take her, we need to go into the fight overestimating her, not underestimating."

"Do you think the two of us could handle her?" Sam asked.

"It's worth a try," Karl said. "But we'd have to make sure our powers don't cancel each other out."

"What on earth makes either of you think it would only be two of you? If you think for a second that I'll let Kylara's body get stolen by a dragon poltergeist, you're crazy! The three of us could do it, especially if you focus on healing us and keeping us charged, Sam. Karl and I might be able to restrain her."

"Three?" Jasmine harrumphed. "There are four of us. Dragons." She snorted.

"I want to help too!" Petalwing buzzed over their heads. "And four plus one makes five!"

The other pixies buzzed around and chorused that they also wished to help.

Petalwing grinned. "All of them makes, uh…one, two, three four, five, six, uh…ten?" she twirled upward. "A lot! There are many pixies and we will help the Big Pixie!"

"Great, then what's the plan?" Tanya asked. "Does it make more sense to contact the Steel Dragon?"

"We can't waste that kind of time," Sam retorted.

"If you all wish to follow the Big Pixie, we must act quickly," Petalwing said. "She left a trace of energy behind when she closed the gate but it is fading. If we wish to follow, we need to go straight there."

"Then that's where we go," Sam said and took his dragon form again.

Tanya and Karl nodded and both transformed as well. While Jasmine climbed onto Midnight's back and he strapped her securely with cords of shadow, Tanya took seeds from some of the swamp plants and a few small pieces of vines or twigs—cuttings, Sam had heard her call them.

He had nothing to do to prepare except think about Kylara. That put a light of passion and hope in his chest that made him glow.

"Are we ready?" Petalwing asked cheerfully as if they were going out for ice cream.

"Let's do this," he said.

She and the other pixies opened a gate to the real world and led the three dragons and the mage through to a fight against a goddess and enough dragons to make any attempt to defeat them laughable.

CHAPTER THIRTY-FOUR

When Kylara opened her eyes, she saw nothing. She was in a place of darkness. It was warm there and comforting, like being under a blanket with a mug of cocoa after a long day climbing mountains on a chilly day. A faint hum in the background was soothing as well like a melody playing below her range of sound. She could feel it vibrating her back to sleep. The air smelled pleasantly of cinnamon and chamomile tea.

Tea—something about chamomile tea pierced her senses.

She sat bolt upright in the darkness. Her mind raced through the last events she remembered. The cult of Tiamat had arrived at her school, they had attacked her and "given" her more powers, and Kishar had turned the headmaster to stone. She recalled how she had left the school to protect her friends and how the other dragons had all attacked her at the pond. Tiamat had entered her body, the memory a stark reminder of how she had lost.

That meant this place of darkness was not a place at all but a prison in her mind. Suddenly, the darkness was no longer enveloping and comforting but stifling. It did not feel warm but stuffy. The sound made her feel nauseous and the smells of tea and cinnamon seemed cloying and fake like someone was piping them in to cover something rancid and it was barely working.

Kylara reached for her light powers and created a ball of white light in front of her. It ripped through the darkness but bounced back to blind her. She was in a deep hole and every surface reflected the light at her as if she were in a pit of mirrors. Instinctively, she closed her eyes and tried to adjust to the brightness but even through her closed eyelids, the brilliance of the room was painful. She finally turned the light off.

After a deep breath, she tried to recall where she had last seen Tiamat. It was so confusing to try to piece it all together—more like a dream than an actual battle. But that made some kind of sense if she was trapped inside her mind. That was where she must still be, then—trapped in a prison that Tiamat had spun of her memories.

Did that mean she could simply wake up and it would all go away? She pinched herself with diamond-tipped claws. Nothing happened beyond a twinge of pain and she sighed. She had not expected it to work but it was still a disappointment that it had not.

Irritated, she drew another deep breath—an uncomfortable sensation given that she hated the fake smells in the air—and tried to puzzle this out. Tiamat must know about her powers. It meant that she would have designed this prison to work against them. She could feel no moisture in the air. There was no wind to call or seeds to grow into plants. She had a sense that if she tried to simply destroy the walls, she would only hurt herself.

After a moment's thought, she decided to try to feel around with her dark powers. Tentatively, she created tendrils of dark and sent them out in all directions like the roots of a tree. She was indeed in a kind of cell—a round room that she sensed was a long way down. Her shadows found no holes in the walls and no cracks although one spot seemed a little different.

Kylara stood and walked toward it in the darkness. It was

frustrating to not be able to comfortably use her light powers. After years of having them always available to her, she felt quite useless in the dark. Still, she ventured forward carefully and reached out to the orb she had sensed with her inky dark tendrils. She made contact and discovered that she knew exactly what this was—a doorknob.

She twisted it and felt a space open in front of her, one completely identical to the one she was in right now. With a frown, she launched her tendrils of darkness into the room and after a few minutes of probing, she found another doorknob. She opened it to reveal yet another identical pit.

What did that mean? Tiamat had created this place in her mind so why bother to make doorknobs and multiple rooms? It didn't make any sense—well, not unless Tiamat had to do it. But why would that be? Maybe her captor couldn't simply imprison her in a corner of her mind. She might eventually find a way to break out. But this way, she could direct her attention. Instead of allowing her prisoner to find a crack, Tiamat had given her one. Which meant this wasn't a cell she was trapped in but a maze.

But mazes—even the Labyrinth itself—had solutions. She could get out of there. It would not be easy given that she was effectively blindfolded and powerless, but she had to try.

The young dragon mage did not think that using her shadow powers was the way to escape, however. It was the first thing she had done that worked. She had been able to sense the doorknobs with the tendrils of dark, which made her think it was what Tiamat expected her to use. For that reason, she didn't want to use it.

She sat and wondered what else she should try. The momentum power might be a good option, but what would happen to her if she obliterated everything inside her head? Would she end up as a vegetable forever? Was all this merely an illusion?

Kylara took a deep breath and decided to try. This was a

prison, after all, or part of a prison anyway. Maybe she could break a few walls and find her way back to herself.

Before she could change her mind, she turned her skin to diamond, called on the power, and ran toward a wall. She crashed through it, kept running, and broke through another, and another. For a split second, she thought she saw something ahead—her dorm at the Lumos School? But then everything shattered around her.

The sound of breaking glass rose to a cacophony as diamond shards rained on her. Terrified of the sound and the pieces striking her skin hard enough to draw blood—after all, diamond could cut diamond—she flared her light power which only made everything worse. Instead of being surrounded by merely the sound of broken glass, she could now see a thousand...ten thousand...a million pieces of glass falling and reflecting light.

She fell back and shielded her eyes from both the light and the falling shards. The glass fell for far longer than should have been possible. She had seen six-story apartment buildings collapse and her prison defied normal reality to have the amount of diamond-hard glass that fell. But finally, the noise stopped. She opened her eyes and realized she was again in the middle of a dark room. A quick exploration with her shadow tendrils told her that she was back where she started.

Brute force was not the way out of this. But why would it be? Tiamat was the mother of all dragons, or at least she claimed to be. Kylara still was not sure what she believed but she knew that a spirit or ghost or whatever had invaded her body and that a number of people had said this was because she had absorbed so many dragon powers.

Brute force was the most basic of dragon abilities. Even in their human form, dragons were inhumanly strong, and that did not even include those who could turn to stone or bend the elements to their will. Tiamat would have built this prison with the intention to stop force, so trying to force it open was not likely to work.

But didn't that also mean that no dragon power would work? If her captor had spawned all the dragon powers—and given that she was currently trapped inside her mind by the dragon, she was inclined to believe that she had—wouldn't she have thought of a way to thwart all of them?

Kylara sighed. She didn't know how long she had been awake but she was tired. The stuffiness of this prison-maze-corner of her mind felt more comforting now. Perhaps she should simply lay down. Although where she wanted to lay down was her dorm room. That was where she felt safest.

The thought triggered another possibility and she pushed to her feet. What if she could go to her dorm room? She had the ability to open gates and that was a pixie power, not a dragon one! She did not think she could gate out of her mind and appear in her actual dorm room as some kind of specter—nor did she want to, as Tiamat might simply steal her body permanently—but maybe she could go there in her mind.

She called upon the pixie powers, opened a gate, and grinned as she peered through it at her dorm room. It had worked.

The dragon mage stepped through and reappeared in the same pitch-black cell.

Immediately, she opened another portal, this one to the U at the Lumos School. She stepped through and again, she reappeared in the same place. If anything, going to the U had felt like even more of a failure. When she had tried to go to her dorm, she had felt something of the room. She could almost hear Tanya complaining about not knowing what to wear and could almost smell the coffee Jasmine sometimes brought for late-night study sessions. The U had been even more insubstantial.

Kylara cursed and the sound echoed off the panes of diamond glass that ringed her cell. Of course Tiamat had thought of this power. Kishar had banked on the ability to get the cult to the pond. It seemed doubtful that the ancient dragon wouldn't be able to use it now that she wore her body like a glove.

What else was there to try? She could not see how anything else would work. If she could only understand why the dorm room had felt more substantial than the U had. Was it because she liked it more?

It was worth at least an attempt. She tried to think of her most favorite place. A few came to mind—the dining hall of the Lumos School and the sky over her mom's land, but she eventually settled on a mountain stream that ran through the mountains where she'd grown up. It was always ice cold as it was fueled by snowmelt. She had spent many happy moments there. It was the stream that had carved the Straits, the tricky section of switchbacks where she had practiced how to fly with agility and where she had first met Sam.

She opened a portal and stepped through. This location lingered a fraction of a second longer than the dorm room had but still vanished quickly. Before it was completely gone, she tried to focus on a specific memory of this place. Her mind alighted on when she had inadvertently caused Sam to crash into one of the walls. He had caused an avalanche and might have died if she had not saved him. She could see him and feel the worry she'd felt. But then she remembered that Sam was fine and she reappeared in the dark cell.

Why had that place stuck in her mind longer? Was it because of Sam? Part of Kylara wanted to think that it was, but if it was Sam, she didn't understand why seeing him hurting would have made the emotion linger. She hadn't even meant to think of him hurting and had thought about him in flight, not him crashing. Yet the pain of that part of the memory had been more powerful than the pleasurable parts—like a flare to guide her and keep her out of this cell.

What if it was the intensity of that emotion that made it last longer? It made sense. Seeing Sam had been a bizarre experience for her. She had found him handsome, so there was that, but he was also the first dragon she'd ever seen. That had made her doubt her mom and distrust him but also be interested in him at the same time. What would happen if she tried to teleport herself to a memory that was even more intense?

Although she had many to choose from, there was one that stood out above the rest.

Kylara took a deep breath and opened a gate to her mom's land. "Get in the jeep, Kylara! Now!"

For a moment, she was swept up in the memory.

Her mom popped the hood, cursed as she burned her fingers on the radiator, and dumped coolant inside the poor vehicle. It had a leak—a small one—that Hester had planned to fix on the weekend.

"Ok, let me grab a bag!" Her mom had warned her about this happening one day. Kylara didn't have a bag packed but she knew exactly what she'd take. She turned to go inside—she knew what she wanted—but felt a flash of rage from her mom.

"There's no time to pack, dammit! Get in the fucking jeep!"

Her mom cursing had always stuck with her.

Coming up the mountain road from the town, she saw what appeared to be a storm of fire. A face seemed to have formed in the center of it, one of fire and fury. The face of flame looked hungry.

The memory flashed forward through the first part of their escape.

She scooted into the driver's seat, planted her butt comfortably, and positioned her foot on the gas before she locked her gaze on the road.

"Mom, what is happening?"

"We're under attack, Kylara," Hester's full attention was on the flames coming over the hill behind them. She sounded like she was answering as an afterthought. "You need to drive as fast as possible without wrecking the jeep. You can do this.

That fire is gaining on us. I can't allow it to catch up to the vehicle."

"I'm driving as fast as I can!" she replied.

"You need to get to a Steel Guard station. They'll protect you. They can keep you safe."

Fire and smoke and tears swirled in her vision as Hester swooped in for another strafe across the landscape. The fire formed a swirling vortex of flame and smoke. The twisting tornado of flame lifted off the ground and hurled her mom from the sky.

The dragon struck the ground hard enough to make an impact crater, but she didn't stop fighting. She whipped her tail and righted herself as another rolling wave of fire surged into her. Although she blocked it with her wings, she burned the membrane that connected the bones as she did so. But her scales were diamond and she was a tough old dragon. She blasted the base of the next flames that swept toward her and managed to take away the root of the fire tornado.

Kylara drove away like she had when it had happened. She did as her mother said and fled. Knowing that her mom would survive this did not make it any easier this time, though. She would be captured and held against her will by the girl's family.

Kylara found herself sitting in her jeep, its engine nearly over-heating, while streaks of tears ran through the soot on her face. She let the pain of that day wash over her. She let the time she would spend away from her mom hurt her as it had before. Even more painfully—and contradictory—she mourned her aunt, the woman who had done this to her.

Finally, the tears stopped. She stepped from the jeep and wiped her face. Despite the dilapidated vehicle being on the bleeding edge of death, it continued to sputter. But why would it stop? In her memory, it had taken her out of the mountains and almost to a Steel Guard station.

Only now, she was not in her memory but something close to

it instead. She looked out from the mountaintop and saw the landscape of her mind spread below her. In it, the Lumos School was right next to her mom's land and Tanya's was a little to the west. She realized that her mind had clustered all those places together as they were places of safety. Beyond these were strips of land she had flown over—obviously condensed—that looked like they would take her to different places, mostly those of battle.

In each of these regions, the events that she had experienced there ran over each other, each one transparent until her mind settled on it and the others faded into the background.

She took a deep breath and decided she could work with this. At least she was free of the prison Tiamat had put her in or she hoped she was, anyway. She still didn't have control of her mind yet—let alone her body—but at least she was out of that damn, dark cell that made her want nothing more than to sleep.

It was a start, and she would run with it.

CHAPTER THIRTY-FIVE

They stepped from the portal into a humid jungle sprawled around a massive stepped pyramid. Dragons of unusual shapes, sizes, and abilities were everywhere. At the top of the pyramid, standing in front of what appeared to be a temple, was Tiamat herself. She looked reminiscent of Kylara's dragon form but was also undeniably different. At first glance, she had the same glittering diamond scales and the same strong posture, but the similarities stopped there. Her scales—despite being diamond—were not the cool blue that the young dragon mage's had been. Instead, they sparkled with a thousand colors.

But beyond that, something about her seemed motherly. It was a weird thing for Sam to notice and if he was honest with himself, it made him a little uncomfortable. He had only seen dragons look like this when they were growing a clutch of eggs. It seemed to be Tiamat's natural state, however, and it worked well for her. Even from their position hidden in the jungle, he could feel her aura compelling him to go to her, to praise her, and to help his mom.

He only hoped that compared to the power that poured off the goddess—he couldn't help but think of her this way, even though he didn't want to—that no one would notice the three dragons and a mage hidden in the jungle.

Before they had stepped through, they had all taken a moment to get their auras under control. Feeling anything too strongly would spill into a dragon's aura. That meant they could not let thoughts of Kylara being gone run through their heads. Although the opposite was also dangerous, of course. If they were too hopeful, that might also be detected. Sam got the sense that the Followers were not exactly a hopeful group, not if Kishar was their leader. The rescuers had therefore tried to channel a sense of awe as that seemed to be what Tiamat wanted most.

It had felt weird to culture a feeling like that in the swamp but it was now no longer as difficult to maintain.

There was something impressive about a massive dragon who radiated more power than Sam had even known was possible and also looked like she should have sore joints from needing to lay eggs. The dragons swooped around the stepped pyramid and certainly added to the effect.

"Petalwing," he whispered, "now that you know where Kylara is in the real world, can you go get help?"

"Yes, that's a great idea!" the pixie replied and grinned.

"Great, so…" He gestured for her to get on with it but she only smiled. "Go now, Petalwing!"

"Oh, right—of course!" She opened a portal and was gone. He had hoped to see the skyline of Detroit on the other side but she had been so fast that he hadn't had a chance to see where she had gone.

"All right, what now?" Karl asked as he studied Tiamat. "We can't exactly sneak up there."

"We need a distraction," Jasmine said.

Sam nodded. But what kind of distraction would be big enough to lure away dozens of dragons?

Before he could think of a solution, one of the Followers thrust through the underbrush and discovered them. "What the hell are you doing here?" he demanded. Sam tried to come up with a lie but before he could say anything, the pixies transformed into sparks and streaked into the dragon's face.

He roared in pain and fell back, felling a massive tree.

Tanya was quick to summon the roots from the same tree to grow over the dragon. Sam looked at the clearing. The roar of their attacker had not gone unnoticed. Three more who had been watching the perimeter of the clearing now walked toward them.

"Hey!" one of them yelled before Sam streaked a beam of light into his face. The dragon clutched his eyes and screamed.

"Nice move, golden boy. You made a beam of light that points directly to us," Karl snapped but he didn't sound angry. His voice was eager instead.

"Tanya, watch our backs?" Sam said as the dragons who circled the pyramid shifted their focus to the scuffle breaking out on the edge of the jungle.

She nodded and the trees closest to them bent inward. Branches interlocked and vines grew between them to create a wall of solid, woody growth behind them. It would be difficult to attack them from behind but it would also make escape impossible. But escape wasn't an option. They would not leave without Kylara, period.

Karl launched a web of inky tendrils across the ground between them and the approaching dragons.

One bounded forward and fired barbed growths at them from her wings. She stepped in the webbing of shadow and Karl pulled it back with sufficient force that she fell with a bone-crunching sound.

Sam caught another in the face with a beam of light as he inhaled. The golden dragon had no idea what would have come out of his throat but he knew it would not be fire. Thankfully, he would never find out. The dragon toppled and clawed at his face.

Two others descended from above, each of them with two pairs of wings. They moved with an agility Sam had not known was possible until Jasmine threw a wall of energy up that one of them pounded into and shattered his delicate wings. He tumbled and landed heavily as the other flew close enough to force the golden dragon to engage in hand-to-hand combat.

He was surprised how well he held his own against his adversary. He had grown accustomed to losing against Kylara and fighting to a draw with Karl, but it seemed all that practice had paid off. While he wasn't able to drive the dragon back immediately, she was not able to land a blow on him either. When fighting against such odds, however, a stalemate was a loss for the side with fewer fighters.

As Sam defended himself and tried to overcome his opponent, more dragons rushed to join the growing fray. Karl was able to snare a few of them but his powers were not unlimited. Some pushed through and those he pinned to the ground struggled to break free. With each new dragon he snared, those he had already captured came closer to breaking loose.

Jasmine was one of their greatest assets. After centuries of oppressing mages, dragons were simply not accustomed to fighting them. Their breath attacks often dissipated against shimmering blue shields. When their wings were struck by spears of the same energy, they plummeted from the sky.

Sam flared his eyes and blinded his opponent, but before he could make any forward progress, another dragon attacked, this one with claws that broke away into splinters that lodged in his skin like cactus thorns. They were doing all right and holding their position thanks to the fact that Tanya prevented them from being surrounded. But merely holding their position would certainly not do a damn thing against Tiamat.

The golden dragon did not know whether to count it as good luck or bad when the earth began to rumble and tear beneath their feet.

He vaulted up to avoid falling into the massive, earthen trench that opened beneath him. Karl remained where he had been and his tendrils stretched with the expanding gap so he balanced atop them like a spider on a web. He had made a platform for Jasmine as well. Somehow, despite the ground vanishing beneath her feet, she managed to stay focused on the battle.

Tanya, though, was not so lucky. The enormous gash in the earth had ripped her defensive shield of plants in half. Sam had not been the only one to realize that surrounding the five of them would pitch the odds of the battle against them. As she toppled into the jagged fissure, a slew of dragons attacked her.

She would have to hold her own against them, though. They all attacked with sprays of acid, blasts of wind, or odd breath weapons. None of that was as dire a threat as the dragon who had moved the earth itself, though. If it thrust the two parts together again, the young dragon could be crushed.

"Karl, we need to find whoever moved the ground!" Sam ordered.

"I'm a little busy here!" Karl replied. He was in flight now, a dark dragon in the middle of a thousand streaming tendrils. Another opponent attacked him with the same powers—his father, Lord Midnight.

The golden dragon tried to focus his attention on the source of the earthquake but it was difficult with the fight raging between father and son. He knew the earthquake dragon would have to spend time recharging his power. Otherwise, he would have already crushed Tanya.

"You betray your bloodline!" Lord Midnight roared at Karl.

"You're a blind old fool!" his son replied and combined a dozen of his tendrils into one twisting cord of shadow that he launched at his father like a drill.

The older Midnight caught it and split the ends of it like it was nothing more than a pretty braid. "You were always weak, Karl. Always. And now I discover that you've given up courting the Sum of All Dragons and instead, let this mage wench ride you like a horse? You're an embarrassment." He fired a tendril of his own.

Karl blocked it but as soon as he did, it split into a dozen pieces. He tried to block these but each time he did, they separated into a dozen more. Despite his efforts, he was outmatched and Sam still had not found the earthquake dragon. Did he step in to help Karl—who was already in a dire situation—or did he help Tanya, who might still have minutes before she was truly in danger?

He did not have to make that decision, however. Jasmine acted first. She cut through Lord Midnight's web of shadow with a blade of telekinetic energy. Thankfully, she had trained with Karl enough that she knew exactly how his powers worked. She severed the tendrils of darkness at their root and all the connected pieces simply puffed into nothing.

Karl seized the moment and surged forward, powered by three pairs of wings. He collided with his father and drove him into the dirt, lashed him in place, and tightened the bonds until the older dragon, deprived of oxygen, faded from consciousness. Sam expected to feel hatred or betrayal coming from Lord Midnight but pride filled the dragon's aura before he passed out.

This did not escape Karl's notice, who snorted at his unconscious father. "The old man always did say he respected power."

"You should have kicked his butt a long time ago," Jasmine said.

"Nah. I could never have done that without you."

Sam felt a rumble and finally saw the dragon he'd been seeking. His eyes were the color of stone and focused on Tanya. His scales looked more like pebbles and rocks than something reptilian. The most obvious clue that he was indeed the dragon responsible for shaking the earth was that his feet were all sunk into the ground. He opened his mouth and a roar issued from his throat, low at first but growing louder as the earth shook more violently. A fissure opened at his feet and moved toward Tanya.

Sam had no doubt that if it reached her, it would collapse the trench around her.

He simply could not let that happen and focused his energy into the back of his throat. His scales stopped glowing—starting with the tip of his tail and claws and moving toward his head—until all his power was focused on the ball of light in his throat. He roared and the ball erupted, although—being made of light and traveling at the speed of light—it did not so much as shoot across the battlefield as disappear from his throat and reappear in his adversary's face.

It struck the earthquake dragon and shattered like an egg to blast its target with not only light but heat, ultraviolet light, microwaves, and even gamma radiation.

The dragon screamed and toppled sideways. His energy had already been channeled into the ground, however. The fissure streaked forward then turned, moved toward the pyramid, and opened a hole under one of its corners. It didn't fall, of course, but the entire structure settled a foot or two into the hole and Tiamat—still at the top and seated calmly like a mother watching her children play—lurched a little.

"Bring them to me!" the mother of dragons bellowed.

Sam raced toward Tanya but in the chaos of the earthquake, she had flown free from the pit. They landed and squared off back-to-back. Karl and Jasmine joined them as dozens more dragons circled ever closer.

If the odds were stacked against them before, they were now absolutely staggering.

It was at that moment that a portal opened and the faculty from the school—led by Kor, the grizzled dueling instructor—poured out into the battle.

"Is this good? This is good, right?" Petalwing asked and flitted about as a ribbon of sparks.

"Very good!" Tanya shouted and the pixie grinned.

Kor, a handful of other dragons, and Professor Sharra with the mage security team joined the battle.

As they engaged the cultists, Sam looked at the top of the pyramid. Tiamat seemed distracted. Rather than watching the fight, her eyes were distant, her tail twitched, and her claws scratched at the stones of the temple.

She roared and unleashed a huge gout of flame—bigger than any he had seen and even bigger than the biggest bombs he had seen humans make—into the air.

He did not know what was going on up there or inside the dragon's head, but he knew he had to get there fast if he wanted Kylara to have any hope of still having a body when this was all over.

CHAPTER THIRTY-SIX

Tiamat did not know how the Sum of All Dragons had escaped—
or why she would want to—but she knew it the moment that she
did. Did the girl not understand that she risked immortality itself
by trying to fight against her spirit inside her? She could have
everything she wished—an eternal dream, limited only by her
imagination—but instead, she wished to throw away that which
she intended to give her?

The Mother of All Dragons didn't understand it but she
would deal with it. She would think an eternity of dreams would
be preferable to being turned into a mindless husk of one's
former self, but she had never pretended to understand the wills
of humans. The Sum of All Dragons was ultimately a human.

However, the timing couldn't be worse. Some meddling inter-
lopers had found her temple in the jungle and had chosen this
exact moment to attack. Their purpose was inscrutable and ultimately irrelevant, of course. They would lose and their blood
would be spilled, exactly like hers had been so long ago, but she
did not wish to risk too many of her Followers in a fight.

Still, she could not help that now. She had to deal with the rat
scrambling around inside her body. And it was hers. She had

made dragons. That meant anyone who used their powers used her powers. It was unfortunate that the Sum of All Dragons did not see it this way but she would be forced to see reason or—at the very least—be made incapable of reasoning ever again.

Tiamat ordered her Followers to attack and looked inward.

The girl ran through her memories. It was a clever escape from the place where she had imprisoned her, the goddess could admit. Not that it would matter.

She swooped over the desert where Kylara ran and brought a bank of clouds with her that turned the dry sand to a muddy wash in seconds. The dragon mage—in her human form, foolish child—looked up with terror in her eyes. Tiamat turned to shadow, plummeted, and materialized moments before her claws gored the child.

Although she drove into her with every ounce of force she had, her claws did not puncture the human's soft body. In fact, one of them broke.

The ancient dragon looked at what should be the dead mind of the girl and saw she had wrapped her human body in diamond. It was curious, to be sure, but not something she could waste time on.

The girl's eyes blazed with light and she blasted Tiamat's shadows away.

She laughed and brought lightning down.

Rather than recoil from the attack, the child made a shrub grow in the blink of an eye. Taller than her, it redirected the blast of lightning.

Kylara—Tiamat had to admit the girl was clever enough to warrant using her name—raced across the desert. She gave chase and used the winds of the storm to catch up easily. Moments before she caught up to her quarry, the girl transformed, leapt skyward, and bulldozed into her with one of her favorite new powers—that of momentum.

Tiamat had been unprepared for it, so when the diamond

horns struck her, she was knocked aside and careened away before she landed awkwardly.

She stood and faced a being made of pure water. It surged into her, covered her entirely, and tried to drown her. It might have worked if she were not an aquatic dragon above all else. She simply breathed as the water tried to crush her. It was odd, though, as controlling water like that was not one of her powers.

Curious, she used a dragon's more familiar ability of making water take the form of a dragon to force the water away. No sooner did she do so than a being of air attacked her. Was it an elemental? A being from the spirit realm given form? But how could that be?

Tiamat reached out with her aura and felt the source.

"Clever girl!" she bellowed and used her ability to augment the sound of her voice so that wherever the girl was hiding, she could hear her. "Using the memory of your aunt to make spirits? It might have worked if we were in my mind but we are in yours. You cannot hurt me with those."

The Mother of All Dragons lifted the boulder where the memory of the girl's mage aunt was hiding and sliced her in half with her tail. In an instant, the elemental spirits faded to nothing and were gone.

"So, you admit this is my mind, not yours?" Kylara roared before she drove into her with the power of momentum. Again, she had been unprepared and was hurled across the desert land- scape and into a pile of boulders.

The girl was better with her powers than she had thought. She pushed to her feet but her adversary was already upon her and lashed out with tendrils of shadow and blasts of light. It was a clever choice to alternate those two attacks, as each needed to be blocked with the other. Despite this, she was not able to strike the goddess, not even with all her dexterity. Every tendril she sent forward was obliterated with light and every beam of light was swallowed by shadow.

The girl fought well and with a ferocity Tiamat had not expected from such a young person, but it was not enough. The ancient dragon blocked her languidly, then inhaled and blasted her with freezing breath to encapsulate the smaller dragon in a block of ice.

But Kylara did not give up. Instead, she heated herself and melted the ice from within. As she did so, she used the water to push thorny plants from the ground. Her adversary burned these away but some of them popped and spattered her with hot acid.

No, she realized, it wasn't the cactus but the girl. She had sprayed her with acid while she fought. She truly was trying her very best. Tiamat would enjoy taking her apart.

The young dragon mage had thought that using memories would give her the edge against Tiamat, but she had been wrong. When that failed, she had turned to combinations of powers, but she could not seem to break through her captor's defenses. She had thought that the light-dark might work and had been certain that she could get the acid to ignite and burn her opponent, but both attacks had been fruitless.

"Why not live in this dream, girl? Why bother with all this?"

"I could ask the same of you!" Kylara retorted and yanked the screws out of her mother's house lower down the mountain. She pelted the ancient dragon with pieces of metal, but she didn't even seem bothered when she blocked them. Instead, she simply flicked her tail like an annoyed cat and forced the metal spikes to turn into discs that fell to the earth. For some reason, she could no longer get them to work but that was fine. She had hardly any experience with the metal powers and it became obvious that she would have to win this with skill.

"I did dream, girl," Tiamat said and sprayed acid at her that burned when it touched until she was able to breathe ice at it to nullify it. "I dreamed of this day. It is your turn to sleep now and perhaps, in a thousand years or so, I will give you a day out."

Kylara roared and dug in with her momentum ability to launch herself at her foe. It was the only ability she had managed to land a strike with. Perhaps she could combine it with something else.

The ancient dragon was knocked back and the dragon mage flared her light at the last moment, hoping to blind, disorient, and injure the dragon at the same time. She tumbled from the force of the blow and rubbed her eyes.

But the injury only seemed to last for a moment. Tiamat regained her feet and powered toward her with the same ability. She tried to dodge but her adversary lashed out with a shadow tendril and redirected her into the path of the attack. A rib broke when it struck her and another when she careened into a pile of boulders.

She stood, breathing hard. What was happening made no sense to her. She was hitting Tiamat—and hitting her hard— yet the dragon did not seem to be weakening at all. She, on the other hand, needed time to heal. Unfortunately, it was time she did not have.

Tendrils of shadow exploded from the soil around her feet. She lanced them into nothing with beams of light from her eyes but she was not able to obliterate all of them. One circled her front leg and yanked it out from under her. Another caught her face and threw her into the ground so hard that she tasted blood when a tooth broke.

Kylara was afraid. She felt completely and utterly terrified, like a mouse trying to fight a cat. Her mind screamed that she was an idiot to leave that warm place with the soothing lullaby. She even felt like she missed the smell of tea.

Her teeth gritted, she pushed to her feet. None of those feelings were hers. She couldn't shake them and still felt the terror Tiamat wanted her to feel, but thanks to her time with

Amythist, she at least knew where the feelings were coming from.

"You are not my master!" she screamed and made every scale in her body glow with radiant light. The shadows that bound her to the earth evaporated into nothing and she was free. She braced herself for another attack but it did not come. She launched skyward and looked down to where her enemy stood and watched her.

The dragon didn't even seem winded. Her comparison to a cat and mouse seemed even more apt. She was fighting for her life but it had become very clear that Tiamat was merely playing with her.

"Oh, child." The Mother of All Dragons shook her head and lightning streaked from the sky and struck the dragon mage. The pain of being struck by lightning—even for a dragon who could control it—was indescribable.

Screaming, she plummeted.

When she opened her eyes, her adversary stood over her. Her eyes—like her scales—sparkled in a thousand colors. "If I am not your master, who is?" she asked her.

"My friends, my mom, and the people who need me." She spat acid at Tiamat's face.

The dragon expected the attack and had prepared herself for it. The corrosive bile did nothing to her.

"Child, you sound like a servant."

"What's wrong with that?" She tried good old-fashioned fire breath, but Tiamat blocked it with the back of a claw.

"If you wish to serve, serve me." The goddess stepped back and a tornado descended upon Kylara and lifted her off her feet. She tried to redirect the flows of air but before she could, the nails she had tried to drive into her enemy struck her. They were no longer discs of metal, but chains. These wound around her wrists and neck but didn't connect to each other. Instead, they pulled in opposite directions.

The dragon mage writhed as Tiamat increased the pressure and pushed her higher with the tornado. She exhaled flames, then ice, and finally, acid. All of them were sucked up by the tornado and each struck the girl in turn.

She started to black out as she was pulled apart. At least she now understood what would happen if she died while inside her mind. Her body would live on under the control of Tiamat.

As much as she wanted to resist, she found she could no longer withstand the other dragon's aura. As acid corroded her scales, as fire and ice competed for which could cause more damage, and as wind and metal tried to pull her to pieces, she could do nothing but cry tears that were lost to the storm. She was defeated and was nothing. While she was the Sum of All Dragons, it meant absolutely nothing. She should never have left the darkness and should have stayed where it was warm and safe.

"Please!" she begged. "Please, let me dream!"

"Oh, child. Do you truly think that is still an option after all you have proven yourself capable of?" Tiamat chuckled. "No, no. You will be broken into shards and sprinkled across the wasteland of your mind. You will watch as I destroy that which you loved. It is not a punishment, my child, but a lesson. You should never disobey your mother."

CHAPTER THIRTY-SEVEN

"Do you have a plan, kid?" Kor shouted at Sam as he fired silver barbs from his tail at a dragon who had the ability to control metal. Despite his target redirecting the barbs before they could strike him, he was not dissuaded. He seemed to see the power of the other dragon as a personal challenge.

"I need to get up there."

"You want to challenge her?" The Silver Bullet snorted but he looked impressed. The dragon he fought against threw a few of his barbs back at him and he intercepted them with his forearms. They clattered harmlessly away.

"That's Kylara. Tiamat…I don't know…stole her body or something. I have to get her out."

"We have to get her out," Tanya said and pushed into the conversation.

Their instructor looked at them. "I suppose your friends will want to go too?" He threw three more spines. The first two were deflected but the third somehow overwhelmed the dragon's powers and pierced its eye. It screamed, fell back, and clawed at its face. "Vector-based power." He smirked. "I pushed one spine

up and one down. Those powers balanced each other out and…"
He winked.

Karl and Jasmine fought a dragon who could create lances of
stone that lunged from the soil, although Karl watched the
exchange between Sam and Kor out of the corner of his eye while
he dodged. Jasmine hurled the sharpened pillars of stone away
with her telekinesis.

"They certainly will. She'll need all our help," Tanya told the
instructor.

The Silver Bullet took a moment to survey the battlefield.
Everywhere they looked, dragons either battled dragons or
rained destruction on the mages. But—much like Jasmine—they
did not quite seem to know how to defeat the mages. They hurled
acid or fire or ice at their tiny, squishy enemies, who knew how
to block all this with their shields. The cultist dragons would then
fly on, thinking the mages were dead, only to be attacked from
behind by the very same opponents they had strafed with fire.

Sam—for all his combat experience—could not make much
sense of anything. It seemed to be utter chaos to him—more like
dozens of one-on-one fights that spilled over into each other
instead of an actual battle. Kor, however, was able to make sense
of everything.

"Get to the jungle, then give me one hundred and twenty
seconds before you go up the south side of the pyramid."

"Right!" Sam said but had to add, "The south side?"

"That's points off your grade." The old dragon snorted. "That
side is at her back right now. Got it? One hundred and twenty
seconds is two minutes, by the way."

"We know that!" Tanya snapped.

Kor shrugged. "Maybe you do. Golden boy, though—"

"Two minutes, south side. What will you do?" Sam asked.

"Leave that to me." The Silver Bullet grinned like a kid in a
candy shop. "Professor Sharra, mount up!"

"Gladly!" The professor lifted herself with her telekinesis and settled on his back. They raced away like a bullet.

"One hundred and ten!" Kor shouted over his shoulder and goaded Sam into action.

"Karl, Jasmine, take cover!" He shot a tight beam of light at the jungle to show where they would go.

Midnight nodded and flew in that direction. For a moment, Sam was concerned about the dragon they had been fighting but Kor swooped down and grasped her by the scruff of her neck, lifted her off her feet, and disconnected her from her earth power.

Karl used the opportunity to wrap himself in shadow and vanish into the jungle. Sam and Tanya stepped under the cover of the canopy a moment later.

"What's the plan?" Karl asked as he emerged from shadow, now in his human form. Jasmine said nothing, her gaze focused on the battlefield. It did not seem like they had been followed. There was too much happening for any dragon but the one directly fighting them to have noticed, and their instructors had taken care of that.

"We have about ninety seconds to move through the jungle and climb up the back of the pyramid to attack her from behind," Sam explained as he transformed into his human body and pushed through the thick undergrowth.

"The back? What is that supposed to mean?" Karl grumbled. "What if she moves?"

"We're supposed to go to the south side," Tanya explained and used her plant powers to force the underbrush to make a path for them. Suddenly, the way ahead was clear and the canopy above their heads was thicker. They could move much faster and hopefully undetected. He increased his pace.

"Well, why didn't you say that?" Karl scoffed.

"Because who the hell knows what south means?" Sam hurried on and used his dragon-enhanced speed to race through the jungle a little beyond the perimeter of the clearing. As they moved, the sounds of battle grew slightly more distant.

"I have shadow powers, golden boy. That means knowing where the sun is and what the light is doing is important. Kor must be planning to create a distraction on the north side of the tower, then."

"Sure, whatever, but hurry." Sam stopped at the back—the south side, he reminded himself—of the tower. From their hiding place inside the vegetation, he could see that Karl was right. Kor and Professor Sharra were creating one hell of a distraction. They didn't stop to engage any single dragon but instead, swooped around the battlefield, launched silver spikes everywhere, and bludgeoned everyone with waves of telekinesis.

Every single one of the Followers of Tiamat now pursued them. Those who got close enough to attack were harassed by other dragons from the Lumos School or someone from the mage security team. Their pursuers grew closer all the time, however, and Sam knew the distraction would not last much longer.

"Let's go!" he shouted and burst from cover the moment Karl and Jasmine caught up to him and Tanya.

The four of them raced across the open space between the jungle and the pyramid. Sam—in the lead—transformed into his dragon shape and the other two dragons did the same. Before he had time to wonder how they could get Jasmine to the top of the ziggurat, she lifted herself by her robes and rocketed up the side. He didn't fly but instead, bounded up the stepped pyramid and took the massive levels in twos or threes.

In moments, the four of them reached the top.

Karl launched tendrils of inky darkness that bound the mother dragon's legs. Tanya went to the roof of the temple—no doubt to drop seeds to grow and use in the fight—and Sam blasted Tiamat in the eyes to blind her. Jasmine struck the dragon's chest with a massive telekinetic push.

Between being disoriented, having her feet bound, and the force of Jasmine's strike, Tiamat landed heavily and fell to the next step of the pyramid.

Vines burst from the top of the structure and cascaded over the edge to bind the dragon goddess.

"Let Kylara go!" Sam ordered, still on the top step, and looked at her with his eyes glowing.

The dragon did not seem to even notice him. Her eyes were focused on something distant and her pupils danced as if she could still see despite the flash of light he had struck her with.

Tanya's vines bound her tighter and tighter. They sprouted thorns that dug between her scales and sawed into the goddess's flesh as they constricted.

Tiamat's consciousness seemed to return to her. She looked Sam in the eye—no longer blinded—and the vines around her turned black, wilted, and were covered in frost. As quickly as they had frozen, fire incinerated them. She was free.

"I would almost think you planned this," the Mother of All Dragons hissed enigmatically, struck Sam with the tip of her diamond-tipped tail, and flung him from the first step of the pyramid down to the fourth.

He righted himself and climbed into the action again despite his head spinning.

Karl attempted to strike their adversary with tendrils of darkness, but he was thwarted at every attempt. Worse, the dragon did not even seem to be particularly challenged by the fight. Instead of only using light powers to obliterate the binding shadows, she used a combination of light, fire, and bolts of lightning from above as if this were not a fight for her but merely a well-practiced training exercise.

Tanya lashed out with plants that grew in the cracks of the ziggurat, but Tiamat's use of her powers was too smooth. Between fire and ice, the plants had little chance of success.

Jasmine tried to pound the dragon with telekinetic blows.

These looked powerful in that Sam could see where each blow struck from the indentation it caused. But their enemy had the same diamond scales Kylara did. If she bruised beneath her scales, she did not show it.

The golden dragon leapt into battle. His claws and teeth glowed with radiant energy but he was not able to penetrate her defenses. She was not a particularly skilled physical combatant—which seemed to imply that she did not have access to Kylara's knowledge, only her body—but that didn't make fighting her easy.

He was used to having his claws and bites blocked by claw or tail, not by walls of ice, balls of fire, or scraps of floating metal. While she might not be a trained brawler, she certainly knew how to defend herself. A dozen powers spun around her to hold his physical strikes at bay as well as Karl's shadows and Jasmine's telekinesis. Tanya's plants seemed to have been proven to be irrelevant long before.

They fought their hardest and barely managed to maintain a stalemate. And that was with Tiamat not fully engaged. Sam had been in enough duels to tell that she was not mentally present in the fight. Like Kor showing moves to a first-year, she seemed to operate from a distance. She was distracted, probably by Kylara. He had a feeling that if she turned her full attention to any of them, she would win handily. Not only that, but he also got the sense that if they kept fighting, they would tire long before this cult-proclaimed goddess would.

Which meant they needed to change the rules of engagement.

"This isn't working!" Karl seemed to have reached the same conclusion when a weaponized icicle stabbed through his shoulder. He fell back and gasped in pain.

Sam did not know what to do. He had to keep fighting to save Kylara but he also had to heal the other dragon.

"Your friend needs help!" Petalwing buzzed into Tiamat's face and made the dragon's attacks miss temporarily, even if they did not stop. He infused Midnight with light energy to super-charge his healing power.

That was about all the time the pixie was able to give them, though. Tiamat sprayed the creature with ice, slowed her, and whacked her out of the air with a flick of her tail. Petalwing's tiny body was nothing compared to a dragon who could augment her momentum. She catapulted away like a miniature meteor and careened into the ziggurat so hard that pieces of rock flurried.

The pixie fell forward, landed on her hands and knees, and coughed blood. She smiled, though, like this was all a game. "I bet I can do that two more times!" she said, her teeth bloody.

"No!" Tanya shouted and Petalwing obeyed.

"Karl, hold her off!" Sam shouted as he went to the diminutive creature.

"It's a tall order but sure, why not?" Karl and Jasmine brought a web of darkness and shields up. The ancient dragon was able to break through both powers but together, they managed to keep what attention she gave to the battle off Sam.

"Petalwing. The Big Pixie is still trapped inside there."

She nodded. "I know. I could feel it. How do we help her? This fighting seems hard."

"Do you think it's possible to power Kylara's spirit inside the body? Or would Tiamat simply take the energy?"

The pixie rubbed her tiny little chin in thought, then shrugged. "I don't know. She is the one who can absorb powers, not Tiamat, so it might work. But then again, Tiamat is exceptionally strong so maybe she would gobble it." Petalwing beamed. "It sounds fun, though! Why not?"

Sam could match the shrug but not the happy little grin. *Why not, indeed,* he thought darkly. They couldn't fight Tiamat, but maybe Kylara could from the inside. The worst-case scenario was that he would simply feed more power to the already super-powered goddess and doom the world to her subjugation. If that happened, he would probably be allowed to live as the one who had given her the edge she needed. Maybe she would let him talk to whatever was left of Kylara in a hundred years or something. Given that the alternative was to let the goddess beat them to a pulp without any real effort, it seemed the only option.

"I'll try to heal Kylara!" he told Tanya.

Before she could protest—he could feel from her aura that she fully intended to do exactly that—he rushed toward Tiamat.

He didn't try to land any strikes so the dragon did not block him. He was able to get close beside her and put both his dragon hands on her before he felt excruciating pain in the back of his neck.

His plan had been that he would have time to pump some of his healing energy into Kylara's body. Before he was able to, however, Tiamat bit him.

She clamped her jaws and his tail spasmed. Her teeth had punctured a nerve and until it healed, his tail was effectively paralyzed.

"Kylara!" he called while he still could. "Come back to us!" Without waiting for an answer, he sent out all the magic he could muster and turned his entire body into a gleaming beacon of healing energy.

Tiamat laughed, the sound choked and harsh since her jaws held his neck.

Her aura insulted him and made him feel foolish for thinking he could do anything for his friend. He felt like all he was doing was making their enemy more powerful but also like he was an insignificant speck and the energy he tried to use was like a firefly compared to the sun. She was strong and he was weak— like he was an insect and she was the goddess prophesied to return.

In the next moment, a tendril of shadow touched his leg and another power poured into him. Karl was giving him some of his energy. A seed landed on his back and began to grow, and he felt Tanya's power enter his body. Jasmine somehow used her powers to augment his own. Another strange sensation rippled into him when Petalwing infused him with power as well.

Through all of it, he felt Tiamat's aura most of all. She laughed at their pathetic, mortal attempts to overthrow a goddess. He tried to remain focused but she made him feel like all he was doing was making her more powerful—like this was all in vain and he would be punished rather than killed quickly.

Sam gritted his and teeth ignored the aura.

"This magic…is for…Kylara!" he channeled the magic flowing into him and lit up like a sun.

CHAPTER THIRTY-EIGHT

The tornado of dragon powers stopped but Kylara was already beaten. She fell from the sky, too weak to catch the air with her wings and too tired to think. Tiamat caught her in her jaws like a mother cat catching a kitten. She might have found it humiliating if she had the capacity to think but she simply accepted it. The reality was that she was too broken to fight or to even stand.

"Your friends care about you," her captor remarked, dropped her on the dirt, and planted her talons squarely on her chest. The girl looked past the dragon to the sky. Two huge holes had appeared. For a moment, she wondered if her tormentor's control was shaking, but the thought vanished quickly. Tiamat was too powerful to lose control. The holes had appeared because she had created them. She was allowing her to see out into the real world.

The Mother of All Dragons had not lied about her friends. Karl, Sam, Tanya, Jasmine, and even Petalwing attempted to stop the dragon.

"They do not understand what I am," Tiamat explained to Kylara while she battled with her friends outside in the real world. "They think this is like any of the other fights they have been in when it is not."

Sam raced toward the two holes in the sky and pushed past his adversary's defenses. Despite her exhaustion and her place beneath the dragon's claw, hope rose in her chest.

It was immediately dashed when Tiamat snapped her jaws on the back of his neck. From inside her mind, Kylara could taste his blood and feel bones crunch beneath the massive teeth. If he were any creature but a dragon, he would already be dead. Only his healing power kept him alive and it would only last so long.

"Kylara!" he called and the words echoed across the desert landscape of her mind. "Come back to us!" The holes in the sky filled with light as he sent healing power through his body and out of his scales. It poured off him and despite being trapped inside her body, she could almost feel it.

Tiamat looked at the sky above them. Tendrils of light like bolts of lightning but in slow motion pushed through the holes. The girl stretched toward one and the effort made one of her captor's talons dig deeper into her shoulder.

She flinched when Tiamat bit harder. The holes in the sky shook furiously as Sam thrashed from the pain of her bite.

The Mother of All Dragons only laughed. She roared and the lightning bolts of healing energy retreated. Most of them faded to nothing. Where before, there had been over a dozen, there was now only one.

But still, Sam refused to give up. Somehow, he called on another well of power and the tendril of light extended slowly again as if it had to drill into Tiamat's consciousness. Despite this, it drew closer to Kylara.

It was not only Sam's energy, she realized. The light, tiny vines and leaves that sprouted could only be Tanya's work. In the tiny shadows these leaves provided, a characteristic inky darkness strengthened the beam of energy. The three of them were trying to reach her and to help her, even though she was defeated.

But she couldn't be, she told herself grimly. She could not give up on her friends when they were so close. She reached up—pain from Tiamat's talons be damned—and tried to take the power they offered.

The ancient dragon looked at her as if she were a child who had urinated on her shoes. "Oh, did you want some of this energy?" she asked rhetorically. The end of the rope of power was barely a few feet above her head now.

Kylara summoned every ounce of strength she had and stretched toward it.

Tiamat thrust her into the earth and laughed. "You truly do not understand. You are the Sum of All Dragons. That means you are pieces cobbled together to serve me. You may be the Sum, but I am proof that the whole is worth more than the parts."

And with that, she caught hold of the strand of energy as if it were nothing more than an errant kite string. The girl felt Tiamat's power double, then triple. Soon, her scales glowed and the flowers on the plants near them began to bloom. She reached beyond her captor for some part of it—even a smidgeon or a speck of shadow—but she was still alone and still too weak.

She began to black out again from the pain, the blood loss, and her own failure.

Sam's voice snapped her back to the present.

"This magic…is for…Kylara!"

She felt her friends' magic like a tidal wave inside her. It poured into her and deepened the reservoir of magic in her chest. She didn't know how it was possible until she realized that the magic flowed through Tiamat and into her. More and more streamed into her, strengthened her, healed her, sharpened her reflexes, and empowered her aura while it augmented her in every way.

The talon on her chest no longer weighed so heavily. Kylara

shoved upward and Tiamat's eyes widened as she was lifted and toppled back.

The goddess righted herself and glared at her but took a moment to stare in horror at the girl and the space above her. When the dragon mage looked up, she realized that the tendril of light, shadow, and plants was now tethered to her like an extension cord on a chainsaw. She felt unstoppable.

"It's time to give me my body back," she said.

"It was I who made your body possible in the first place!" Tiamat retorted and lunged at her.

She exhaled and a wall of ice formed in front of her enemy. The dragon drove through it but she had expected that. She sprayed acid that spattered on the goddess's round chest and made her scales blacken and hiss as the dragon screamed in pain.

Kylara bounded forward and filled herself with the power of momentum seconds before she bulldozed into Tiamat and launched her into a tumbled and uncontrolled flight across the landscape. "You are not welcome here," she stated plainly when the dragon's progress was stopped by a pile of boulders.

"How dare you speak to a goddess this way?" Tiamat called bolts of lightning down.

In response, the dragon mage summoned fragments of the metal her adversary had used to bind her, then formed them into a tall spike that caught the lightning and sent it into the ground. "You are not welcome here!" she said.

The ancient dragon launched spikes of stone from the earth at her. She shattered them with a flick of her diamond tail. While she knew that on some level, doing this hurt, but with her friends' power augmenting her, she healed almost instantly. The bruises under her diamond scales did not remain for long.

Tiamat exhaled an inferno and she raised ice to stop it.

When her enemy fired beams of pure light, she absorbed them with shadow.

"You are no longer welcome here!" Kylara roared and

launched a tangle of shadow tendrils at Tiamat. They caught the dragon and bound her, but she was wily and sprouted thorns that cut through the bonds.

The Mother of All Dragons exhaled a shadowy mist and she summoned a maelstrom of wind that blew it away. She was able to hold her adversary now, but she could not seem to defeat her. How did she press for victory? As she threw powers at her foe that she did not even know she had, she tried to think about how she had been imprisoned.

She felt a stab of fear in her chest and realized that—once again—Tiamat attempted to control her with her aura. Was that the key to this entire thing? Was that how she could make her leave?

Kylara focused on her aura and filled the desert with confidence, bravery, and hope. She had meant it only to drive Tiamat's negative emotions away, but something far stranger happened. The dragon was knocked back like a boat hit by a tsunami and suddenly, the young dragon mage was alone in the desert.

Immediately, she reached out and tried to grasp her body but still could not.

That meant her enemy was still there, but where?

The desert dissolved and she now stood in Detroit where she had failed the pixies. Those feelings of worthlessness began to overwhelm her but before they could, her friends' confidence in her flowed through the beam of energy that still connected her to the sky.

She had not failed there, she reminded herself firmly. On the contrary, she had defeated Mort. She had not done it alone but had done it with the help of her friends. Those same friends were helping her again. With a sound like the sky itself being torn apart, Tiamat exploded out of a building and drove into her.

Kylara flew back from the force of the blow. She powered through the outer wall of a building, a dozen interior walls, and out the other side. Her enemy was already there waiting for her.

She swung her diamond-studded tail but the girl saw it coming and grasped the dragon with shadow.

The two fell together, biting, clawing, and spitting unthinkable things at each other. Ice, fire, acid, wind, light, shadow, and even a swarm of biting insects all slammed into her. She threw all of it back at her adversary until the two of them pounded into the dirt.

"Do you remember this place, Kylara? Where you failed the pixies."

"I saved the pixies," she replied, pawed the ground, and surged into an attack. "And you are still not welcome here!"

She bulldozed into Tiamat, who rocketed through a building and out the other side. In the next moment, the girl was in the sky and the ancient dragon was below her, falling toward the surface of a frozen lake.

The goddess shattered the ice and sank to the bottom. Kylara hovered above where she had vanished and dared to wonder if this was all over. She could still feel her friends' power energizing her.

The edges of the lake melted, then the center. Steam rose off the water before it began to bubble. Soon, the entire lake was at a rolling boil. A moment later, the water was all gone and Tiamat stood at the bottom beside the recreated fishing hut that Cassandra had built beneath this lake before it had been destroyed.

"This was where you failed the worst. This is where you defined your entire wretched, miserable life." The Mother of All Dragons breathed fire on the hut and obliterated it.

Kylara landed across from her. She approached slowly and transformed into her human form. The beam of energy flowed into the crown of her head and she knew that without the strength of her friends, she would lose. She also knew she could never have come this far without them and would still be trapped in a deep, dark pit if even the thought of them had not been enough to motivate her.

But, for perhaps the first time in her life, that did not bother her. Of course she would not have been successful without her friends. What did success mean without people you cared about to share it with? Needing her friends' help was not a weakness but a strength—perhaps her greatest strength of all.

"I was a baby when I first came here, Tiamat," she said. Before, using the dragon's name had frightened her but it now seemed commonplace. She realized that her enemy must feel more alone than she did.

"A baby whose family was slaughtered," the dragon retorted.

"A baby who was rescued by someone who cared about her," Kylara replied. "I may be the Sum of All Dragons, but I'm also a sum of all the people who have helped me in life. I would be nothing without them. I guess I'm like you, Tiamat. Without your Followers, you would also be powerless."

Kylara felt terror in her heart but it was different than before. It still came from Tiamat but now, it seemed less focused. Where before, it had felt like a spear stabbing into her heart, it now felt like a bomb detonating and burning everyone in the vicinity, her enemy included.

"You are not welcome here!" She fired a blast of energy. It started as an amalgamation of all the powers she had absorbed but as it traveled across the bottom of the lake to strike Tiamat, it became a weapon of pure magic.

It struck the ancient dragon and she reeled. Still, she was not defeated.

She reared and launched a blast of magic in retaliation. It glowed with a thousand colors—exactly like her scales—and collided with Kylara's beam.

Tiamat roared and her magic pushed closer to the girl. It went from ten feet to five, to two, to barely a few inches past her fingertips.

The young dragon mage somehow knew that if that beam touched her, this fight would be over. She would be utterly destroyed and scattered across her mind, and this body would belong to her enemy. But the converse was also true, she realized. If she could get her beam to strike her adversary, the dragon would finally obey.

Kylara planted her feet, felt her friends' power flowing into her, and forced her magic toward her foe. A great shower of sparks spattered in all directions—burning, scarring, or freezing pieces of the lakebed around them—as she pushed the other magic back.

"Impossible!" Tiamat screamed.

"You need to ask for help," she said. "My friends are helping me. That's giving me an advantage."

"I am a goddess!" the dragon screamed and her beam of magic pushed harder.

But the girl's energy did not budge and there was no reason why it should. It was augmented by her friends and she would not fail them. She pushed her magic with all the force at her disposal and it erupted with showers of sparks and waves of different kinds of magic as it chewed through Tiamat's beam.

"No! This is not how it's supposed to be! Why do you fight when I could give you everything?"

"I already have everything anyone could want," Kylara replied. She found that maintaining the beam of energy didn't take as much work as it had at first. "I have friends who care about me, a mom who loves me, and adults I trust who want me to succeed."

Tiamat flinched as if she had slapped her. When she did, her magic faltered and the dragon mage's rainbow beam connected with her chest.

The dragon screamed as the entire world seemed to fall apart.

In one moment, Kylara was at the bottom of the lakebed and in the next, the landscape was gone completely. She hovered high above the map of her mind and could see her mother's land in the desert, the fishing hut where she'd been born, the Lumos School, the cities she had fought in, and all the places between.

The goddess fled between them all and tried to find a place to bury herself in her mind. She did not allow it although she did not understand why she still attempted to fight. If she needed a place to live, why not ask for help? She might have considered letting her stay if the dragon came to her willingly, but trying to burrow into her memories would not do.

A great beam of light shone onto Tiamat. The dragon looked into it and screeched like a rat in a trap.

"Do you need help?" Kylara asked.

"Give me your mind, girl!" the dragon pleaded.

"I will not," she said and shook her head.

The Mother of All Dragons turned her back on her and tried to burrow into a facsimile of Professor Sharra's classroom. The girl turned the brightness of the spotlight up. Tiamat could resist no longer. The light from her beam seemed to desiccate the last of her energy.

The ancient dragon collapsed onto the floor of the classroom —the very same classroom where Kylara and her friends had learned to work even better together all semester long—and began to evaporate. Her scales burned away first, then the tips of her claws, followed by her tail and wings. Her body went next, then her skeleton, so all that was left was a skull that screamed at her for daring to disobey her.

Finally, she was gone, and the dragon mage flew higher and faster until she was the sky itself, the entirety of this world.

CHAPTER THIRTY-NINE

Kylara opened her eyes in the real world. Incongruously, she had Sam's neck in her jaws. She released him and felt a horrible gagging sensation in the back of her throat. Startled, she fell back and exhaled a great plume of smoke that coalesced into the form of a dragon.

She scrambled to her feet and inhaled a breath of air, ready to transform it into one of her myriads of powers. Tiamat would not come back into her body. Not now and not ever. But the dragon's spirit seemed to have no interest in returning to the Sum of All Dragons. She flitted away as if even being near the girl burned her.

The dragon mage could tell she was defeated so she turned to Sam, who lay on the ground, completely motionless aside from the halting rise and fall of his chest as he tried to draw air. She placed her dragon hands on him and returned some of the energy he had given her. The healing light flowed through his body but his scales did not glow. Instead, the wounds on his neck and spine mended. His breathing became more even and his eyes fluttered open.

"Ky...you came back to me."

"You make it kind of hard not to with the spotlight and every-thing." She smiled.

Sam looked like he wanted to say more but had to focus on healing his wounds. Besides, there was still the spirit of Tiamat to worry about.

Jasmine had mounted up on Karl and the two of them flew with Tanya after the misty spirit of the goddess. He launched cord after cord of inky shadow, but none of them could gain purchase on her spirit. They either passed through as if there was nothing there at all or—occasionally—made a swirl as if she still had the wherewithal to dodge the attacks.

The mage's shield powers brought no better results. She tried to create sphere after sphere to encapsulate the spirit, but Tiamat continued to evade her. If even the tiniest part of her was outside the sphere, the telekinetic powers did not hold her. She was able to flow and escape. They were too high for Tanya to use her plant powers, but she kept close, slashed at the cloud of spirit, and sprayed fire breath that did nothing to slow Tiamat.

"I'll be right back, Sam, all right?" Kylara said.

"I have something I want to say—"

"It'll have to wait."

His aura felt like he wanted to protest but he was still too weak. Instead, he laid back and closed his eyes.

Kylara took to the sky. She did not know how she could stop Tiamat but she knew that if anyone had the power to do it, it would be her. She drew on every ounce of speed she had and used wind to augment her speed, extra wings made of shadow, her momentum power, and more. But her adversary had already put too much distance between them. She would reach the edge of the jungle before she could reach her. If that happened, she might escape!

Before the fallen goddess could enter the jungle, however, Kishar jumped out in front of her. Her dress was torn and her hair in disarray, but she was still breathtakingly beautiful. "I offer myself to you, Goddess Tiamat! I have followed your path my entire life. Let me be that which she would not!"

Tiamat's spirit form tightened like a swarm of bees coming into a new tree.

The First Walker closed her eyes and spread her arms to bare her chest while she displayed a look of bliss on her face. "My heart belongs to you, Tiamat, it always has."

The goddess' spirit pounded into her, but rather than flowing into her chest, it forced her mouth open and poured into her throat and nose. Kishar's eyes widened with pain as more and more of the spirit flowed into her. She looked like she might asphyxiate but a second later, Tiamat's spirit was gone, completely buried inside her.

She fell to her knees and bent over to place her hands on the soil as if bracing herself to throw up. Her eyes closed, she took a long, deep breath of air and threw her head back violently as a dragon's talon reached out from her throat.

It was a horrible sight to behold. Later, Kylara would regret not turning away but in that moment, she still tried to reach the spirit with every trick she had and did not think of the nightmares this moment might give her in the future.

The talon stretched out of Kishar's throat. Its wrist was as wide as her mouth and the forearm was even thicker. The woman's jaw seemed to come unhinged to allow Tiamat out— like a python but in reverse.

Next came the upper arm—wider still and muscled, with a spike on the elbow that might have pushed out of Kishar's eye socket had it faced the other way. Even the arm was larger than the First Walker. To see her on her knees with the massive dragon appendage protruding from her throat was horribly disconcerting to witness.

The talon descended and planted itself on the ground and— much more quickly—the other arm slid out of the woman's throat and planted itself on the other side of her. The two arms pushed against the ground and each other and a cloud of dark mist—some part of Kishar's power—appeared around her body, perhaps to give her more flexibility as the dragon climbed out of her.

Tiamat's head came next. Kishar was hardly recognizable as human now, merely a stretchy mess of skin and fabric that no longer obeyed any of the laws that bodies did. More mist poured from her as the goddess forced her rainbow-scaled head into the sky.

When her torso tried to emerge from Kishar's throat, something happened to what was left of her host. She seemed to turn inside out and suddenly was gone as if she'd folded into the dragon's legs and tails. The horror of transformation was completed.

The Mother of All Dragons stood before them. The woman's form was gone. In its place was the same rainbow-scaled and curvaceously motherly form of Tiamat.

Kylara landed in front of her. "If I could defeat you when you controlled my body, alone and frightened of you, I can do so again with my friends. I'm no longer afraid."

The goddess inhaled as if she wished to taste the thick jungle air, then shook her head. "There will be time for you to challenge a god later," she said. "For now, I bid you farewell."

"You wish," she said and moved toward her.

The ancient dragon growled and wisps of dark mist poured from her nostrils. It was the same petrifying power Kishar had possessed but it moved much faster. Before she could even take a step, the mist had wreathed Karl, Jasmine, Tanya, and even Sam, all the way at the top of the pyramid.

"I can undo whatever you do to them," she said, not sure if it was true but hoping it was. It had to be.

"You can, child, but how quickly? Can you turn them all back before I break one of them?" Tiamat barely inclined her snout upward at her three friends who were airborne.

Kylara clenched her teeth. She might be able to catch one of them, but all three? "What do you want, Tiamat?"

"To meet again," the goddess replied and opened a gate behind her. She stepped through and it closed behind her and the mist was gone.

It was over and somehow, she and her friends had won.

CHAPTER FORTY

With Tiamat gone, Kylara became the focus of attention. Karl, Jasmine, and Tanya landed and circled her, ready to defend their friend from anyone stupid enough to think they could beat the dragon who had defeated a goddess.

She scanned the sky but after what happened to Kishar, it seemed that whatever cohesion the Followers of Tiamat had once had was now gone. The staff from the Lumos School still gave chase but if it was hard to defeat a dragon in combat, it was almost impossible to stop one who wished to flee, especially if they had unusual powers.

Still, Karl, Jasmine, and Tanya did not let their guard down, not until every cultist had been chased over the horizon and Kor and Professor Sharra returned to declare the area secured. The security mages wasted no time and erected a sphere of shielding power around the pyramid and surrounding jungle. The calls of parrots and the din of insects became more distant. It had seemed like a lifetime, but they were safe again.

"Kylara...are you all right?" Jasmine asked. She undoubtedly had a better sense of how secure they were because she could read the mage energy in the same way that dragons could read each other's auras. Tanya was still focused on the jungle, surely listening to every tree, vine, and shrub for any sign of a dragon moving. Karl had a web of shadows stretching from them as well. Between the two of them, Kylara doubted that even a grasshopper would be allowed to move about freely.

"Yeah, I'm fine, thanks to you." She smiled at her friends. They returned it but she could read their auras—Karl and Tanya's anyway—and could tell that they still felt concern for her. "I felt your power inside my mind and was able to drive Tiamat out, thanks to that energy you sent." They did not seem at all mollified by her reassurances.

Confused, she looked down and finally saw what they saw. Her body was the same shape and her scales were still made of diamond, but they were no longer the color she was so familiar with. They were a dark-blue now, bordering on black, except for where the sunlight struck them in just the right way. She raised her arm, rotated it, and stared as every color of the rainbow danced through the scales. Tiamat's scales had looked the same. She must have absorbed them when the dragon had possessed her.

Now that she was free, she could also feel that those colors represented the many powers she had absorbed. She still had ice breath, the momentum power, the ability to move metals, and everything she'd had before the cult had begun their attacks. However, there were more inside her that she had not even touched on—powers that would take weeks to unravel. She did not know if she had received all of them from that horrible moment at the pond when the cultists had all attacked at once or if Tiamat had somehow given her more when she had possessed her.

"I'm still me." She smiled. "Can't you feel my aura and tell?"

Tanya laughed. "I can feel your aura, but that's what's weirding me out!"

That amused Kylara. She had thought that it would be overwhelming to feel everyone's aura without the protection of the amulet, but—after what Tiamat had done to her—it was nice to feel other people's concern.

However, focusing on the auras of the dragons around her called her attention to the aura that was the most concerned for her.

"Excuse me," she said, pumped her wings, and took flight. She reached the top of the pyramid quickly and landed beside Sam. He still lay on his back but was in his human form now. That was a good sign as it would allow his dragon body to continue to heal and would hurt less.

He smiled at her and although he noticed her iridescent scales, he did not seem put off by them like her other friends did. He merely smiled the same old brilliant smile of his.

"Hey," Kylara said.

"Hey," he replied and pushed into a seated position.

She sat next to him. "Are you all right?"

"Yeah, thanks to you."

"Right back at you," she said.

They both chuckled and looked out across the landscape. Kylara felt turmoil inside her, desire and caution warring with each other. She did not know if the feeling was hers or Sam's.

"There's something I've been meaning to ask you," he said after a moment.

Ah, so the feeling came from them both.

"Yeah, shoot," Kylara said and immediately regretted the choice of words. She could feel something wonderful in his aura and had responded like she was a teacher and a student had asked her a question after class.

"Kylara…I…that is…you're amazing." He smiled his dazzling smile and a part of her seemed to melt. "I wondered if…I mean, I wouldn't want anything to change between us, and I want you to know that even if you say no, I'll still have your back. I swear that."

"If I say no to what?" she prodded.

Sam drew a deep breath. "Kylara, will you go out with me?"

Her grin felt wide enough to split her face. "I thought you'd never ask."

He smiled despite the fact that she hadn't specifically said yes. She supposed he could tell from her aura and from the fact that she was probably glowing. "I was waiting for a calm moment but realized that with you, that would never happen so…"

"So, you waited until after you had rescued me from a prison inside my mind created by an ancient goddess?"

"You don't have to say yes!" he blurted.

"Samuel Lumos, I would love to go out with you."

Sam reddened and again, Kylara found herself regretting her choice of words. He had only now asked her out and she was already saying "love" to him?

He took her hand gently. Despite him being in far worse shape than her, she could feel his healing energy flow from his hand into hers. She returned it with her reserves. They sat there like that for a moment, simply enjoying the warmth of each other's hand, and let their energies soothe and warm each other.

"I'm happy you said yes," Sam said and turned to her. His eyes were beautiful golden orbs that matched his golden hair perfectly. He was amazingly handsome but he'd always been that. How had she never noticed his mouth before? The way his lips twitched slightly before he grinned? They looked so warm. Kylara leaned toward him, closed her eyes, and drew a deep breath. She had never kissed anyone before. Would she feel Sam's healing power through his lips? His tongue? Would their auras sync?

Unfortunately, she did not get the answer to any of her questions.

"That's quite enough of that!" the Silver Bullet snapped when he landed on top of the pyramid with the two of them. His silvery dragon form had fresh scars but Kor did not look as if he minded. If anything, he looked like he wore the new wounds with pride—although it was hard to tell because he looked at the two of them as if they were vermin that had snuck into his pantry. "Your professors are here and this is a school day, therefore field trip rules apply, which means no fraternizing!"

"Yes, professor," Sam said quickly. He always was a rules-follower, although Kylara noticed that he did not release her hand and his aura showed no other emotion besides joy.

"And you, Miss Diamantine? I don't care if your scales have learned how to do a jig, you will show respect to your professors."

"I thought you didn't like to be called a professor," she quipped.

"And I didn't think you liked detention, but you'll spend the next two weeks regrowing the landscaping in the U. Funny how these things work, isn't it?" Kor grinned. She could read his aura and knew that he was not mad but rather incredibly proud. He was not about to show that, though, while they were still on a battlefield, even if the enemy had retreated.

"I should get us back," she said and finally slipped her hand out of Sam's as she stood. She couldn't wait to touch him again.

"We have enough mages to help with that," Kor pointed out. "But we're not about to start the evacuation without you. Are we ready?" Something about the way he asked that question that gave her pause.

Was she still the same dragon? She knew she looked like Tiamat and that the goddess had used her body as her own. What did that make her? She felt like the same person but she decided it was naïve to think that everyone would treat her the same way. That made Kor's attitude toward her all the sweeter, though. He had known she was a powerful duelist longer than almost any other and he knew now that she was even more powerful. Still, he tried to treat her like a regular student.

Kylara decided she would do the same. "Yes, sir. I think we're up for it."

"Good. Then get your tails down there and let's get home. The humidity here is horrible."

She thought that her return to the Lumos School would feel triumphant, but as soon as they returned, she was reminded of why she had left in the first place.

Lady Amythist still stood in the U, petrified in stone.

An immediate pang of regret stabbed through her. With everything that happened, she had almost forgotten what had happened to the headmaster.

"Kylara, if there's anything you can do..." Professor Sharra said imploringly.

Kor looked at her and said nothing. His bluster meant all the more to Kylara now. He would have had every right to have slapped her around and dragged her back to school immediately, given that Amythist was in this condition, but he had not. Instead, he had made it clear that he was still a teacher and she a student. In a way, that eased the pressure on her. If she failed, she knew he would take the blame and not let her do so.

Or he would try, anyway.

Kylara reached inside and felt through her new catalog of powers for the right one. It was so hard to tell what was what with so many currents running through her inner river of magic. "I'll try my best but I don't know if there's a time limit, though."

Tiamat had said something to Lord Midnight about him being able to survive for centuries. Was there any truth to that? She decided there was only one way to find out.

Cautiously, she approached the petrified statue of the headmaster and exhaled.

Nothing happened.

She had not channeled the right flow of magic, she told herself and took a deep breath to try again. This time, she tried to think about what she needed to do. When she had battled

Tiamat, she had been able to call on whichever power she needed almost without thinking. She knew she had the instincts to do this—or she told herself she did, at least.

Again, she exhaled and tried to melt the stone but created fire. She choked the flames out as soon as they had left her, not wanting to burn the statue. But the flames had no effect. They did not break it nor did they set the headmaster free.

Kylara felt panic begin to build in her chest. She directed light at it, but this was merely swallowed by the dark stone. Next, she tried wind and wrung mist from the air—much like Kishar's mist but not as dark. It did nothing but cover the statue in little drops of dew.

"Headmaster, please!" she begged and rested her head against Amythist's. She could almost feel her in there but she did not know how to get her out. Could she use the acid power to melt the stone? It might damage the statue, though, and then Amythist would be lost forever. Still, Kylara had to try something. She was the only one who could—

"Remember, intention is everything." Petalwing flitted around her head before she could do anything too rash. "You cannot do a thing unless you intend to do it. If you want to play tag with a butterfly, you first have to want to play tag with a butterfly."

The young dragon mage couldn't help but smile at the absurd little pixie. She had almost sounded profound. Still, she was right. Intention was how magic worked. That was why practice was so useful to her. It allowed her to focus her intention better but intention was always at the root of her abilities. It was this that let her create shadow or light, or make plants grow, or let her share a moment with a friend. Intention was everything.

So, rather than trying to create a specific kind of magic to do a specific task, Kylara focused on helping the headmaster. She thought of everything Amythist loved. Her mind sifted through images of hot cups of tea, puttering about her over-cluttered office, moving through her garden, and trying to coax plants to life that had no business growing in the desert. All these things required the old dragon to move, of course. If she wanted to give the ability to do any of those things back to this person who had helped her so much, she would have to un-petrify her.

She felt her intention with every cell. Without holding back, she allowed the desire to help to consume her and the need for the magic to do as she asked to suffuse every part of her so she could help one of the people who had helped her.

Kylara took a deep breath, held it, and when she exhaled, a tiny trail of black smoke puffed from her nostrils. She caught hold of the sensation that came with the small dark cloud, reached into the river of her magic, and grasped this particular current. Like a person building a windmill, this was the part of the river she would use to help.

Calmly, she inhaled again and when she exhaled this time, a dark mist emerged from her nostrils. It ignored the desert breeze —she could feel this with her storm powers—and instead, flowed around the statue of the headmaster. It surrounded Amythist, obscured her, and eclipsed her, so not even she could see her.

From the dark interior of the cloud, a purple tail lashed out and smacked her.

"Headmaster!" she said, shook the blow off, and grinned. She would have suffered far worse if that were the price to bring Lady Amythist back.

"Miss Diamantine?" The old dragon asked as the air cleared around her. "But…where is Kishar? Where are the Followers of Tiamat?"

"They're gone, ma'am. It's…a long story."

"And you had some part in it, I see." Amythist gestured at her newly colored scales.

"I did, ma'am. I'll explain everything."

"That's right, you will. Right now, young lady."

"I don't know, Amythist. I think it can wait." Kor sauntered up and wrapped his wings around the headmaster in a dragon's hug.

"Kor?" The old dragon seemed flustered. "To what do I owe this…outpouring of emotion?"

Kylara grinned inwardly. It was the first time she had ever sensed embarrassment in the headmaster's aura.

The Silver Bullet drew back and smiled warmly at Amythist. "You've been our rock since you got here, headmaster, but it's good to know that you won't be one forever."

"What is that supposed to mean?" the headmaster demanded but there was no time to give her an answer.

Professor Sharra, the mage security team, the dragon professors who had battled the temple, and every student who had seen what had happened to their beloved headmaster could wait no longer. They raced forward and clamored to pat the woman's tail and to lay their hands on her as if they needed to prove to themselves that she was all right.

Kylara stepped back, content to be out of the spotlight for a moment. She had never felt anything like this. Although she had been in crowds before, it was never without her pendant and never in a crowd that was so singularly focused on one simple emotion—joy in the return of someone they loved. The feeling of so many people feeling the same thing, of celebrating together, of being so overjoyed that they jumped up and down, blew fire into the air, and shot sparks from their fingers was the most amazing thing she had ever felt.

Until someone took her hand in a warm grasp that was firm but gentle. She looked at Sam. "That was seriously slick." He grinned.

"Thanks. I had a ton of help," she said.

"Humble. I like that, you know," he said.

"I'm the humblest." She winked.

Sam snorted and shook his head. "I wanted to try to kiss you but after that…well, I wouldn't want to encourage you."

"Oh, I don't need any encouragement," she said.

She discovered then that she could, in fact, feel Sam's light through his lips and it was a wonderful thing.

Kishar no longer knew why she had done what she had done. In the moment, she had wanted to help her goddess. Yes, she had thought that in doing so, she might earn more power for herself, but it was altruism that fueled her decision to welcome Tiamat inside her.

That lie had lasted for about a second before the ancient dragon saw right through it. With the goddess inside her mind, there was nothing she could keep from her. She could not hide her ambitions, her motivations for being the First Walker, or her fears.

And she could not hide all the dragons she had frozen in stone from her.

"It is a lucky thing indeed that none of them were shards of my power," Tiamat chastised from the very top of the deep dark pit she had been placed inside.

"It was not luck, Your Grace, but an interpretation of your will! I would never have done anything against you."

Pain flared in her body. It came from everywhere and nowhere. But she could deal with pain. It was Tiamat refusing to show herself to the woman who had given the goddess her mind and body that hurt the most.

"Do not lie, Kishar, not to me. You are quite skilled at it but you cannot lie to yourself any more than you can lie to me."

"I did not lie!"

"You so nearly killed Pakennen, child. Do not deny it. It was luck that spared him, nothing else. Your love of power is out of control, child. But do not worry, your mother will teach you better."

"Yes, please, teach me, oh Mother of All Dragons. Teach me to be better!"

But exactly like every other time, Tiamat was gone. Kishar was left alone at the bottom of the dark pit. She had long since given up on trying to escape and was worried that trying to do so might damage her mind.

And no matter what the goddess said, she knew her mind was her greatest asset. Her power was unusual, yes, but she had amassed powers by convincing others to do what she wished, not through brute force. Lies were a part of that, of course, as was knowing when to tell the truth.

She would be honest with Tiamat for as long she had to but that did not mean she did not have secrets that the goddess had not uncovered. Kishar had followed this path a long time and she knew this was merely another waypoint on her journey. She would rise again. Like the goddess herself, she would sleep until that time came.

The woman lay down, closed her eyes, and let the darkness take her, confident that at least her dreams were her own.

KEVIN'S AUTHOR NOTES
MARCH 9, 2021

Good news: I moved!

After spending a few years in a really nice apartment building in Boston, my wife and I moved to a new spot. This one is an apartment in one of those old brick Beacon Hill buildings Boston is so famous for. It's funny how strange and how *good* it feels to get back to a more 'normal' sort of apartment.

It hadn't really hit me before just how bland and basic the high-rise style apartments are. Like, they're all the same. Not just within a building, but they all more or less blend together even from one building to the next. It's like someone decided what a good apartment 'should' look like, and then everyone copied it.

Well, the new place is nothing like that. It's got a steel spiral staircase, a wonderfully large kitchen, brick walls, hardwood floors, windows that open onto the street... In almost every way that the old place lacked character, this place has it. Oh, and it's cheaper, too, which is terrific in a time when almost everyone is tightening their belt a bit, us included.

I have a bird feeder hanging in the window and get to watch birds every day. I certainly couldn't do that in the old place! I'm not sure what it says about me, that I appreciate this old, quirky place so much more than the shiny new one, but I'm happy, and at the end of the day I guess that's what matters, right?

OK, so after reading book five — I assume you're done! — who's stoked for the big finale?

Next book, we get to see how all of this wraps up. It's a fun conclusion to this series, and I can't wait to share it with you. The next book, "The Sum of All Magic", is going to be a capstone of Kylara's tale. Although we *will* of course see her and her friends again in the future.

After that we're moving on to Galen's story, the ongoing tale of his adventures. Plus, his stories will let us learn a ton of new information about the dwarfs.

Hey, I wanted more than anything else to say 'thank you.'

When Michael and I got together in Las Vegas to chat about ideas for co-authoring a series together, both of us had a lot of fun with the concept planning, and the whole process has been fun — and sometimes educational — as well. But this universe has gone on to be so much more than we thought when we came up with the idea. We went from fifteen Steel Dragon stories (bundled at launch into five super-size volumes, because we wanted to see if readers would enjoy their books that way) to six Dragon's Daughter books, and now there are going to be six books in this new series as well. All told, that'll be a twenty-seven book universe, which is pretty impressive. It's certainly more books than I've done in any other universe!

And we certainly wouldn't have continued writing all these books without you.

Steel Dragon was slated for at least nine books, but there was no guarantee we'd keep going beyond that. Your enthusiasm for the story inspired us to tell more tales of Kristen Hall. The incredible reaction we got from the completed Steel Dragon series led us to continue writing more tales, and more...

I don't know if Galen's story ("The Dragonclaw Sword" series) will be the final volumes of the Children of Tiamat universe or whether we'll do more stuff after these are done. That's sort of up to you. Because as writers, we're creating things for you. We make these stories to delight, to entertain, to inspire. So long as you're enjoying them, we'll keep telling them.

So thank you. It's an honor to bring these adventures to you, a pleasure coming up with new and dreadful events that can threaten our heroes, as well as cunning plans they create to get themselves back out of trouble again. And none of it would ever be possible without you, the reader.

You're why I get to do this every day, and I won't ever forget that.

I still love to hear from readers, so if you want to drop me a line, I can be reached at kevins.studio@gmail.com; I can't promise to reply to every email, but I will get to as many as I can.

Thank you for reading our story and these author notes in the back.

From Kevin: "I'm not sure what it says about me, that I appreciate this old, quirky place so much more than the shiny new one, but I'm happy."

Not to fear, Kevin, your friend and collaborator is here! (Okay, you might want to fear just a little.)

Please note, I am WHOLLY unqualified to be saying anything about whatever related to what this really means. I'm just having fun and suspect Kevin gets the right but not the obligation to do the same to me. So here goes:

What it says is you are where you live. If a quirky place over a shiny new one feeds your soul? You are quirky, and unfortunately, not new.

Like…you are getting old, my friend. Real Old. Seen any gray hairs?

That many?

Ouch.

Have you mumbled under your breath about the stairs yet? No? You will. Give it time.

(I'm older than Kevin, so maybe this is just me providing a warning. Just roll with it.)

You see that brick you are fond of? The reason it appeals is any mistakes when you hit or scratch it, it just adds more character. The wife will not notice more character. In a brand-new shiny place, they are called "honey-do" list items. Like, "Honey, fix that scratch you made on the wall when you were flying your drone in the house."

Once again, this might be me remembering my past. I don't know if Kevin HAS any drones. I do…and I have not flown the latest drone inside the house.

Yet.

Finally, living in an older house feels more comfortable to those of us who are getting older. Brick provides a sense of permanence that shiny new paint on thin paper walls does not provide.

And if the house feels permanent, we subconsciously realize that the dragon called Age will have a harder time attacking us, which helps.

Because in our minds, we are still running across the cosmos, saving galaxies.

It's just a thought, and I have to say, you started it. <Smile.>

Ad Aeternitatem,

Michael Anderle

Book 10 - Clad in Steel

Book 11 - Brave New Worlds (2019)

Book 12 - Warrior's Marque (2020)

<u>The Ragnarok Saga (Military SF)</u>

Accord of Fire - Free prequel short story, available only to email list fans!

Book 1 - Accord of Honor

Book 2 - Accord of Mars

Book 3 - Accord of Valor

Book 4 - Ghost Wing

Book 5 - Ghost Squadron

Book 6 - Ghost Fleet (2019)

<u>Valhalla Online Series (A Ragnarok Saga Story)</u>

Book 1 - Valhalla Online

Book 2 - Raiding Jotunheim

Book 3 - Vengeance Over Vanaheim

Book 4 - Hel Hath No Fury

<u>Blackwell Magic Series (Urban Fantasy)</u>

Book 1 - By Darkness Revealed

Book 2 - Ashes Ascendant

Book 3 - Dead In Winter

Book 4 - Claws That Catch

Book 5 - Darkness Awakes

Book 6 - Spellbinding Entanglements

By A Whisker (short story)

The Raven and the Rose - Free novelette for email list fans!

<u>Dead Brittania Series:</u>

Dead Brittania (short prequel story)

Book 1 - King of the Dead

Book 2 - Queen of Demons

Raven's Heart Series (Urban Fantasy)

Book 1 - Stolen Light

Book 2 - Webs in the Dark

Book 3 - Shades of Moonlight

Other Titles:

Over the Moon (SF romance)

Midnight Visitors (Steampunk Cat short story)

Demon Ex Machina (Steampunk Cat short story)

The Coffee Break Novelist (help for writers!)

You Must Write (Heinlein's rules for writers)

www.ingramcontent.com/pod-product-compliance
Lightning Source LLC
Chambersburg PA
CBHW050529110726
47899CB00005B/1645